WISHFUL COWBOY

HOPE ETERNAL RANCH ROMANCE, BOOK 5

ELANA JOHNSON

ISBN-13: 978-1-953506-33-7

WISHFUL COWBOY

CHAPTER ONE

L uke Holt lay in the bed where he'd slept for a few months—the last few months of his prison sentence. Axle lay on his feet, the warmth from the dog's body seeping into Luke and making him sweat. He hadn't gone to bed with the pooch, but the dog wandered back and forth between the two bedrooms connected by the Jack-and-Jill bathroom.

He listened for the sound of Slate's breathing, but he couldn't hear it. It was still odd, even nine months later, to not be in the same room with over a dozen other men and all the noises they made in their sleep.

Luke blew a fan at night, mostly to combat his body's natural furnace tendencies. But also to mask any sounds that might wake him.

He'd slept better here at Hope Eternal Ranch than he had anywhere else since leaving. He frowned, not sure what that meant. He'd never thought he'd stay here the way everyone else had. The problem was, there wasn't much for him out in the world either.

"At least there's no snow in Vegas," he muttered as he rolled over. Axle got up and moved, padding up the length of Luke's body, turning, and leaning right against his back. Luke didn't complain, because it sure was nice to have another living, breathing thing so close to him.

The dark gray light filtering into the room told him it wasn't quite dawn yet. He wasn't getting up yet—and he wouldn't get up when the sun did. He didn't work here anymore, and as today was his last full day in Texas, he and the rest of the boys from River Bay were going fishing.

Fishing.

Such a mundane thing to do. But Nate had requested it as his Christmas gift, and no one in the group could deny Nathaniel Mulbury. Least of all Luke.

With his eyes closed, he thought of the first time he'd met Nate. His first night in prison. He'd been a fighter before, and it was his natural instinct to have conversations with his fists instead of his words. He didn't have to talk to his opponents. He didn't have to care how they felt. All he'd cared about was winning.

He'd done a lot of that, and he believed his prison sentence to be an injustice to him. He still felt that way, and if he dwelt on it for too long, his anger caused his fingers to clench and his jaw to tighten. Then all Luke wanted to do was start swinging.

He deliberately breathed in and pushed the air out. *Can't change the past,* he told himself. *Accept what's happened, and move on.*

He was getting much better at actually doing what he thought. Since seeing Slate overcome the demons in his past, Luke figured it was time for him to practice what he'd been preaching.

Yes, he didn't think he was guilty of any crime. But what he thought didn't matter.

Nate had taught him that, on that very first night in prison. Luke had picked a fight, because he always felt better when the pent-up energy inside of him flowed out through a jab or an uppercut. Nate had pulled him off a guy half his size and barked right in his face.

"That's not what we do here, champ. Get control of yourself."

Luke had gone right after Nate too, shoving him back and taking a swing at that pretty face, but Nate was a bigger man, and had been in prison longer, *and* he had three guys right there willing to take blows for him.

Ted, Dallas, and Slate.

Luke had faced down all four of them, wondering how they'd formed such a strong brotherhood in prison. How they'd formed a bond at all. He wasn't great at that, but he'd been willing to try.

Luke had been the last in the group, and he still wasn't sure how great he fit. The crew had been there for Family

Day for Dallas when his wife had filed for divorce and dropped her kids off at her sister's.

They'd come to visit Luke and Slate when they were the last two left. They'd come and picked them up on their release day.

Ginger had petitioned to have Luke in the re-entry program. He felt a debt of gratitude for her he hadn't for another person other than his friends in prison.

So maybe you should stay here. He pushed the thought away. His family lived in Las Vegas now, and he had enjoyed being closer to them. They'd moved while he was in River Bay, and his Family Days had consisted of Nate's brother and Dallas's wife. Ted never did have much family come to the facility, and neither did Slate.

They both seemed to be thriving now, though. Heck, Nate and Ted had fallen in love by the nine-month mark of their releases, and Luke felt like it was just one more way he was failing.

He tried so hard. Tried and failed, almost all the time.

His mind cleared, and he managed to go back to sleep. He woke when a woman said, "Go on, Axle, you naughty thing. You're not supposed to be in here."

He knew the voice, but his eyes were sluggish to open to see her face. In the next moment, the blanket got torn from his body, and the fan he used blasted cold air across his bare torso.

That got his eyes to snap right open. He grunted too, and that was when Hannah Otto said, "Oh, I'm so sorry."

Luke sat halfway up, his heart pounding in the back of his throat. "Hey," he said.

"I didn't know anyone was in here," she said. "And Slate said he needed a blanket, and..." She trailed off as her eyes moved from his face down his body.

Luke knew he had a lot of muscles. He worked purposely to get them and keep them. He'd loved boxing, and at least half of that was because of the physical conditioning it required.

He liked to run, and he liked to lift weights. With all the muscle he had, it was no wonder he was like a walking furnace—or that he only slept in a pair of thin gym shorts.

Hannah stared at him, her mouth hanging open, and the moment turned awkward. Luke reached for the blanket she still held in her hands, and it came loose easily. He covered himself up as she blinked her way back to the land of the living.

He didn't know what to say or do. He'd entertained a fairly massive crush on the woman standing in front of him while he'd lived here at Hope Eternal Ranch.

But Hannah had been dating Bill Buckingham at the time, and Bill was one of Luke's roommates in the Annex. When they'd broken up, Luke had started to form a plan with Jill to ask Hannah to dinner, but in the end, he hadn't.

In the end, he'd gotten a job with a construction crew and knew he wouldn't be staying in town. He didn't think it fair to start a relationship with Hannah that he couldn't finish, and he'd never asked.

He met her eyes and found her face red and getting redder fast. Without a word, she spun and left the bedroom, the slam of the door behind her making him cringe.

He sighed and looked up to the ceiling. "Really?" He didn't have any other words for the Lord. Out of all the people who could've come in and disturbed his sleep, it had to be Hannah?

She was dating someone else now, and Luke wasn't surprised. She was easily the most beautiful woman he'd ever met in his life, and he was honestly surprised she hadn't been taken a long time ago.

He wasn't as surprised that he was still single. He'd never really wanted a girlfriend growing up, because his older brother had had one, and she was so much *work*. Luke had enjoyed wrestling in high school, and then he'd gotten into boxing immediately afterward.

He hadn't gone to college, and he'd never wanted to. He liked working with his hands, and he'd thought construction would be a good career for him. The work was hard, and he had to get up early, but he didn't mind either of those things.

His father was a part-owner in a real estate development firm, and Luke had been working for him since Thanksgiving.

Someone knocked on the door, and Luke said, "Just a sec." He jumped up from the bed, left the blanket behind, and pulled a T-shirt over his head before opening the door.

Slate stood there, looking over his shoulder as he said something to Nick and Connor down the hall. When he turned back to Luke, he said, "I'm an idiot." He stepped past Luke into the bedroom and started pacing.

"Why?" Luke asked. "What happened?" Slate felt like the little brother Luke had never had, though he was technically older than Luke. He closed the door and watched his friend go back and forth.

He'd done this in prison too, when he needed a couple of seconds to work out his thoughts. It was amazing to Luke how much of a person was ingrained in who they were, and also how much a person could change.

"I forgot Jill and I were going to her parents for brunch in the morning."

Luke frowned, the dots not lining up. "Okay."

"I can't drive you to the airport."

"Oh." Luke smiled and ran his hands through his hair. "It's fine. I'm sure one of the other boys can."

"They can't." Slate stopped pacing and faced him. "When Jill reminded me last night, I asked everyone. Ted and Emma are going to San Antonio to see Missy's other mom. Dallas and Jess are leaving for Montana tonight. Ginger has a horse she's taking through a birth, and she wants Nate there, because she's getting bigger, and she's worried she'll need to take a break, and someone has to be there with the horse..."

Slate hung his head as Luke's mind spun. Everyone had such busy lives...except for him.

"There are tons of cowboys here," Luke said. "I'll find someone to take me."

"You don't need to do that," Slate said. "I found someone."

When he wouldn't say who, the unrest in Luke's soul stirred. "It's not Bill, is it?"

"No." Slate scoffed. "Give me some credit."

"Why aren't you saying who it is?" Luke asked, squinting at Slate. "There's no credit, unless you somehow got me a ride on a spaceship or something so the drive will only take five seconds." Luke hated driving in the car. He felt like it was such a waste of time.

"You like this person," he said.

"Is this a guessing game?" Luke's patience was already thin, and he hadn't even showered yet. "Just spit his name out, Slate."

"It's not a him," Slate said. "It's a her. It's Hannah."

Luke opened his mouth to respond and only a guttural squeak came out.

"She seemed really happy and excited to do it," Slate said in a rush.

"That's not happening," Luke growled, the words coming out coated with gruffness and maybe a little distaste. "I can get my own ride to the airport." Heck, he'd call a cab before he rode for an hour with Hannah Otto. The woman had just fled his room without a word; riding in the car together for even five minutes would be akin to torture—for both of them.

No way. Wasn't happening.

CHAPTER TWO

Hannah Otto pressed her palms into her hips as she slid her hands over them. These jeans were amazing, delivering everything they'd promised they would from the ad she'd tapped on. They had some sort of magic material in the waist and hips, and they'd slimmed her by at least five pounds. Probably ten.

The flowery shirt she'd paired with them actually lay mostly flat against her stomach, and she stepped into a fashionable pair of cowgirl boots she'd never wear around the ranch. She was a part-time cowgirl at best, and she was truly happiest curled into the couch with a bowl of caramel popcorn and the largest diet cola someone could bring her.

She loved horses and dogs, goats and chickens. She didn't mind her daily chores of making sure the small animals on the ranch got fed. She even knew how to mend fences, as the goats at Hope Eternal seemed to have a special knack for breaking things. Every morning was an adventure as she walked out to the paddock as the first rays of sun warmed the path beneath her feet.

Hannah had learned to like getting up early, just like she'd learned to like her barrel-sized and shaped midsection and her impossibly thick hair. In high school, she'd shaved the bottom half of her head—everything in the back below her ears—in an attempt to have the same amount of hair as other girls her age.

"All right," she said with a sigh. She turned and picked up the keys to her car, which she'd only gotten a few days ago. She'd only driven it back to the ranch, and she realized as she went into the kitchen that she should've gone out yesterday to practice.

Her nerves needled her, but she managed to pour herself a large amount of coffee into her thermos, add sugar, and a healthy splash of cream. She reached for her purse, which held all of the essentials, and headed outside.

She'd expected to be early, because she was always early. Always ready before everyone else. And yet, she seemed to have fallen behind all of her friends. She put away her jealousy, because it could act like a poison, spreading through her whole system before she even had time to breathe. The antidote worked in a far slower way, and Hannah hated how off-kilter her envy could make her feel.

"Ready?" Luke asked, and Hannah flinched away from him, dropping her keys in the process.

"Oh." Her humiliation had no end, as she was constantly making a fool of herself in front of the man. Things between them had been much easier before Jill had told her Luke was going to ask her out. She'd gone out to the cabin construction site several times and had intelligent—or at least cohesive—conversations with him.

Since her break-up with Bill, though, everything between her and Luke had shifted. He never had asked, and then he'd left the ranch.

"Here you go." Luke had bent and retrieved her keys while Hannah stood there mute. She'd done the same thing yesterday, but at least she'd had a good reason then. The man had muscles everywhere. Muscles on top of muscles, and while she'd never seen him work outside without a shirt on, he obviously went shirtless at some point, because his skin had been golden and beautiful.

The familiar heat that had assaulted her yesterday made a reappearance, and she was grateful she'd thought to double-down on the deodorant.

"Thanks," she said, taking the keys. "Let's see... unlock..." She found the right button the key fob and pressed it. The car made a satisfying clicking noise, and Hannah beamed at Luke like she'd done an amazing thing by unlocking the car.

"Can you pop the trunk?" he asked. "I just have the one bag."

"Sure." Hannah got that job done too, and Luke lifted his bag into the trunk as if it were empty. He met her gaze as he rounded the trunk to the passenger side, and Hannah opened her door to get behind the wheel.

The new car smell filled her nose, and she managed to get the engine started. "Okay." She flexed her fingers on the steering wheel and looked at all the controls. "This is a brand new car for me. I literally got it a few days ago."

"It's nice," Luke said, sliding his seat back to accommodate his longer legs. "Why did you need a new car?"

"Oh, uh." She laughed lightly and wished she'd pulled her hair up for this drive. An hour trapped in the car with this man. What in the world were they going to talk about? "I had a little mishap a week or so before Christmas, and my old car got filled with river water."

"Filled with river water?" Luke chuckled, and Hannah dared to look at him. Their eyes met, and the ice broke into tiny shards. She laughed with him. "That doesn't sound like a little mishap, Hannah."

He drawled her name out like a true Texan, and this time, the warmth filling her body was comfortable and wanted.

"I sense a good story," he said, buckling his seat belt. "You can tell me on the way." He was so calm, and Hannah wondered how he did that. He probably didn't have feelings for her anymore. That was how.

Too bad hers hadn't disappeared, despite her relationship with Chuck Knight. They'd only been seeing each other for a month, but he'd kissed her on the second date, and she could admit that she liked Chuck a whole lot.

They had a decent level of electricity between them, but nothing like the spitting, crackling lightning she felt when Luke got within ten feet of her.

"I want a good story from you too," she said, putting the car in reverse.

"Oh, I can't promise that," he said with a grin.

"You've been gone for four months," she said. "Surely you've had at least one interesting thing happen in that time." She eased past the cars and trucks parked in the gravel lot and turned around to leave the ranch and go over the bridge covering the river.

She turned toward town and reached for her coffee. "I'm assuming you want me to go first."

"Hmm?" Luke looked up from his phone, clearly distracted. "I hate to say this, but my flight just got delayed."

"Oh." Hannah eased up on the accelerator. "Should we go back? How much of a delay?"

"About ninety minutes," he said. "I was thinking we should go to breakfast." He looked at her, hope in those dark eyes.

"Breakfast?" Hannah squeaked.

"Yeah," he said with a playful smile. "Did you eat already?" He let his eyes drift down her body, though she was sitting, and she could tell he already knew the answer to his question. Of course she hadn't eaten that morning. It was barely light, and she'd showered, curled her hair, put on makeup, and the cutest clothes she owned...for an hour-long drive to an airport.

"I could eat," she said.

"Great," he said. "There's that pancake place that everyone loves."

"You sound like *you* don't love it." She looked at him out of the corner of her eyes and caught a half-shrug. "I'm going to take that as a no," she said. "Okay, I know a place we can go."

"You do?"

"Sure," she said. "I grew up out in the country here. We had to drive forty-five minutes to get to Sweet Water Falls just to buy groceries. Well, we did have a tiny country store, but they sold more supplies than groceries. We could get bread and milk and the very essentials there."

"Did you like it?" Luke asked. "Living out in the middle of nowhere?"

"I didn't hate it," Hannah said. "Not sure I liked it either. It's nice only driving a few minutes to town. Our whole family would go one Saturday a month, and the trip took all day long." She sighed as if she'd actually run a marathon not just gone shopping for apples and shoes.

"I grew up in Beeville," he said. "We lived right in town, and I could walk across the street to a store that had every-thing we could want."

"Stop bragging," she teased, and he laughed. Hannah relaxed even further, and she made the turns that would take them to Madam Croque. She arrived in the parking lot, noting that it wasn't very busy this morning. She loved the old, brick building, all of the vines on the pillars, and the vibrant flowers in the springtime. Now, in the winter, the landscape still held a certain beauty in the form of tall, brown grasses that grew straight up in bundles.

"This place has real food, right?" Luke asked, peering out the windshield.

"I'm offended," Hannah said, putting the car in park. She reached for her purse. "You're going to love this place."

"I'm kind of a diner type of guy," he said. "This looks...fussy."

"I know good food," she said. "And you are not a diner type of guy. You like good food, right?"

"Yeah," he said slowly.

"Put your cowboy hat on then, Luke. You're going to be blown away." She got out of the car, hoping Jared was cooking this morning. He had a way with eggs that no one else did, and Hannah enjoyed his cooking and that he took a few minutes to come out and see how his patrons liked the food.

She reached the door first, but Luke jumped in front of her. "I got it," he said, smiling at her.

"Thank you." She smiled at him, admiring those broad shoulders in that burnt orange shirt. It had a collar and a couple of buttons down the chest, with thick fabric that still seemed to stick to the ripples in his muscles.

He wore jeans and work boots, with a belt and a buckle that indicated his Texan heritage. With the cowboy hat, he almost looked like he belonged at Hope Eternal. The boots gave him away, though Hannah had seen him ride a horse and he certainly knew how.

Inside, Lana said, "Hannah, how are you?" as she grinned and picked up two menus. "Two?" She didn't bat an eyelash as Luke came to her side. "This way."

"You know her?" Luke asked.

"I may or may not eat here a lot," Hannah said. She loved the quaint booths, each one decorated with something unique to Texas. Her favorite one bore a table with pressed bluebonnets under a thick sheet of glass.

"I had no idea you were fussy, Miss Hannah," Luke said, his mouth practically touching her ear.

She shivered and giggled, instantly hating how girlish it made her sound. She sucked in the laugh and followed Lana through the restaurant to the Marble Falls booth. This table had maps and trail guides beneath the glass, and Hannah peered at them.

"Have you been out to the Hill Country?" she asked Luke.

"Couple of times," he said, sliding onto the bench across from her. "Look, I should be honest with you."

Emma picked up her menu but kept her eyes on him. "Okay."

"I'm from Beeville, right?"

"Yes," she said. "You said that."

"My mother is a Bee," he said. "She, uh, owns ninety percent of the town, and well, a couple of the bigger resorts out in Hill Country too."

Hannah didn't know why this made him uncomfortable. "Sounds like a lot of work," she said.

Luke blinked at her and started laughing again, and Hannah didn't know what she was doing. This felt like a date, and he wasn't her boyfriend. At the same time, she didn't want to say goodbye to him in another couple of hours.

"It was a lot of work," he said. "My uncle manages most of it now that my family's moved to Las Vegas."

"She must be a black sheep, your mother. Land-owning Texans don't usually up and leave."

"My father wanted to try real estate development, and Vegas was in a huge boom," he said. "That's what I'm doing there now. Working for him." He reached for his water glass, his eyes flitting all over the place before he finally looked at her again.

She got the feeling talk of his job made him uncomfortable. Perhaps it was the conversation about his family. No matter what, it was something.

"Hannah," a man said, and she looked up at Jared. They laughed, and Hannah launched herself out of the booth to hug him. "How are you? I haven't seen you in at least a week."

"Oh, come on." Hannah stepped back and tucked her hair. "It's been at least nine days. Maybe only eight."

Jared grinned at her. "Whatever you've been doing is working." He whistled as he looked down to her toes and back to her face. "You look amazing."

"Thank you." Hannah cocked one hip and put her hand on it. "Now, we want those special crispy potato nachos that aren't on the menu..." She raised her eyebrows, and Jared laughed.

"You got it, Hannah. What else can I get you guys?" He glanced at Luke, and Hannah did too. He wore an expression of wonder, and the buzz in Hannah's veins made her feel beautiful and charming.

"I want the peach sunrise," she said. "And the spinach and bacon soufflé, with the grapefruit segments."

"Makin' me work this morning," Jared said, grinning.

"For you, sir?"

Luke looked like he'd been asked an impossible question. He hadn't picked up the menu, and Hannah just watched him. She was just about to say maybe he needed another minute when he said, "Do you have anything like a western omelet?"

Jared flicked his eyes to Hannah for the briefest of moments. She kept her smile hitched in place. "I have a western omelet breakfast roll," he said. "It comes with a toast cup or fresh fruit."

"I have no idea what a toast cup is," Luke said. "Or a breakfast roll, but it sounds great."

"Comin' up," Jared said, and he walked away.

"He's the chef-owner," Hannah said once he'd gone.

"And you know him personally."

"Yes," Hannah said, smiling at him. She reached for her water glass too, and hid halfway behind it as she added, "I actually dated him for a while." She took a drink immediately afterward, watching Luke.

He looked steadily back at her, and he finally folded his arms and rested them on the table in front of him. "Hannah, if I ever came back to Texas for good, would you...I don't know. Would you consider going out with me?"

Hannah's smile felt like it was made from pure gold. "We're out right now."

"Are we?"

"Aren't we?"

"I thought you were dating someone," he said, leaning back in the booth. He shook his head. "Nah, this can't be a date, because you're not a cheater, and I would never go out with someone who was dating someone else." His eyes sparked with something bright and hot and dangerous.

Hannah swallowed and nodded. "Of course. You're right. I'm seeing Chuck."

"This is just breakfast on the way to the airport with a friend, because his flight got delayed."

Hannah leaned into the table now. "Sounds like a great way to start the day. Now, about these luxury resorts in the Hill Country...can you get, I don't know, discount rooms or passes for your friends?"

A COUPLE OF HOURS LATER, HANNAH PULLED UP TO the curb at the Corpus Christi airport, her face actually aching from how much she'd smiled this morning. Not only that, but her throat was dry and scratchy from all the talking.

"Here we go," Luke said before he got out of the car. She jumped out after him and reached back into the car to open the trunk. He lifted his suitcase out and put it on the sidewalk. He repositioned his cowboy hat and cleared his throat.

Hannah could only watch him war with himself, but she did want to know what he was debating. She was just about to ask when he faced her. With that sexy beard and such a perfectly symmetrical face, he was the definition of handsome.

"Can I tell you a secret?" he asked.

"Yes."

"You can't tell anyone. Not Slate, and definitely not Jill, because she'll tell Slate."

"Okay."

"Not Emma or Ginger or Jess either. No one." He wore a stern expression, and yet Hannah wasn't afraid of him in the slightest. She wanted to know all the intricate sides of Luke Holt, and she really wished he didn't have to go.

"I will not tell a soul," she promised.

Luke drew in a deep breath and blew it out. He looked back toward the doors to the airport and back at her. "I don't really like Las Vegas. I don't like my job there."

"Oh," Hannah said. Whatever she'd been expecting him to say, it wasn't that. "I'm sorry, Luke. Can you do...something about that?"

"I should probably look into it." He reached down to extend the handle on his bag. "Anyway, thank you, Hannah. For the ride and for breakfast." He grinned at her, and Hannah thought he could probably light the whole state of Texas with the brightness of it. He easily drew her into his arms, and she closed her eyes as pure bliss flowed through her.

He smelled like cool water and mint and bacon and pine, and Hannah wanted to bottle him up and take him home with her. Her heart pulsed inside a too-small cage as she thought about him leaving—and she remembered Chuck.

"Anytime," she said, her voice choked and far too low. She stepped back, and Luke adjusted his hat again. He nodded at her once, stepped onto the sidewalk, and headed for the doors.

Hannah stood next to the taillight and watched him go, noting that he never once looked back. When he disappeared, she got behind the wheel of her car and sighed. She had another hour of driving in front of her, and a date with Chuck on the horizon.

Her stomach squeezed, and she knew why.

She didn't want to go out with Chuck now that she knew what she could have with Luke. She knew there was a difference between the two men, and how she felt when she was with each of them.

For the first half-hour, she debated with herself whether she could break-up with Chuck over the phone. They'd only been seeing each other since Thanksgiving, and tomorrow was New Year's Day.

"You can't break-up with him on New Year's Eve," she said, realizing what their date was tonight. But how could she kiss him at the stroke of midnight, knowing she wanted him to be someone else?

"But that someone else doesn't even live here," she said. "You don't even know when you're going to see him again." Could she really ruin what was a good, fun relationship with Chuck for what could be nothing with Luke?

"Nothing," she told herself. Right now, she had nothing with Luke, and something with Chuck. She didn't want to be alone, and she could build off of something. She couldn't work with nothing, and she didn't call Chuck on the way back to the ranch. She could kiss him—she'd enjoyed kissing him previously—that night and continue to get to know him.

Something is better than nothing, she repeated, hoping it wouldn't become a mantra for why she was staying with Chuck.

A reason for not admitting her feelings for Luke.

CHAPTER THREE

L uke panted as he got out of the ring, his fingers tight inside his gloves. "I'm done," he said to his partner, Chris. "You finish it out." He leaned against the ropes, trying to catch his breath. He wasn't sure why he was so winded today.

Probably because you already ran five miles this morning, he thought. He had to do something to keep himself busy and out of his parents' house. Even in February, the sun breathed plenty of heat onto Las Vegas. He ran at dawn, and he dressed in the suit his father wanted him to wear for the appointments they had that day. He'd been working with his dad in the real estate industry for the past two and a half months, and if Luke let himself think too hard about it, he had to admit he didn't like it very much.

He simply didn't know what else to do.

He disliked lounging around the huge house his parents

had bought last year, so after work, he put his exercise shorts back on, and he headed over to the gym.

His father owned this establishment too, and it seemed like everywhere Luke looked, his own failures stared him in the face.

"Nice," he called to Chris as he made contact with Alex's chin. The other man's head snapped back, and Luke knew exactly what that felt like. His vision swam for a minute as he came back to center, and if Luke had allowed a hit like that to land on his chin, he'd have been in a rage right now.

His blood pumped a little faster, and it wasn't even him.

Alex swung wildly, which was what Luke used to do in his early days in boxing. Now, he knew enough to lace the fury tight and let it out at the right time. Several more men came over from their workouts to watch Chris and Alex, and Luke glanced over at a couple of them.

Not many people had been super friendly toward him, but Luke nodded at the guy next to him. He missed Nate and Ted, Dallas and Slate, powerfully in that moment. His friends from prison always acted happy to see him, because they genuinely *were* happy to see him.

They'd do anything for him, and he'd do anything for them.

As he focused back on the fight, he thought for at least the hundredth time that he didn't belong here in Vegas. He'd hated the months he and Slate had spent in Colorado too. Really, in the past decade, Luke's happiest days had been spent at Hope Eternal Ranch.

He frowned as Chris danced backward, his gloves coming down. "Stay high," he called, and the trainee got hit gloves back into a defensive position.

Luke did love boxing with his whole heart and soul, and he'd been flirting with the idea of entering a few amateur fights. He hadn't been able to bring himself to do it yet, and he knew why: He didn't want to tell anyone. Not anyone in Texas, especially Nate, and not his parents.

Boxing was the reason he'd gone to jail, and Luke couldn't imagine anyone thinking him going back to the sport was wise. Luke *knew* it wasn't wise.

He groaned with a couple of other guys when Chris took a hard body hit, but Luke realized most of the men here were cheering for Alex. That only made him want Chris to win all the more, because Luke loved a good underdog.

The fight settled into more shuffling, and Luke's mind wandered again. He used to watch fights just to analyze how the athletes moved their feet, how a match could go from winning to losing with a single breath. One little slip, and the competitor could have him on the ropes. One moment of hesitation, and he could find himself flat on his back, wondering what had happened.

He wasn't anywhere near as strong as he'd once been, and Luke knew he never would be again. He wasn't going to take steroids again. Ever. He and Slate had bonded over their similar addiction to drugs, and they'd made a pact in prison. Luke wasn't going to break it now, not after Slate had faced his demons head-on and won.

He couldn't help thinking, though, that if he did get back in the ring, would he ever win without the steroids?

Doesn't matter, he thought. *You're not fighting again.*

The real question was: What was he going to do with his life?

He looked around and realized what a pathetic existence he had. Hanging out with near strangers in the gym, cheering for a man who was out-matched, all in an attempt to not be at home.

He turned away from the match before it ended, because he suddenly didn't care. He'd been looking for something to give him direction in his life, but he realized now he needed to *take* a step in the direction he wanted to go.

And he didn't want to be here.

"Holt," someone called, and Luke turned toward the voice.

Every muscle tensed as Damian Vasquez and his posse approached. Luke knew better than to show fear to these men, and he knew he'd faced far scarier things than any of them. A man saw things in prison, even a low-security facility, that changed him.

Damian scanned him down to his trainers, and Luke started peeling the tape off his gloves. "You wanna fight?"

"No, thanks," Luke said. "I'm done for the night." He put a tight smile on his face as Damian closed in. Luke stood over six feet tall, but he worked hard not to puff himself up and make himself look bigger. Damian had plenty of height too, and more weight than Luke.

Luke had steered clear of Damian, because he knew who ran the rings here at the gym, and it wasn't him. It had been, once. When Luke's parents had left Texas in favor of Vegas, his dad had moved the gym too. A lot of the guys here had relocated too, including Damian.

He'd stepped into Luke's shoes when Luke had gone to River Bay, and he'd followed the man's career for a few months before he'd realized how unhealthy it was to keep looking at life beyond the walls.

"There's an amateur fight this weekend," Damian said, glancing to the man on his right.

Luke looked at him too, taking in the squinted eyes and dark demeanor. "I'm not interested in entering a fight."

"Why you here training every night then?" Damian took an aggressive step forward.

"Just working out," Luke said coolly. If he told his dad how the guys at the gym treated him, he'd get them to straighten up. Luke would never do such a thing, though. He was thirty-two years old, for crying out loud. He wasn't going to go running to daddy because some guys at the gym weren't nice to him.

He started to walk away from Damian, hoping the man wouldn't find him disrespectful. He said nothing, but Luke felt his eyes on him all the way to the locker room. His heart pounded as he ducked around the wall and pressed his back to it.

He took a deep breath in, and then pushed it all the way out. "You've got to get out of here," he whispered to himself. "You're not going to find yourself here. You're only going to find trouble."

THE NEXT MORNING, LUKE FOUND HIS PARENTS SIPPING coffee at the breakfast bar. "Morning," he said.

"Hey, honey." His mother looked up at him with warm, milk-chocolate-colored eyes. Luke had gotten a tad darker features from his dad, but he could see his mother in him when he smiled. "Sleep good?"

Luke usually lied and said yes. Everything was fine. Another day. Another five miles through the neighborhood. Another day of selling homes. Happy, happy, smile, smile.

He shook his head. "Can I talk to you guys for a minute?"

That got his father to look up from his tablet. He glanced at Mom, and Luke sat at the bar too. He hadn't gotten himself a cup of coffee yet, because his adrenaline buzzed in his teeth as it was.

"I don't think things are working out here," he said slowly, trying to find the right words. "I'm trying to like the job, Dad, but I don't. I want to stay in shape, but I can't keep going to that gym." He shook his head, so many scenarios running through his head, the same way they had last night.

"I'm going to find myself right back where I was before I went to prison," he said quietly, imagining himself to be the strong, quiet Nathaniel Mulbury for only a moment. Nate never said anything that didn't need to be said, and the words were always precisely in the right order. "I don't want that."

Mom reached over and touched his hand. "You're not the same person."

"Exactly," Luke said, looking up at her, almost begging her to understand. "I *can't* be that person again. I can't. I'm not going to prison again." He wouldn't. He couldn't.

Silence fell over the breakfast bar, until finally Dad said, "Real estate isn't for everyone."

"What will you do?" Mom asked.

Luke shook his head, wishing doing so would make his thoughts spark like lightning. Then maybe an idea would emerge. "I'm not sure."

"There's always something to do in Beeville," Mom said. "I can call Uncle Casey and find out if he needs someone."

Luke nodded, though he didn't see himself running one of the resorts his family owned. He wasn't the friendliest of guys, and customer service didn't seem like one of his strengths.

"What do you want to do?" Dad asked.

"I liked the ranch," Luke admitted, the words flying from his mouth without him thinking too hard about them.

"All my friends are there..." He let the words trail off, because he didn't know how to finish them.

"Wolf Mountain is near there," Mom said. "They have horseback riding, Luke. And cabins. It's almost like a cowboy experience."

Luke looked at his mother and smiled. "Mom, it's a five-star resort. Just because it's in Texas doesn't make it a cowboy experience." He laughed, because his mother had no idea what a working ranch looked like. Hope Eternal wasn't even the ranchiest of ranches. They did a ton of commercial activities with school children and the community to make their money, where some ranches literally raised cattle and sold the beef.

She laughed with him, and even Dad joined in with a chuckle or two.

"I don't know," Luke said into the new silence. "I just don't feel...right here." He hadn't told his parents about the conversation with Damian from yesterday, and he wouldn't. He'd made a decision, and he'd stuck to it.

His phone blinged with a tone that went from low to high, and that signaled that one of the boys from prison had texted.

He flipped his phone over and swiped on the message from Ted. The picture loaded and came into a perfectly clear portrait of Ted...and his brand-new baby.

"Oh, wow," Luke said, something warm and electric flowing through him at the same time.

Just like the picture didn't have any blur in it, Luke suddenly knew exactly what he needed to do.

He turned the phone so his parents could see it. "That's Ted. Remember I've told you about him?"

"Oh, look at that darling baby," Mom said, her voice soft and pitching up. She pressed one palm to her heart. "She's darling."

She was, and as Luke looked at the picture again, another message came in. *We named her Francine, after Missy's second mom. We're going to call her Frannie. She's missing her Uncle Luke.*

He picked up his phone and stood. "I have to go back to Texas," he said, looking between his mom and dad. Mom nodded as if she knew he'd go back all along.

Dad didn't seem terribly happy, but he said, "You do what you think is right, Luke. We'll support you."

"Thank you," he said, stepping around his mother to get to his father. He hugged him tight, wishing he could articulate all of the things he felt for his father. "I want to make you proud, but I'm not a good real estate agent."

"You did everything I ever asked of you, son," his father whispered. "If you're meant to be a cowboy, go be a cowboy."

Luke released his father and drew his mom into a hug. "I love you, Mom."

"I love you too, my sweet boy." She held him tight and patted his back. "I wish I could tell you exactly what to do to make you happy."

"I wish that too," Luke said. In fact, he wished a whole bunch of things. He wished he hadn't had to give up boxing. He wished he'd never gone to prison. At the same time, if he hadn't, he'd never have met Slate, his very best friend in the whole world. He wouldn't have Ted to send him perfect pictures of his new baby that had cleared Luke's mind and given him a reason to return to Sweet Water Falls and Hope Eternal Ranch.

He wished he knew what tomorrow would bring, and he wished he had the guts to text Hannah Otto and let her know he'd be back in town soon.

But just like waiting for his future to make itself known hadn't worked, Luke also knew that wishing didn't do much for him. He went upstairs to his bedroom, and he started packing.

"Action," he muttered. "Do something, Luke. Don't just stand there, waiting to get hit."

CHAPTER FOUR

Hannah could not believe the perfect package Emma and Ted had brought back to the ranch. Her eyes filled with tears as she took the tiny pink bundle from one of her best friends. "Oh," came out of her mouth, and she couldn't look away from the tiny face.

The baby had her eyes squished closed, and she was all pink skin and dark, dark hair. "So much hair," she said, smiling as she balanced the newborn in one arm and lifted her other hand to feel the silky hair.

She looked up at Emma, who wore an identical look of adoration to her husband.

"She has hair everywhere," Ted said with a grin. "That's my fault." But he didn't sound upset by it.

"She's a little like a kitten," Emma admitted. She couldn't stop smiling either, and Hannah sank onto the couch with little Frannie cuddled right into her chest.

A sense of contentment settled over her, and she wanted a baby of her own so very much. She wanted a life where she could hold a baby all day and do nothing else. She knew that wasn't entirely reasonable, or entirely something she'd really do. But Frannie smelled like powder and fresh air, and right now, Hannah just wanted to hold her while they both slept.

Having a herd of naughty goats who couldn't seem to behave themselves didn't help her current mood, and she sighed as she let her eyes drift closed.

"There's something boiling over over here," Nate said from the kitchen, and Hannah's eyes shot open.

"Shoot." She stood up, refusing to relinquish Frannie back to her mother, and bustled into the kitchen. The West Wing boasted a massive kitchen and dining room, and Hannah's breath came quick by the time she reached the pot of pasta she'd put on the stove.

Nate stirred it with the wooden spoon she'd left behind, and she flashed him a grateful smile. "Thanks." She took the spoon from him, easily swishing it through the water with the baby in her arms.

Nate gazed down at the baby, and Hannah made a quick decision. "Would you?" She passed him the baby before he could protest, though alarm registered in his eyes.

"I can't—"

"You're going to be a dad in little more than a month," Hannah said. Nate met her gaze, and when he looked back at baby Frannie, he wore a brand new softness in his eyes and around his mouth.

"See?" she said, turning her attention back to the pot. She drove the spoon down to the bottom of it to make sure she got any stuck pasta off and smiled. "You're a natural already."

The baby grunted and snuggled right into Nate's chest, and Hannah swore she heard him sigh in contentment. Whether he did or not, Hannah knew he'd be a very good father, because she'd seen the love and attention he gave to his brother's son.

Nate had had Connor for a few years now, and everyone on the ranch loved the little boy, but no one more than Nate. Hannah had no idea what it would be like to lose a sibling, as she had two older sisters she couldn't get to stop calling and texting her.

Did she want to go to lunch on Wednesday?

Could she watch Maisey and Diane for a few hours on Saturday?

Why couldn't she come on Sunday for dinner?

Honestly, no one could understand why she didn't want to drive forty-five minutes to be assaulted with questions about who she was dating, when she'd get married, or why she'd broken up with the last guy she'd been with.

She'd stopped texting her sisters the moment a new man asked her out, and she'd stopped telling Mama about them right from the beginning. Now, Hannah waited at least three months before even mentioning she'd started seeing someone new.

She hadn't mentioned Chuck at all, and they'd been dating for three and a half months. She probably should, because Chuck treated her like a queen, and telling her family about him would open doors Hannah had kept closed.

Purposefully closed.

She frowned as the image of the handsome cowboy who'd come to the ranch last year blitzed through her mind. Luke Holt.

She hadn't told her family about Chuck, because she still hoped Luke would come back to the ranch.

Ridiculous, she thought. It had been months since he'd left, and while she'd seen him over the New Year holiday, they didn't speak often. *Hardly ever* would be a more accurate description of their level of conversation.

Hannah hadn't been able to drive him from her mind, though, and she could admit she hadn't even tried.

She brought the spoon up and separated one noodle from the others to test how done it was. She'd dumped the pasta in the boiling water only moments before Emma and Ted had walked through the front door at the West Wing, and she'd forgotten to set a timer.

The rigatoni barely had any bite left, and she quickly turned off the flame and lifted the pot off the burner. She hadn't gotten out the colander yet, and she cursed herself for getting distracted. At the same time, a baby was a worthy

distraction, and she set the pot in the sink and turned to get
the colander out of the cupboard.

With the pasta draining, she stepped over to the slow
cooker to check on the marinara and meatballs. She'd put
that together this morning, in anticipation of Ted and Emma
bringing their baby back to the ranch today.

Everything looked ready in the slow cooker, and she
took out her phone and sent a text to the group string.
Dinner's ready. Come when you can. There's plenty for all.

Before she knew it, the back door opened, and voices
filled the space. Hannah scurried about getting down plates
and setting out forks. She opened three bags of Caesar salad
and mixed it all up.

Ginger came to stand beside her. "This looks amazing,
Hannah." She put her arm around her shoulder, and
Hannah grinned at her. She leaned into her friend's hug,
because she enjoyed the human touch.

"This is going to be you in a month."

Ginger put her hand on her very pregnant belly and
smiled. "Maybe."

"Maybe?" Hannah asked. "What do you mean?"

Anxiety blipped in Ginger's eyes. "I just mean...I'm
silly, of course." She tried to laugh, but it honestly sounded
like a strangled croak. "Most women survive childbirth.
Heck, Emma's done it twice."

"Survive childbirth?" Hannah stared at Ginger, trying
to make her words like up. "You're worried you won't
survive?"

Ginger swallowed. "It's irrational, I know. Some people do die giving birth."

"Ginger, you're going to be at the hospital," Hannah said in a firm voice. "There will be a lot of doctors and nurses, and you're going to be fine."

The redhead nodded, and Hannah couldn't quite believe the normally strong, powerful, and knowledgeable woman was scared of having a baby. She wanted to wrap Ginger in a tight hug and reassure her over and over.

"Hey, beautiful," Nate said, sweeping his arm around Ginger and stealing her away. He surely told her she'd be fine, and Hannah understood having unexplained fears. After all, she lived in fear every day that she'd never find the right man for her, no matter how many dates she went on and how many men she went out with.

"All right," Jill said, setting a huge tray of garlic bread on the counter. "Quiet down. Quiet!"

The chatter in the house stopped then, because Jill had a loud voice and a fun, vibrant personality. Everyone loved her, and she loved everyone she met. She and Slate Sanders, Luke's best friend, had gotten engaged just before Christmas, and Jill wanted a spring wedding with a lot of flowers. Bluebonnets, poppies, lilies, roses, daisies, everything. Those had been Jill's words.

They'd selected a date in late April, to make sure both babies had come, and that life would be somewhat normal before Slate and Jill left the ranch for their honeymoon. The time between seasons was one of the busiest, but

Ginger had assured Jill that she could have her spring wedding.

Hannah wanted her to have it, even if it made her throat tighten and squeeze as if she'd swallowed a capful of vinegar.

"All right," Jill said, looking at Hannah. She smiled and nodded, as if to say, *Go on, now. Tell 'em what we've got.*

Hannah smiled back at her, feeling the world narrow. Jill still lived in the West Wing, but in just two more months, she'd be gone. Only Hannah would be left, and she wasn't sure she could survive in the huge house alone.

She'd told herself over and over that her friends lived nearby. Heck, Ginger and Emma lived in cabins only a hundred yards from the West Wing. Jess and Dallas lived in town, but it only took ten minutes to get there. Jill and Slate had claimed a cabin too, and Hannah wouldn't truly be alone.

She would be, though, and she knew it.

Talk about irrational fears, she thought just before opening her mouth. "It's nothing fancy, but one of Ted's favorite foods is spaghetti and meatballs, and I heard Emma say more than once that she could eat garlic bread for every meal." She smiled at her friend, working hard to keep the emotion out of her voice.

"I added the salad just to pretend like we're going to be healthy around here." She smiled at the group of cowboys and cowgirls who'd come in off the ranch, as well as all the women who'd once lived right here in the West Wing.

"Come eat," she said in conclusion, and the noise swelled again.

Hannah got out of the way, because she never led the group through the line. Rather, she'd go nearly last just to make sure the food didn't run out.

Jill kept the garlic bread coming, and Hannah opened a couple more bags of salad before she picked up a plate. The tangy, salty scent of her grandmother's marinara met her nose, and a smile graced her face. She twisted a beautiful pile of spaghetti on her plate and added three meatballs.

She'd skip the salad if it didn't fit on her plate, and for today, she wouldn't feel bad about it. She had a body-shaper and a couple of pairs of pants that slimmed her as well.

Hannah turned toward the large dining room table and stepped toward an open spot. The noise swelled, and Ted and Nate both stood at the same time.

"There he is," Ted boomed, his loud laugh joining the fray of sound. He looked past Hannah to someone over her shoulder, and Nate laughed too.

Slate twisted and looked, and he got up too, saying, "Luke. You made it."

Luke.

Hannah's heart leapt into the back of her throat, and while every system in her body sped up, she seemed to be moving very slowly. Her legs trembled, and her hands shook, and as she turned around, she dropped her plate of spaghetti.

The shattering of the plate silenced everyone, and about that same second, Hannah's eyes met Luke's.

Lightning struck her from head to toe, and then Slate swooped in between her and Luke, hugging his best friend and breaking the connection she'd always felt to the sexy cowboy ex-con.

CHAPTER FIVE

L uke had been welcomed back by his family when he'd arrived in Las Vegas, but it simply wasn't the same joy, love, and rush he felt from the cowboys and cowgirls and others at Hope Eternal Ranch.

Jill exclaimed about how thin he was, and Slate stood back and said, "Nah, he's probably gained weight. Muscle mass." He grinned and slung his arm around Jill, both of them smiling for all they were worth.

Ginger hugged him tightly, her baby belly between them, and then Dallas stood there with Jess and the kids.

"Uncle Luke, look," Remmy said, and he scooped the little girl right up into his arms. He could feel Hannah's gaze on him, but he didn't dare meet her eyes again. Even that brief moment a few minutes ago had been enough to sear him right through. His nerves still buzzed, and the whole world had narrowed to just her.

"What is it?" he asked Remmy, looking at the object in her hand. It seemed to be a rock she'd painted, but he couldn't read the letters.

"It's my pet rock," she said. "I named him Stony."

"What a great name," he said, setting her back down. He wasn't the best with kids, but with the ones he knew, he got along with okay.

He glanced around for Connor, nearly getting knocked down by the blond boy as he barreled toward him. He grunted as he caught him, and Connor hugged him tight with wiry arms. "You're back," he said, and that about summed it all up.

Luke pressed his eyes closed and said, "Yeah, bud. I'm back," in a voice that gave away far too many emotions. Good thing it was so loud and no one could hear him.

He straightened, and Ted stood there. "It's so good to see you, brother." Ted engulfed him in a big bear hug, which made Luke laugh. He hugged Emma and asked about the baby, but she was apparently sleeping in a swing several feet away in the living room.

Luke didn't need to hold her right now, and he faced Nate, a powerful feeling of acceptance moving through him. The guys at the gym didn't possess the same brotherhood that Luke had with these men, and they never would.

The men he spent time with in prison would sacrifice for him. The guys at the gym were only looking out for themselves.

He laughed and stepped into Nate's arms, the two of

them clapping one another on the back. "Come eat," Nate said. "There's tons of food."

Luke surveyed the counter while Nate asked someone for another chair. He picked up a plate, noting this meal had Ted and Emma all over it. Spaghetti and garlic bread. It was simple, and yet the sauce looked homemade.

He knew who would have done that—Hannah—since Emma was the guest of honor. She had won a cooking competition before Luke's time on the ranch, but he'd heard all about it, and he'd sampled Emma's cooking.

Hannah loved to cook too, though, and Luke thought of the breakfast they'd shared a few months ago. Had she thought about it at all? Was she still seeing someone else? He hated that he didn't have all the information he needed, but he told himself he had time to get it.

He turned to the table, and Nate had found him a chair. He nodded to it, positioned right on the end of the table, and Luke walked toward the group. Crowds unnerved him, and he thanked all the stars in the heavens above that Nate had put the chair on the end.

He'd probably done it on purpose.

He sat down, and just like that, he was assimilated into the conversations going on around him. Nate and Ted spoke about the fields that needed to be prepped, and Luke heard a few words about new horses on the ranch. He'd seen some construction down the lane when he'd pulled up, and he wondered if Ginger would assign him to that project.

She hadn't given him a formal assignment yet. She'd

asked him to come see her in the morning, and Luke hadn't needed more than that. In fact, he liked only having the barest of schedules for the day. Otherwise, he got overwhelmed, which was one reason he'd disliked the real estate industry.

Perhaps it was just his father's way of doing things Luke didn't like. He didn't need every minute of every day planned out. He liked more flexibility and the ability to be spontaneous in his activities.

"Are you back for good, then?" Spencer asked.

"I think so," Luke said, twirling up his first bite of spaghetti. The crisp, almost acidic scent of the marinara hit his nose before the food touched his tongue, and he groaned as he tasted the sauce. "This is so good."

Spencer grinned at him. "Don't get used to it. Bill moved out, and we got this new guy, Jason." Spencer pointed down the table to a man Luke didn't recognize. He had a long, sloped nose, and he was currently in the middle of telling an exciting story, if the light in his eyes said anything. Jason seemed like the kind of man that needed to be the center of attention, and Luke's nerves buzzed a little more.

"He literally burns something in the microwave every single day," Spencer said. "The whole Annex smells like smoke and melted plastic."

"Great," Luke said in a deadpan. "Will I be in the basement?" He looked away from the man who'd just finished talking. The table down that way erupted in laughter, and Luke couldn't help smiling.

"No," Spencer said. "Jason took Bill's room, and I moved up into the one Slate was in. You can have the same room back, if you don't mind sharing the bathroom with me." He smiled at Luke, who returned the gesture.

"Fine with me," he said. "You didn't like being in the basement?"

Spencer held Luke's gaze for a moment, something moving fast through his dark eyes. Luke wasn't sure what it was, but it almost felt like…unrest. "Yeah," Spencer finally said. "Or rather, no. I didn't like being in the basement." He picked up a piece of garlic bread, his gaze falling to his plate and then down the table again. "Don't say anything. They're just all…so young."

"How old are you?" Luke asked.

"I'm old," Spencer said. "I'm thirty-nine. That's eleven years older than Jack, and he's now the oldest one in the basement."

Another round of laughter from down the table rent the air, and Luke looked at the crowd down there. Most of them didn't live full-time on the ranch, but Luke had seen the majority of their faces before.

Day workers that came in when Ginger called, or seasonal people she hired on a weekly or monthly basis. If she hired someone full-time, they almost always lived in the Annex.

"This place has got to be almost empty," Luke said,

glancing around the West Wing. When he'd first come to Hope Eternal Ranch, he'd been told the West Wing was off-limits. He hadn't had a problem with it, because he just wanted to keep his head down, get the work done, and finish his sentence out in the sunshine instead of behind bars.

"Almost," Spencer said. "Jill and Slate are going to live in a cabin on the Back Row. Then it'll just be Hannah."

Luke looked down the table to her, and she lifted her eyes from her plate to meet his. It almost felt like she'd cast a spell on him, the energy of it shooting from her and straight into him.

He managed to smile, and she did too. He wondered how she felt about living here alone. The West Wing acted as the hub of activity for the ranch, with many meals eaten here, and offices off the front living room. He'd be here tomorrow to meet with Ginger. None of that changed the fact that she'd live and sleep here alone.

For a while there, Luke had thought he wanted to be alone. Just him and wide open land. Him and the beach. Him and the sky, the air, the water.

He still liked being alone for a little while, but he didn't want to live the majority of his life that way. He did need and want to be surrounded by people he could trust, who trusted him, and who believed in him.

"So, I don't think I heard," Nate said a few seats away, his voice breaking into the trance Hannah had cast on Luke. "Why did you decide to come back?" He glanced at Luke and then Slate.

"Oh, well." Luke reached for his cup of punch and took a big drink. "I...." He became aware of everyone staring at him. At least everyone on this half of the table, including Hannah. She seemed keenly interested in hearing his explanation, and he wondered if that were really true. Perhaps only he could feel the pulsing electricity between them.

"I really didn't like real estate," he said, clearing his throat afterward. "I realized I like working outside. That's why I like construction. But it's too hot in Vegas for that, and too dang cold in Colorado." He grinned at Slate, who nodded in a very exaggerated way.

"I figured, you guys were all here, and Sweet Water Falls is close to the beach." He shrugged, though it was the familial atmosphere and brotherhood that had really brought him back, not the weather. "So I came back. Ginger said she'd find me something to do, and...yeah." He stuffed his mouth with a big bite of bread, hoping the attention would turn to someone else.

It did, because Jill got up and yelled, "I'm getting out the chocolate cake," and that caused an eruption that only cowboys could produce. Luke laughed along with his friends. He finished his meal. He ate a couple of pieces of cake, and a couple of hours later, he found himself in the same bedroom he'd slept in last year, the same blue and gray blanket on the bed.

"I can leave Axle," Slate said from the doorway. His dog had already jumped up on Luke's bed, circled, and made himself at home next to the pillows.

"Where are you?" Luke asked. "I didn't even think of that. If Spencer took your room." He glanced toward the door that led into the bathroom.

"I'm in the cabin Jill and I will live in," Slate said. "It's just out the back door, to the right. Next to Ted."

"Next to Ted," Luke echoed, wondering how they'd all managed to come to this same ranch, on this same spot of land along the Coastal Bend of Texas.

Slate entered the room, a serious look on his face. "It's good you're back."

Luke sank onto the bed, making Axle slide into his back. He chuckled when the dog didn't try to get up but stayed smashed into him. "Yeah," he finally said, looking at Slate. "I never did find myself, but I think I found someone I *don't* want to be."

Slate nodded like that made sense. Luke knew it didn't, but he didn't try to explain further. "We all want you here."

Luke nodded, because he did want to feel like people wanted him around. Belonging somewhere was important to Luke, as much as he tried to pretend like it wasn't. "Is Hannah—?" His voice muted, because he didn't know what to ask. Embarrassment heated his face, and he shook his head. "Never mind."

"She's." Slate ground his voice through his throat. "She's still dating Chuck Knight. They've been going out for a few months now. Maybe four or something. I don't know."

Luke nodded, the answer to his most pressing question

lodging in his throat. It tightened, and he just wanted to be alone.

"Okay." Slate retreated to the door. "I'm leaving Axle with you. See you tomorrow."

He left and Luke barely had time to say, "Yeah, see you tomorrow," before Slate closed the door, sealing Luke in the room with his thoughts and a now-snoring briard.

———

"THANKS SO MUCH FOR HAVING ME BACK," LUKE SAID, hating his tone but keeping his smile on his face. Ginger grinned at him and indicated he should sit. She hadn't even gotten up, and he didn't blame her. She was eight months pregnant, and Luke honestly didn't know how she moved at all.

Luke took his seat, his heartbeat blipping just a little. He wasn't sure why. He knew Ginger; she knew him. She valued his work.

"Let's see," she said, shuffling some papers and a couple of folders. "I know you got in just before dinner last night, and I don't think your boys left you alone for five seconds." She smiled, and it lit up her green eyes. "I'm so glad you're back, if only because Nate's glad."

"Thank you," Luke said.

"Of course, I know what you can do, and I'm not sure if you saw the construction down the road." Her eyebrows went up.

"Briefly," Luke said, his fingers curling into fists.

"Because of Jill's amazing holiday festival, our horseback riding lesson enrollment has increased by fifty percent."

"Wow," Luke said, smiling because he hadn't seen a ton of Jill's festival, but what he had looked fun.

"Yeah." Ginger sighed as she smiled. "It's great, but we don't have the horses or facilities for that. So we're building a new stable, and we've got the animals. They need to be trained, and I need you on both."

"Both the construction and the horse training?"

"That's right." She extended a folder toward him, and Luke wondered it could possibly hold. "Hannah is the overseer of the project, and..." She kept talking, but Luke's ears misfired at the words *Hannah is the overseer of the project.*

"I'll be working for Hannah?" he blurted out.

Ginger paused, her eyes widening. "No, you work for me," she said slowly. "Hannah is overseeing this particular project, and she knows every moving piece. I met with her last night, and we went over your strengths." She glanced behind him. "Here she is."

"Sorry," Hannah said, and Luke whipped around, standing as Hannah Otto entered the room. He felt incapable of staying seated in her presence, and foolishness rushed through him. "Marc called, and he's got a flat tire. I told him I'd send someone to help, and I grabbed Collin as he arrived."

"Is Marc okay?" Ginger asked as Hannah slid into the chair next to Luke's.

She cut a glance at him, a small smile curving her lips. "Yeah, he's fine. Almost went off the road, but he'd just left his house, so he had a wide shoulder."

"Not like out here by the river."

"Right."

Ginger glanced at Luke. "I was just telling Luke that we met last night and reviewed his skills, so that you'll put him on tasks he'll excel at."

Hannah nodded, and Luke could barely hold still.

Ginger focused on him again. "Hannah will let you know what you're working on and when, and you'll pass things off with her."

Luke nodded, his throat so dry.

"Great," Ginger said brightly. "I'll leave you two to it." She nodded with a very final look on her face, and Luke stood.

"Can I talk to you for a sec, Ginger?" Hannah asked, and Luke hesitated too. Then he told himself that Hannah obviously wanted to talk to her friend alone, and he kept moving. The result had him stumbling toward the doorframe. He caught himself, humiliation burning through him, and he escaped the office before he could make a bigger fool of himself.

CHAPTER SIX

Hannah watched Luke leave the office, and she waited a few more seconds to make sure he was good and gone. She faced Ginger, who held up one hand, palm forward. "I know what you're going to say."

"I don't see why he can't work with Jess. He'll obviously be more comfortable." Hannah wasn't sure why she was trying to get Luke onto someone else's team. She wanted to work with him. She wanted to talk to him. She wanted to spend more time with him.

He'd barely said two words to her last night. At the same time, Hannah had felt like he'd come back to Texas just for her. Ridiculous, she knew, but the feeling nagged at her, and she'd barely been able to sleep last night.

She stifled a yawn right now, not looking forward to the next twelve hours. She was far too old to miss so much sleep, and she hoped this wouldn't set the precedent for the whole week.

Ginger hadn't said anything, and Hannah sighed. "You're not setting me up with him, are you?"

"Of course not," Ginger said, her eyes flashing with dangerous fire. "He's amazing with a hammer, and he's good with horses. That's your team, Hannah."

Resignation filled her, and a sigh came out of her mouth. "I know."

"I thought you were dating Chuck."

"I am," Hannah said.

"But you want to date Luke."

Hannah couldn't confirm or deny it, at least not vocally. In her mind, yes, she wanted to go on a date with Luke Holt. She wanted to hold his hand and find out if the sparks she could feel across the distance between them would fill her whole body.

A hint of worry accompanied the thoughts, though, because what if the sparks fizzled? What if she broke up with a really great guy for a chance at Luke, only to find out they weren't as compatible as she hoped?

Her stomach wobbled, and Hannah wished she had another serving of toast. A double-decker stack of toast.

"If it's a problem after a couple of weeks, let me know," Ginger said. "We move people all the time, and I can easily tell him that Jess requested him full-time in the stables."

Hannah nodded and left Ginger's office. She'd been spending more and more time in the office at the West

Wing, because she only had a few weeks left in her pregnancy. The doctor had told her absolutely no horseback riding, and she shouldn't venture too far out on the farm, just in case she went into labor and needed to get to the hospital quickly.

Hannah entered the kitchen and opened the fridge. Her choices lay in front of her: peach cups, grapefruit segments, string cheese, protein shakes, bottled water, and a variety of groceries she'd have to cook to be able to eat.

She didn't want fruit or protein shakes. She wanted a big piece of chocolate cake, and she quickly closed the fridge and opted for the freezer instead. She had mini ice cream sandwiches, and she took one of those and started unwrapping it.

She could eat the frozen treat in five or six bites, and it would be gone before she left the yard. Before anyone saw her eating ice cream before nine a.m.

She stepped out of the garage, at least half of her ice cream sandwich left, and Luke said, "Can I walk with you?"

Hannah choked on her ice cream and jumped a couple of feet away from him. "Oh," she cried out, and she dropped her ice cream.

Luke held up his hands. "Sorry. Just me." He looked down at her treat, and Hannah did too. "Wow, I'm just striking out all over the place this morning," Luke added.

"You're fine." Hannah said, the sun suddenly too hot. She crouched and scooped the sugary snack off the cement. She stepped over to the trash can and dropped the remaining ice cream sandwich in it. "I don't need that anyway. It's far too early for ice cream."

"It's never too early for ice cream," Luke said, that sexy, sly smile coming to his face.

Hannah had to put one hand against the wall of the garage to steady herself. After a moment to gather her composure, she continued back toward him, putting a smile on her face too. "Are you ready for this? Do you remember how long the days were?"

"Anything is going to be better than following my dad around, showing houses to people who can't afford them." He grinned at her and turned with her as she passed him. They started across the lawn to the dirt road behind the house and all the cabins that had been built. The walk always calmed Hannah on the way to work, and she could shed the stress of whatever had happened that day on the way home.

Her nerves settled, and she managed to stuff her hormones back into the box where they belonged. "I bet your parents are going to miss you."

"I don't know," Luke said. "They didn't seem to mind me there, but I..."

She heard the pause in his statement, and she really wanted him to finish, so she stayed silent.

"I feel more welcome here," he finally said.

"Interesting," Hannah said.

"It doesn't make sense, I know."

"I think it does," she said. "Here, you've got these four

men who know you on a deep level. They know the worst of you, and the best of you, and they accept you anyway."

Luke started nodding halfway through what she'd said. "Yeah."

Curiosity burned through Hannah. None of the men from River Bay had said a lot about their time in prison—at least not to her or anyone but each other. She knew the reason why everyone had been sentenced, except Luke. She'd heard some rumors, but nothing from the man himself.

She pulled back on the question, because it felt so personal, and she hadn't spoken to Luke in almost two months. She thought of their breakfast together, and how easy the conversation had been. She'd dropped him at the airport, pure happiness streaming through her.

As the stable neared, a couple of people came out, both leading a horse. Jess and Dallas chatted easily with each other, and Hannah envied their relationship. She knew not everything had always been carefree and fun for them, and Hannah chose to grab onto the rope of hope unraveling inside her.

This was Hope Eternal Ranch, after all. She wasn't going to give up on finding her soul mate just because she'd had a few setbacks.

"Hannah?" Luke asked.

She blinked her way out of her thoughts. "Hmm?"

"He asked you something." He nodded to someone to her left, and Hannah turned that way. Nick stood there, his eyebrows up. He carried a sack of feed in each hand, his muscles straining.

"Sorry," Hannah said. "What?"

"The storage is full, because we've got all the construction equipment in part of the shed." Nick set the bags down and grunted. "We've got a load of goat feed here, and I'm wondering what to do with it."

The grumbling of a truck engine met Hannah's ears, and she realized how zoned out she'd been. She looked over to it, her mind spinning. Shading her eyes from the sun, she peered at the hay barn, the equipment shed, the stable they already had, and the storage shed. Another barn sat behind the stables, but it too housed a lot of the supplies they needed for the new stable.

"What about the empty row where our foals usually are?" Hannah asked. "Our first foal won't be born for another six or eight weeks, and there's got to be space there."

Nick nodded. "I'll go check."

"Talk to Jess," Hannah said. "But I think she'll be okay with it."

Nick waved over his shoulder, already on his way toward the stable. Hannah faced Luke, grinning out of sheer instinct. His handsomeness was off the chart, and Hannah could barely look at him. That, or she wanted to stare for a while so she could memorize every line in his face.

"I think I heard you say you'd been working out in Las Vegas."

He grinned on back. "Is that what you heard?"

Oh, he was a good flirt too.

Hannah ducked her head and reached to tuck her hair behind her ear. Too bad she'd put her hair in a high ponytail this morning and didn't have anything to tuck away. She let her hand drop back to her side. "That truck has to be unloaded, and if we keep them too long, they charge us an extra fee."

Luke looked over to the flatbed, which held at least a hundred bags of feed. In fact, probably exactly one hundred, as that was usually the amount Ginger ordered.

"Is this my first assignment?" he asked.

"I'm not going to give you assignments," Hannah said, his words from Ginger's office streaming through her head. He hadn't sounded thrilled about working *for* her. She also didn't want to be his boss, nor did she want to tell him what to do all day. Ginger filled that role just fine, and Hannah would rather observe from the background to make sure everything got done to perfection, within budget, and according to their timeline.

"I can help unload," Luke said as Nick came out of the stable with a couple of other guys, including Ted and Slate. Luke joined them, easily fitting into the crowd. He still stood out to her in every way, and he always had.

The construction here on the ranch had started only three weeks ago, and they were already behind. Hannah had learned that was just how things went with construction, and she felt like she had to make constant adjustments based on the delivery schedule of lumber, when she could get the cement truck to come pour concrete, and according to the inspector's schedule.

They'd cleared several hurdles last week, and Hannah was really looking forward to making some progress on the stable. She told herself she still had three months before the new students would flood the ranch, but she knew how fast three months could go by.

She moved over to the strip of shade along the existing stable and watched the men unload the truck. In all honesty, she only watched Luke. The way his arms bulged. The sound of his laugh. The look of happiness of his face.

She sure did like him, and she wished she had someone who could tell her what to do. Break up with Chuck to give herself a shot with Luke? Keep her safe boyfriend until Luke had more of a footing in his life?

He was clearly still drifting, and he'd been out of prison for almost a year.

She pushed the judgmental thoughts away, because she had no idea what life would be like after being incarcerated. None of the men she'd known who'd come through Hope Eternal Ranch had been able to return to the life they'd had before, and Luke clearly couldn't either. It was perfectly okay for him to take time to figure out what he wanted to do with the rest of his life.

Before she knew it, the truck growled as it eased away from the barn, and Hannah straightened. Had she literally been standing there that long? The work wouldn't get done that way, and she hoped everyone would just go back to their jobs and leave her to slink out of the shade silently.

Nick and the others went into the stable, but Luke turned and came straight toward her. She couldn't make herself invisible, no matter how much she wanted to, so she stepped out into the sun again. "Thanks," she said.

"Yep." He adjusted his cowboy hat. "Are we headed over to the construction site now?"

"Yes," she said, trying to find her thoughts. "Yes, let's go over there. I've had a couple of guys working on it, but I really don't know what I'm doing." They started around the existing building. "We had a professional design the stable, and we have the blueprints. I'm just not sure if we're following them."

"It looked like a building to me," Luke said.

"I'm going to put you in charge of the construction," she said. "I know Ginger wants you on horses too, but for the first little bit, I need you to make sure we're on track with the building."

"I can do that," he said, glancing at her.

Their hands brushed as they rounded the corner, and Hannah pulled in a breath and put a little distance between them on her next step. She had a boyfriend, and Luke had said once that she wasn't a cheater. She *wasn't* a cheater, and she would never do that to Chuck. She wouldn't do that to herself. She didn't want to *be* that kind of person.

"Luke," she said, deciding she just needed to tell him. "I'm still seeing Chuck."

"Hmm." He kept his eyes on the ground, and Hannah eased up on the pace. He slowed with her.

She took a deep breath. "I think you're great, and I'm so, *so* glad you're back." She smiled at him, but he barely looked at her. He didn't smile in return, and Hannah's heart quivered. She didn't want to hurt him. She didn't want to get hurt.

She also knew she couldn't stand still, in a place of fear. If she wanted to find her soul mate, she'd have to take some risks.

"I'm sorry," she said.

That got him to look at her. "About what?" His dark eyes filled with fire and a challenge.

Hannah's mind blanked. "Um." She glanced toward the equipment shed, where they kept their big machines and did all the vehicle maintenance on the ranch.

"Are you sorry you're with Chuck?" Luke asked.

When she faced him again, she found him two steps closer to her, his gaze sparking with desire. "Because I am," he said. "If you were single, Hannah, I'd ask you to dinner for tonight." He spoke in utmost control, his voice low and soft and somewhat terrifying all at the same time.

A shiver ran up her spine and down her arms, and Hannah's fingers tingled as the energy left through the tips of them.

"*Tonight*," Luke said again. He backed up a couple of steps.

The world breathed again, Hannah along with it. She

hadn't even realized she'd started to hold her breath, but the way her lungs pinched and the hefty drag in she took told her she had.

"I guess you have to ask yourself if the only reason you'd say no is because you're with Chuck," he said, glancing down the length of the stable to the bare wood of the new one. "I'll go see what we're dealing with down here." He walked away, and all Hannah could do was watch him.

Wow, she thought, those shoulders so broad, and his back so strong. Someone stepped next to her, but Hannah didn't even have the wherewithal to turn and see who it was.

"It's a good question," Jill said. "He is *hot*, Hannah, and he'd ask you out for *tonight*." She hit the T the exact same way Luke had, giggling afterward.

Hannah released her breath and looked at Jill. "You were eavesdropping on us."

"Duh," Jill said with a grin. She sobered quickly. "Now what? What are you going to do?"

Hannah shook her head and looked back just in time to see Luke walk through a gap in the frame, his hand on the stud for a moment as he passed inside. "I don't know."

CHAPTER SEVEN

Luke pushed back in the recliner to get the footrest to come up. A sigh came out of his mouth, and he let his eyes drift closed. He'd worked hard today, kicking off his day by unloading fifty-pound sacks of feed. Then he'd been up and down on that structure, checking joints and load-bearing beams.

He'd been pleased to see that the initial construction had been done right, or at least well enough, and he'd spent the afternoon going over the blueprints with Marc, Jack, and Sarah. They all had a decent amount of construction experience, and he'd worked with all of them the last time he was at Hope Eternal.

"Pizza's here," Dallas said as he came through his own front door.

"About time," Slate said. "I was about to chew off my own arm."

"Whatever." Dallas's footsteps sounded and Luke opened his eyes. They felt a little scratchy, and he'd have to get used to the grasses here all over again. His stomach grumbled, and he put the footrest down to join his friends in the kitchen.

"Nate's not coming," Dallas said. "By the way. He doesn't want to leave Ginger home alone." He opened the first box to reveal a supreme pizza with all the meats and veggies. Luke's mouth started to water, though he'd half-expected Hannah to call or text or even stop by the Annex. He'd imagined her proclaiming that she'd broken up with Chuck, and would he take her to some fancy restaurant where he thought he wouldn't like the food?

She hadn't. No texts. No calls. No pop-ins.

"I got the Alfredo one you like." Dallas glanced at Luke. "You're still eating that, right?" He flipped open another box to reveal the mostly white pizza, with chicken, green onions, extra cheese, and Alfredo sauce.

Luke salivated. "Definitely."

Ted wasn't coming tonight either, but Luke appreciated that Dallas had bought pizza and set this up for him. Jess had taken the kids to the mall for dinner in the food court and a movie in the treehouse theater there. They'd be gone for a couple of hours, and hopefully by then, Luke would know all the secrets of the universe.

Dallas took some plates out of the cupboard, and when he turned back to Slate and Luke, he said, "I have some news."

Slate exchanged a glance with Luke, and they looked at Dallas again together. "Jess is pregnant."

"That's great, brother," Slate said, but Dallas didn't even smile.

"You...don't seem happy about it," Luke said.

"I am," Dallas said, the smile finally appearing. "Honest, I am."

"Are you?" Slate asked, reaching for a plate.

"I have an eight and a twelve-year-old already," Dallas said. "Thomas just entered this sort of snarky phase, and he's started arguing with me about the weirdest things, at the weirdest times. Sometimes we can't even get out of the house, because he wants school lunch and not a home lunch."

Dallas sounded beyond frustrated, and Luke knew that had nothing to do with the pregnancy.

"So then, the lunch just sits there, and no one ever eats it, and we throw it away."

Luke wanted to say it was just a school lunch, but Slate said, "Bro, bring it to the ranch. I'll eat that lunch any day of the week." He added a chuckle to the statement, and that got Dallas to smile a little.

"Remmy's still sweet," Dallas said. "I just feel like I'm starting over." He picked up a couple of pieces of the supreme pizza and plunked them on his plate. "Which is good. Of course it's good. I love Jess, and she wants a baby, and we want a family that belongs to both of us." He went over to the table. "I'll feel different in the morning, I'm sure. It was just a rough day."

"We all have them," Luke said, taking three pieces of the white pizza Dallas had bought just for him. "For example, today, right at the beginning of the day, I told Hannah that if she wasn't dating Chuck, I'd ask her to dinner for tonight."

He turned his pizza around and took a big bite of the back corner, which meant he got a mouthful of mostly crust. Then he could chew for a while and not have to talk.

Slate choked on his pizza as he started laughing, and Dallas chortled too. Luke wanted them to tell him what to do about the whole Hannah situation, so he ate and waited.

"What did she say?" Dallas asked.

"Nothing," Luke said. "She didn't say anything." His shoulders slumped and he reached for a can of soda.

"I'm sorry," Slate said. "Maybe she was just shocked."

"Oh, she was shocked," Luke said. "I told her she'd have to decide if she'd say no if she wasn't dating Chuck." He scoffed. "Or something. I'm not even really sure what I said, to be honest. I know I walked away, and she didn't call me back. She barely spoke to me the rest of the day, and I haven't gotten a text, a call, nothing."

"Well," Dallas said. He took another bite of pizza and chewed it thoughtfully.

"Well what?" Slate asked. "I swear, when you do stuff like that, it drives me insane."

Dallas only grinned at him. "I know it does."

"Tell the man what to do," Slate said.

"Yeah," Luke said. "Tell me what to do."

"I'm not going to do that," Dallas said. "If it goes wrong, then I'm in trouble."

"You won't be in trouble," Luke said, the desperation starting to build behind his lungs. He'd felt like this in a few fights too, as he got knocked back against the ropes or buried in the corner. He'd put his head down and punch, jab, and basically flail his way back to the center of the ring.

He couldn't do that here, though he had gone on the offensive with Hannah today. "Oh, holy stars in heaven. I went on the offensive." He looked between Dallas and Slate.

Dallas lifted his pizza and pointed it at Luke, nodding. "That you did."

Luke groaned. "When will I learn?" In prison, he'd had to specifically coach himself to keep his cool. He'd gone off the rails the first night, and that was how he'd met Nathaniel Mulbury in the first place. Ted, Dallas, and Slate stood right behind him, and they'd rescued Luke from himself. Literally. It certainly looked like that wasn't going to stop anytime soon.

"Hey, going on the offensive with a woman isn't all bad," Slate said. "You didn't slug her."

Luke had stepped closer to her, though. She hadn't backed away from him either, and his heart thumped in his chest. He shook his head. "It doesn't matter. I laid it on the line. I can't take it back."

"Hey, I held Jill's hand pretty early on," Slate said with a smile. "We all lay it on the line at some point."

"You did?" Dallas asked, and Slate let the two of them talk about Dallas and Jess's wedding and how the romance between Slate and Jill had started very quickly, accelerated quickly, and they'd be married quickly too.

Only a four-month engagement, and then Luke would lose his best friend.

Lose wasn't the right word, but things changed when a man got married. Luke had seen it enough times to know.

"Just see how she is tomorrow," Slate said. "Don't worry too much. Hannah is a really smart woman, and smart people get wrapped up in their own thoughts sometimes."

"He's right," Dallas said. "Give her some time. Maybe she...I don't know. I have no idea how women think."

That got all three of them laughing, and that alone helped Luke feel better about his behavior from that morning. He still didn't have a solution for what to do about Hannah, but maybe he didn't need to come at the relationship swinging with everything he had.

Maybe he should just put his gloves up and wait for her to make the next move.

HANNAH DIDN'T MAKE A MOVE THE NEXT DAY, OR ANY day that week. Luke got up in the morning. He showered and shaved, though he'd started growing out his beard again. It seemed to grow better in Texas than Vegas, and Luke liked the more rugged look it gave him. He felt more like a cowboy. He just had to get past the itchy stage, and he was nearly there.

Spencer or Nick made breakfast every morning, and Luke wasn't going to say no to a hot breakfast. He always came back to the Annex for lunch, for the air conditioning, and to take a quick nap. On Friday, he'd actually eaten his sandwich in bed he was so tired.

He'd definitely forgotten how much energy and exertion it took to build something. He'd forgotten the strength of the sun beating down on him all the time and the wind whipping up from time to time.

All of that, combined with the constant tiptoeing around Hannah, and he definitely needed a lunchtime siesta at the end of the week.

That evening, he ignored his phone and stayed in his room. He didn't want to be pitied, and he certainly didn't want to see Hannah's boyfriend come and pick her up for a Friday night date. He couldn't think of anything worse, actually, and Luke found himself five days into his life back in Texas wondering if he'd made the right decision or not.

He wished someone would just tell him what to do with his life.

"You know what to do with your life," he said to himself as something played on the streaming service on his tablet. "This." He got up and paced in the bedroom. "This is where you're supposed to be. You know it. You can *feel* it."

Before prison, Luke hadn't paid much attention to his feelings. He couldn't even remember having feelings. There was the high of working out and the pain in his muscles. There was the discomfort of hunger and the buzz of the steroids. He'd experienced anxiety on the steroids, and anxiety when he stopped taking them too.

And oh, the anger. The anger Luke actually liked. He knew how to manage the anger. He knew how much he could take, and it was always another punch, another punch, another punch.

Every blow made him stronger, and angrier, and a stronger, angrier Luke won boxing matches. Winning boxing matches made money, and Luke needed the money to keep training and keep taking the drugs.

He ran his hands down his face and exhaled all the air out of his lungs. "You're supposed to be here," he repeated. He wanted to be here. He liked ranch work and construction, and he loved this ranch. He liked Ginger, and all of his friends were here.

So Hannah Otto didn't like him for boyfriend material. It wasn't the end of the world. Luke wasn't going to leave Texas over it, and he told himself he needed to stop wishing for something that wasn't going to come true.

"Stop wishing altogether," he told himself. "Get out there and *do* something if you want a different result." With that decision made, Luke lay back down in bed and let his mind wander as his sitcom played in front of him. At some point, he fell asleep with the TV on, exactly the way he liked ending the day.

Sunday morning, Luke got up with the sun and dressed in his workout clothes. A river ran along the front of the ranch, and he set out at an easy pace, the warbling of the water his companion. He never ran with headphones, because he didn't trust that someone wouldn't come up behind him and jump him.

Maybe he'd had that happen to him before, and old habits—and fear—were hard to shake. He felt like he could experience the run more if he didn't blast music in his ears, and today, he listened to the breeze, the brook, and the birds in the trees.

By the time he returned to the Annex, the gray sky had turned gold, and the heat of the day had already begun. He felt like today would be the perfect day to lie on the sand and waste time, something he'd always wanted to do in River Bay.

Since he'd been out, he'd only spent a few days at the beach, and he was going to fix that today.

He showered, put on his swimming trunks, and went into the shared bathroom to get a towel. He was rummaging around in the kitchen cabinet for some sunscreen when Connor came flying into the Annex. "Uncle Luke," he called, running right past where Luke stood in the kitchen. He chuckled as the boy's cowboy boots slapped the hard floor. "Uncle Luke?"

"I'm right here," he called and Connor came back into the kitchen. "You ran right by me, buddy."

"I didn't see you over there in the corner."

"You were flying," Luke said. "Like Flash."

Connor grinned and hugged Luke around the middle. "Wait. You have your swimming suit on."

"Yeah," Luke said, finally finding the can of sunscreen. He held it up. "I'm going to the beach today."

Confusion crossed Connor's face. "Dad says we have to go to church."

"Hm," Luke said. "I bet he does."

"I was comin' to see if you wanted to sit by me."

"At church?"

"Yeah."

Luke didn't think it had been Connor's idea to come over and ask Luke to sit by him at church. That had Nate and Ginger written all over it, and while he'd gone to services in prison from time to time—and he'd even gone the last time he was in Sweet Water Falls—he didn't consider himself a religious person.

"Why don't you go ask your dad if you can come to the beach with me?" Luke grinned at Connor, sure the boy wouldn't do that.

Indecision raged on his young face, and then he marched out the back door. The moment it closed, Luke wished he hadn't said anything. He didn't want to get Connor in trouble, and he could just imagine the stoic man's face when his son came in and asked to go to the beach with Luke instead of going to church with his family.

He didn't even have his phone so he could text Nate, and his own heart pounded a little harder in his chest. He found a paper grocery sack in a cupboard and put the sunscreen in it. He rolled up his towel and added it to the bag too. After rummaging through the fridge, he found enough to make sandwiches and have a few snacks for the day, and he'd just put them in the bag as the back door opened again.

This time, a pair of big boots accompanied the small boots, and Luke faced Nate and Connor. "You're goin' to the beach?" Nate asked.

"Yep," Luke said. "I really can take him."

Nate looked down at his son, his eyebrows drawn into a deep V. "Tell 'im."

Connor swallowed. "Could we go to the beach after church?"

Luke crouched down in front of the little boy. "Sure, buddy. You can come after church. I'll let you know where I am, and your daddy can bring you." Luke looked up and saw Nate shaking his head. He straightened, his own determination to stay out of the chapel as hard as the look in his friend's eyes.

"I can't bring him," Nate said. "Ginger."

Luke nodded. "Maybe Slate will come. I'll let him know."

"Okay, son," Nate said. "We'll work on finding someone

to take you to the beach, okay?" He put his hand on Connor's shoulder and turned him toward the back door. Connor said something, his face tipped up toward Nate's, but Luke couldn't hear what. They left, and Luke's guilt cut through him.

He could easily sit through a sermon and then go to the beach. He simply didn't want to. He picked up his brown bag of beach supplies and headed out the opposite door, wishing he'd timed his departure for the beach either earlier or later than everyone going to church.

Another wish that didn't come true, he thought. Then, *there's always next week.*

Luke knew what time people left for church now, and he could easily avoid the rush to get off the ranch.

CHAPTER EIGHT

Hannah kneaded the steering wheel, thinking she should be back in the kitchen at the West Wing, pounding her frustration into a nice, sugary dough. Cinnamon rolls. That was the sweet treat she needed to make it through another week with Luke so close it hurt.

At the same time, she knew what she needed to do if she wanted him to be so close it felt good.

She needed to break up with Chuck. He'd called last week and asked her out. Hannah had made up an excuse about not feeling well, about things being so hectic on the ranch, and about wanting to be on the ranch to hold Emma's new baby.

In reality, things were hectic on the ranch. She didn't feel well, because she knew she needed to break up with her boyfriend. And she had held baby Frannie for a good hour before she started to fuss and cry to the point that Hannah had to take her back to her mother.

That hour had been wonderful, with a snuggly, sleeping baby against her chest and Emma's twelve-year-old making mint brownies in the kitchen behind her. Missy loved to bake, and Hannah loved to eat what she baked, so they had a pretty amazing friendship.

So it was that Hannah had Connor, Missy, and Petunia —Emma's teacup piglet—in the back of her sedan, all of them on the way to the beach. She couldn't deny Missy, not when she'd be eating the most amazing brownies with the exact right amount of mint flavoring in the frosting for the next two weeks.

Her mouth watered just thinking about taking a pre-cut brownie from the freezer and having that first bite. She knew exactly how long to let it sit on the counter to warm up a little bit—eight minutes—and still get the frozen center and plenty of snappy, cool mint on her tongue.

"Almost there," she said, swallowing as she realized her mouth had started to water. "You guys have to keep an eye on Petunia if the tide is high. I don't want to be responsible for losing your mama's prize pig."

Missy giggled and shook her head. "Petunia can swim. She'll be fine."

"Can pigs swim?" Hannah asked.

"Of course they can," Missy said. "They're actually really good swimmers, Miss Hannah. We put Petunia in the pool every summer."

Hannah smiled at the girl. "Okay, but you're taking the blame if she drowns."

"All right," Missy said, looking at something Connor held up to show her.

Hannah did love the kids, and when it had come down to her to take them to the beach or they couldn't go, she hadn't had the heart to deny them. She'd told herself for the half-hour it had taken them to get ready to leave that she wouldn't stay. Luke was here, and he could easily fit two kids in his truck to bring them back to the ranch.

At the same time, she wore her swimming suit under her clothes, and who did that if they were simply dropping people off? She wasn't going to swim either, as it was barely March, and even though the sun shone brightly and the temperature on the dash read seventy-five, Hannah could pretend to be too cold.

She wasn't sure she wanted Luke to see her in her swimming suit either. She'd bought a new one at the end of last season, as that was the best time to get a good deal on something expensive. Right when it was about to stop being used.

The black suit didn't have a stitch of color on it—very slimming—and held up all the right pieces with thick straps that went over her shoulders and right up behind her neck. She liked that, as she had a bit of a hump on the top of her spine, and the last thing she needed was an open back on her swimming suit.

Her nerves hit her again as the kids giggled in the back

seat. She glanced in the rearview mirror, reminding herself that this trip was for them.

Yeah, right, she thought, going back to gripping the steering wheel as she drove the stretch of highway along the Gulf Coast. They arrived at the beach, and she said, "Everyone out," in the most cheerful voice she could muster. Nate had texted her where Luke would be, and she started scanning for him the moment she stood from the car.

She had the man's number, so having Nate relay all the information about which beach he'd gone to, and where he sat on it seemed so silly to her. She'd typed out at least a dozen messages to him over the past week, but she'd sent exactly zero.

She lifted her huge canvas beach bag from the trunk, having packed it to the brim with towels, snacks, water, her tablet, extra flip flops, sunscreen, and bug spray. So much for just dropping the kids at the beach and calling it her service for the day. Who had she honestly been kidding?

Connor bent over the trunk and came up with the sand toys, and Missy reached in for the floaties. "Got every-thing?" Hannah asked, still scanning the beach for any sign of Luke. There weren't too many people here, and he shouldn't be too hard to spot.

"Got everything," Missy said.

Hannah turned back to the car, hoping the children hadn't seen her frowning out over the beach, trying to find the tall, tan, talented, and utterly tantalizing Luke Holt. She closed the trunk and clicked the fob to lock the vehicle. "Let's find Luke."

"He's right there," Connor said, pointing.

Hannah followed his finger, and sure enough Luke walked toward them. He wore a bright blue pair of swimming trunks and a cowboy hat. Oh, and a smile as wide as the ocean. No shirt. No shoes. He was dressed down and casual. Relaxed and oh-so-handsome.

Her pulse went positively crazy, and she felt sure he'd see it beating in the vein in her neck.

"Howdy, friends," he said in an exaggerated accent. Connor ran toward him, and Luke lifted the boy up into the air, sand toys and all. "You made it." He glanced at Hannah. "How much did you have to pay Hannah to drive you?"

"They didn't pay me," she said as she and Missy approached at a more human pace.

"Oh, that's right," he said, the smile sliding right off his face. "You like giving people rides to places you don't want to go." With that, he set Connor down, took the boy's hand, and turned his back on her.

Hannah's chest squeezed as they walked away, and her eyelids fluttered in several fast blinks.

"What did he mean?" Missy asked. "You wanted to come to the beach, right, Hannah?"

"Of course, sweetie," Hannah said, but her voice pitched up too much. How dare he say such a thing in front of the kids? How was she supposed to react now?

"Okay, let's go," Missy said, making to follow the boys.

Hannah let her go too, seriously debating leaving. She could throw her bag in the front seat, text Luke that he was in charge of the kids, and just drive. She had snacks and water. Heck, she had enough food for three people for hours. She could drive and drive and drive, and she'd be fine.

Deep down, though, she knew she wasn't fine.

Missy turned back when her feet first touched the sand. "Are you coming?"

Hannah lifted her phone, an idea forming in her mind. "I just got a call. Here. Take the bag." She put the non-existent phone call to her ear, feeling a bit bad for lying to Missy. Sometimes adults had to lie, and she figured this fib wasn't hurting anyone.

She passed the heavy bag to Missy, who nearly crumpled under its weight. "Holy moly," she said. "What is in this thing?"

Hannah was used to people making fun of her for the weight of her purses and bags. Her older sisters had been doing it forever, and even Jill had said something a few times. Of course, Jill could literally reduce the contents of her purse to the size of a credit card. She lived by the motto that there was hardly anything she need besides her phone and her driver's license.

Hannah existed on the complete opposite end of the spectrum, and she never went anywhere without a bag full of supplies. The nail clippers she carried had come in useful many times, as she liked to remind Jill. So did the sanitizing wipes, the aspirin, the bandages, the Chapstick, and the half-pint bottle of water.

Once Missy had nearly reached the spot where Luke had spread his towel on the sand, Hannah hurried back to the car and got behind the wheel again. With the air conditioner running, she stared at her phone.

She navigated to Chuck's name. Their last few texts sat there, and they were her excuses for why she couldn't see him that weekend.

Her thumb hovered over the phone icon, and Hannah looked up and out the windshield. In slow motion, she could see her life playing in front of her, reflected in the glass. She'd attended enough therapy sessions to know she wasn't crazy, and that her ideal life would be projected out of her mind and into this fantasy on the hot glass.

She saw herself bringing her own children to the beach to meet their father. He'd been here for a couple of hours without them, because he simply needed a whole day of rest and relaxation before he could face another week.

Luke greeted her right where he had on the sidewalk, but instead of saying something cutting and sarcastic, he welcomed her with a kiss and a smile. He took both of their children's hands in his, saying, "Let's give Momma a minute to herself."

"I want Luke," she whispered. She looked down at her phone. "Now or never."

She tapped the button to connect the call.

CHAPTER NINE

L uke watched Connor hit the water and try to maintain his balance. He laughed as the boy toppled over, face-first, into the waves after only a few steps. The best part about this beach was that the waves didn't roar to shore, but sort of lapped at it like a lazy dog trying to get a drink.

Missy followed Connor with more caution, and she went out further before she lost her momentum in the waves. She stood taller and had longer legs, which made it easier for her.

Luke employed every ounce of willpower he had not to turn around and check for Hannah. Was she going to stay? Had she really just dropped the kids off without a word?

"You were mean," he muttered to himself, and Petunia looked up at him. "No," he said to her. "I didn't offer you any food."

How he'd come to be sitting on the beach, babysitting someone else's children, with a twenty-pound piglet on his lap, he couldn't fathom. A year ago, he'd been watching his back, wary of a new inmate, and counting down the days until he and Slate could leave River Bay in the rearview mirror.

He patted the pig, who put her cool snout right against Luke's chest. He looked down at her again. "Can I just apologize? Hannah will forgive me, right?"

Petunia gave a soft sound halfway between a snort and an oink, and Luke really wanted that to mean *yes* in teacup piglet language. He looked out to the brilliant gulf again, and let the warm wind wash over his bare skin.

"I have to apologize no matter what." He'd like to do it face-to-face, as he'd hurled the jab at her that way. It would mean more than a text, but the minutes passed, and Hannah didn't come sit by him.

He finally twisted around to see if he could catch a glimpse of her. Perhaps she'd needed to use the restroom or blow up a big floatie to spend the afternoon drifting in.

He couldn't see her, and annoyance flashed through him again. Nate had texted an hour ago to say, *Church just got out, and Connor invited Missy to the beach too. Hannah's going to bring them. That cool?*

That's cool, Luke had said. His pulse had spent the next sixty minutes in various stages of erratic, and he hadn't meant to be so hurtful to Hannah. The truth was, he was hurting, and when he felt like he currently did—like someone was trying to remove his stomach with a spiralizer —he shouldn't be around people.

He should've told Connor he was just looking for vitamins or something, and he'd thrown on his swimming trunks because he needed to do laundry.

Better text her, he thought, and since Luke had really been trying to act on the little thoughts he got throughout the day, he pulled out his phone and shifted Petunia in his lap. She snuffled at him louder now and even nudged the bag of potato chips.

"Can pigs eat potato chips?" he asked her, and she wore such a look of hope in her eyes that he decided she could. He pulled out a chip and fed her the sour cream and cheddar snack. Then he focused his eyes on his phone and quickly typed a text to Hannah.

I'm sorry for saying what I did. Thank you for bringing the kids to the beach, and I really appreciated the ride to the airport last year too.

Regret lanced through him, and he quickly pressed the *send* button before he could go on and on about his faults. He could beat himself up silently until she answered.

Every few seconds, he checked his phone. No text. Nothing. Not even a like or smiley face. In fact, the text only said delivered, not read.

She probably had both hands firmly on the wheel as she drove back to Hope Eternal. Luke hoped with everything he had that she'd see his text and respond. He even started to pray for such a thing.

He checked his phone a few more times before tossing it in the brown paper bag that held everything else he'd brought to the beach. He kept one eye on the kids, because the last thing he needed was to tell Nate and Ted that some harm had come to Connor or Missy because he'd fallen asleep on the job.

He watched the gulls flying above the gulf, and he wished he could be a bird. Simply spread his wings and fly away, taking in the grand picture below him and seeing the whole future in front of him.

A sigh came out of his mouth right as someone asked, "Is this spot taken?"

He looked up to find Hannah standing there, a beach chair looped over her forearm. She wore a cute little tank top that showed off her shoulders, a pair of shorts that barely reached mid-thigh, and a floppy beach hat the color of her lips—bright pink.

Luke jumped to his feet, keeping Petunia tucked in his arms like a football. "I'm so sorry," he blurted out. "That was just mean, and I didn't mean it, and I'm so glad you stayed." He gestured up toward the sidewalk where he'd met her and the kids. Unfortunately, Petunia was still in his arms, and she squeaked and oinked as he waved her around.

"Give that pig to me before you drop her," Hannah said, and they switched items. She cuddled Petunia right against her chest, stroking the animal like it was a fluffy bunny and not a stubbly, hairy pig. "Will you sett up my chair for me, please?"

"Yes." Luke looked at the chair and unfolded it, setting in the sand very near his towel. He kept his eyes down as he made sure the seat locked into place, and he added, "I really am sorry, Hannah. It's been a rough week for me, but that's no excuse for saying what I did." He met her eye, though it was hard to see behind the lenses of her sunglasses. "Did you get my text?"

"As I walked down here, I read it," she said. She lifted her chin slightly. "Apology accepted."

Relief rushed through Luke, and he grinned at her. "Thank you." He indicated she should sit first, which she did. He took up his spot on his towel next to her, stretching his long legs out in front of him. "You didn't have to stay," he said. "I'm okay with the kids."

"If I stay at the ranch, I'll work," she said. "I don't want to work today."

Luke nodded. "It's hard to get away from sometimes. My dad is like that."

They settled into the sound of the waves, the wind, and Petunia's little snuffles. Luke searched his mind for something to say and came up blank. Talking to Hannah had been so easy in the past, and he hated that it felt a little bit hard today.

"Do you like to swim?" he asked, glancing over at her.

She took the opportunity to hand him the piglet. "Can you hold her for a second?"

"Sure."

Hannah rewarded him with a smile, and he barely had

Petunia securely in his arms before she reached down to her waist and started to peel up her tank top. Luke stared, his mouth turning drier and drier with every inch of her swimming suit that got revealed.

In the end, Hannah shook out her hair and draped her shirt over the massive bag Missy had carried down to their spot. "I'm not a huge swimmer," she said. "I do want to soak up the sun though." She scooted forward in her chair and leaned back, sighing as she tipped her head heavenward. "Ah."

Luke had no idea what to say. Her swimming suit barely revealed more than the tank top had, but somehow it felt more intimate. He wasn't even wearing a shirt, and the sun suddenly felt ten times as close to his skin as it had a moment ago.

He finally tore his gaze from her and found Connor and Missy still floating in the water a bit to his left now, the waves pushing them from their original position.

"Would you tell me a story?" Hannah asked.

"What kind of story?" Luke asked.

"Well, if we're going to go to dinner tonight, I have a specific one in mind."

Luke whipped his attention back to her. She wasn't looking at him, though her voice had carried a certain coyness he hadn't missed. "Dinner?"

She turned her head toward him and reached up to adjust her hat. "I broke up with Chuck," she said. She looked like a fashion model with those big glasses, the straight, dark hair, and the pretty pink lips.

He licked his, thinking about kissing her already. "When?" he asked.

She indicated to the world behind her. "Just now." She drew in a breath, and her nerves hit him across the couple of feet between him. "I saw you, and I...I don't know, Luke." She looked away from him, but he couldn't tear his eyes from her.

His muscles tensed, and he needed her to continue.

"I feel something with you that I haven't felt with anyone else before." She lifted her closest shoulder in a sexy mini-shrug. "I want to know what it is. I want to grab onto it and explore it. I want to *see* it, and feel it, and taste it."

Her eyes met his again, and Luke could feel the exact same thing coursing through him. He swallowed, not quite sure if he should say he felt that way too.

"So." She drew in a big breath and pushed it out. "That's my story for you. I'm hoping you'll be comfortable enough with me to tell me what happened that...why you went to prison."

Luke's defenses and barriers flew into place. He pulled his gaze from hers, icy fingers spreading through his body to his blood vessels and veins. Of course she'd want to know that. People were always curious about how and why someone went to jail.

Just tell her the truth.

The thought came to his mind unbidden, and Luke

seized onto it. "You might not like the story." His voice came out ragged, and he cleared the emotion from his throat. "What if you don't like it?"

She reached over and touched his forearm. Lightning struck him with the prick of her fingernails, and he sucked in a breath. His eyes moved to the point of contact as his chest and stomach vibrated.

"Yeah," she said. "Feels like something, right?"

"Definitely," he murmured.

"If I don't like it, Luke, I'll work through it," she said. "Just like you've had to."

He looked at her again, really looking past the lenses and past the pretty face and past anything on the exterior. "You're incredible," he said.

A smile curved that mouth, and that only made him want to kiss her more. "Start talking, cowboy." She reached up and tapped the brim of his hat, then leaned back in her chair and let her hand fall back toward his.

He threaded his fingers through hers, marveling that he felt so comfortable and so charged with her touch. He hadn't had a girlfriend for a long, long time. He wasn't even sure he'd ever had a woman he'd classify as his girlfriend, and he suddenly felt very out of his league.

Hannah dated a lot, and she probably had a very strict set of things she liked about a man.

"Okay," he said as she breathed in, indicating she'd say something. "Before I went to prison, I was a boxer."

"Really?"

Luke glanced at her, finding her eyebrows up. "Really. You think men work out for muscles like these for no reason?" He shook his head. "No. I needed them in the ring." He looked back at the water, hoping the tranquility of it would carry him through this story. "I *loved* boxing."

"You don't do it anymore?"

"No." He shook his head, thinking of the gym in Las Vegas. "My dad owned a gym in Beeville. I worked out there. I had a private, personal trainer and a manager. I was good. I won a lot." He cleared his throat, the images in his mind seemingly belonging to someone else. How had their memories been implanted in his head?

They fuzzed around the edges, and Luke let them take their time leaving. "I worked out hard, but it's not enough. Everyone takes steroids. So." He cleared his throat again. "I did too. They really took me to a new level, and I won even more."

Hannah said nothing, and Luke didn't know what he wanted her to say. He stroked Petunia and kept going. "One night, I won a tournament in a knock-out. That means I hit the other guy so hard, he couldn't get up and continue the fight. It was the pinnacle fight of my career so far, and my manager was talking about going pro, moving on to bigger and better circuits, with more prize money, all of it."

He stared out at the sky now, unseeing. "Then, I got hit with the manslaughter lawsuit. My opponent died." His throat clogged, but he kept going. "His family filed a lawsuit against me, claiming I was in the wrong weight class because

I'd lied about my weight. They said I could've and should've stopped hitting him before he couldn't get up again. They claimed I wasn't even present at the end of the fight, but was swinging to kill in a steroid-induced rage."

By the time he stopped speaking, Luke's voice came out in a whisper.

"Wow," Hannah said, her hand tightening in his. "You got convicted of murder?"

"No," he said quickly. "No, nothing like that. The judge wouldn't even accept manslaughter. Their lawyers dropped it to involuntary manslaughter—which means, yes, I killed the guy, but unintentionally—and I was convicted of that. It means I acted recklessly, and because of my actions, someone died."

"I see."

"It's a federal felony, which was why I was in River Bay. But I got low security because of the involuntary part. I got a forty-month sentence, and I had to submit to drug tests every day for the first year."

With the story out, Luke felt a weight lift right off his chest. Off his shoulders, out of his mind. He hadn't even known he'd been carrying such a heavy item for so long.

"It was a hard time for me," he said. "It still is, sometimes."

"Why's that?"

"I don't think I did anything wrong," he said. "People get hurt in boxing all the time. Men and women suffer from brain damage, broken bones, the whole gamut of injuries. *They're* not going to federal prison for over three years."

A sense of injustice and indignation started to fill him. "I can't get that time back. I don't have a career anymore. I feel...I don't know." He didn't want to say what he really felt, because it sounded pathetic to say *he* was the one who felt cheated of something.

Another man had *lost his life.*

Luke still had his. He could still walk around, breathe, eat, celebrate birthdays with his friends and family.

He clenched his mouth shut, not about to tell her how he really felt. He'd work through it, just like she'd said.

"I'm sorry," she said quietly. "Life isn't perfect, and humans aren't perfect."

"That's the truth," he said.

"We do the best we can. Most of us, at least."

Luke nodded, craving the carefree feeling he'd had a few minutes ago. As the seconds ticked by, the tension bled out of his body. Eventually, he felt more like himself, and he asked, "Where do you want to go to dinner?"

"You have to plan that, Mister," she teased.

"Give me a hint," he said with a smile. "I know you eat out a lot, and you have favorite places." He looked at her, finding a beautiful smile on her face. "I haven't been in town long enough to scope out anything good."

"Okay," she said. "I'll choose the first time." She met his eye, and Luke sure did like Hannah Otto. He also knew now that she expected him to have a plan for their dates, and his stomach lurched. Luke rarely had a plan for anything.

"Dutch Baby is amazing," she said. "They serve breakfast all day, and they have this hash that—mm mm. It'll change everything you've ever thought about potatoes."

Luke laughed, because Hannah did love off-the-wall restaurants with unique food. "I've heard that before," he said dryly.

"Tell me you didn't like that breakfast roll at Madam Croque," she challenged.

He laughed again. "I liked it fine."

"Mm hm," she said knowingly.

"I mean, *life-changing* is a little bit of a stretch," he teased. "As is saying one dish is going to change how someone thinks about potatoes. That's all I'm saying."

"I hear what you're saying, Mister Holt. You're just wrong." She giggled, and Luke liked this easier conversation. She was really good at flirting, and Luke fell into the rhythm of it naturally too.

As his chuckle faded, he glanced out into the water and didn't see the kids. "Do you see Connor or Missy?" He released her hand and got to his feet, shading his eyes with one hand and setting Petunia on the sand with the other.

Just then, a scream filled the air, and Luke jerked toward it. Missy ran toward him, and he took off at a sprint toward her. "Where's Connor?" he demanded.

She sobbed and pointed toward the water. "He went under," she said in halting words.

Horror gripped Luke's throat and squeezed. He couldn't see Connor or even where he might have been. Just waves and waves and waves.

"Luke," Hannah called behind him.

"Stay with Missy," he said over his shoulder. "Call an ambulance." He bent down and took Missy by the shoulders. "Missy," he said calmly—freaky calm. "Where? Can you show me where?"

She quieted and turned toward the gulf. "Straight up from where I ran. We were there, and then he just went under."

Straight out.

Hannah arrived, and Luke passed Missy to her. He met her eyes for one moment in time, noted she had her phone to her ear, and took off at a sprint for the water.

CHAPTER TEN

"I don't know," Hannah said for the fifth time. "She said he went under. We don't know where he is, but he's been under for a few minutes. We need some medical help."

"Okay," the emergency operator said in a firm, gliding voice. "I have an ambulance and two police units on the way."

Hannah kept Missy right against her side, the sniffling girl shaking her. She stared at the water where Luke had splashed out while the operator asked her a question. The words made no sense inside her head.

"Hannah?"

Her name entered her ears and she blinked. "Yes," she said. "I'm here."

"What's your son's name?"

"Connor," she said even though he wasn't her son. She

couldn't imagine going back to the ranch and telling Ginger and Nate that something bad had happened to Connor. She couldn't get her feet to move, and she couldn't think past the next two seconds.

She blinked. She breathed. That was all.

She'd really be terrible in a crisis, and she watched as Luke broke the surface of the water, took a mighty breath, and went straight back down again.

A crowd had started to form near and behind her, and she hated the buzz of whispers. Luke just had to get Connor and get him back up. Right now. He'd been under too long as it was, though Luke had noticed almost immediately that he'd disappeared.

Still, a minute was too long for an eight-year-old.

Tears ran down her face, and an older gentleman put his arm around her. "I'll pray with you," he said in a kind voice, and Hannah nodded.

He began to voice the prayer, and Hannah pressed her eyes closed and just thought, *Please*, over and over and over.

A roar went up from the crowd, and she yanked her eyes open again. It took her a moment to realize Luke had emerged from the depths of the water—and that he had Connor in his arms.

"Thank heaven," she whispered as she rushed forward. Several others did too, and one man laid a towel on the sand right where the water met the earth.

Luke stumbled the last few steps, his chest heaving as he sucked at the air. Two people surged forward and caught

Connor as Luke went to his knees, and they laid him on the towel. His eyes were closed, and everything about him looked...dead.

Hannah sucked back a sob, and she kept Missy pressed into her side.

"Back up," someone said, holding his hands out to move people back.

"I'm going to do CPR," a woman said, looking at Luke.

He nodded, still trying to catch his breath in the soft surf washing ashore. Hannah passed Missy to the older gentleman with, "Will you please stay with her?"

He nodded, and Hannah stepped around the people in the front and through the water to Luke. She put her hand on his shoulder and said, "You got him. He's going to be okay."

Luke said nothing, and they both kept their eyes trained on Connor. The sound of a siren in the distance met her ears, and Hannah wondered what she'd done with her phone. Fear like she'd never known filled her as the woman placed one hand on Connor's chest and pumped a couple of times. She counted out loud, her voice sinking into Hannah's eardrums, where it would stay forever.

Nate should be here, she thought. She couldn't imagine how he'd deal with this. Losing his brother and his son? Tears filled her eyes again.

The woman leaned over Connor and covered his mouth and nose with her mouth. His chest rose as she breathed for him, and she jerked back in the next moment as Connor started to sputter.

"Dear Lord," Hannah said. "Thank you." She rushed toward the boy, because he needed a familiar face to be the first thing he saw.

The woman turned Connor onto his side as he expelled the water in his lungs and stomach. He coughed and started to cry, and Hannah gathered him right into her lap. Luke joined her, stroking Connor's hair and whispering, "You're okay, buddy. It's okay."

The paramedics arrived, and Hannah passed Connor to Luke. "You do not leave his side, okay?"

He nodded, and all the life that had turned numb suddenly roared back to full color. "I'll talk to everyone." She stood and took the woman who'd performed CPR for Connor into a tight hug. "Thank you so much." She wept as she looked at the woman. "Tell me who you are, so I can tell his parents."

"You're not his mom?"

She shook her head. "They'll want to thank you."

The woman visibly shook, tears gathering in her own eyes. "I don't need it."

"Still."

"She's my wife," a man said, the same one who'd backed everyone up. "She teaches babysitting classes, including CPR."

"I've never had to do it on a live child," the woman said,

her voice fragile and brittle. She stepped into her husband's arms, and his jaw jumped as he clenched it.

"Her name is Tamara Weeks. I'm Gill."

"Thank you so much." Hannah hugged them both again, then stepped around a couple of people who hadn't left yet.

She opened her arms to Missy, who ran to her and clutched her tightly. She'd gotten so tall this year, and Hannah marveled at her strength and quick thinking. She stroked her hair and whispered, "You were so smart to scream like that. You acted so fast. You saved him."

Missy sobbed into her, and Hannah looked up to the older gentleman. "Thank you for your prayer and your help."

He only nodded, his eyes quickly going back to Connor. "He'll be okay?"

"The paramedics are here," she said. "I think he'll be okay."

Two men walked down the beach, catching Hannah's attention. She gently unwrapped Missy's arms from around her and said, "Time to be brave, munchkin. Let's go talk to the paramedics."

She met them when they were still several yards from Luke and Connor. "He went under in the tide," she said. "We're not sure how long he was under. Luke got him up, and Tamara Weeks performed CPR. He spit up a bunch of water, and he was crying."

"All good signs," one man said. "You're?"

"Hannah Otto," she said. "My friend and I brought the kids to the beach for their parents."

The paramedics reached Luke and Connor, and they started examining him. Listening to his heartbeat. Asking him questions. Taking his temperature.

Hannah's stomach rumbled, as she'd brought a lot of food and hadn't eaten any of it yet. Missy quieted at her side, and Hannah started looking for her phone. Someone signaled to her, and held up her device, and she went to retrieve it.

"Thank you."

The man smiled at her. "I knew you didn't even know you'd dropped it."

"I didn't."

He handed it over, and Hannah returned to Missy. She typed in the names of the people who'd helped, as well as everything else that had happened. She wanted to be able to remember the kindness of strangers, and Nate and Ginger would want every detail they could get.

Eventually the paramedics said they could take Connor to the hospital or not, and Hannah met Luke's eyes.

"I don't think he needs to go in an ambulance," Hannah said. "Let's call Nate and Ginger and see what they want us to do."

He nodded, and they shook hands with the paramedics and cops who'd come to the beach. The commotion died down, and with it, Hannah's adrenaline.

"Can I call?" Luke asked, extending his hand toward her, indicating he wanted her phone.

"Yes." She had no idea what she'd say to Ginger. Luke had Connor in his arms, the boy's legs wrapped around his torso and his head resting on his shoulder. He could still hold a phone to his ear, but Hannah dialed for him and handed him the device.

"Nate?" he asked.

She nodded, and an entirely new face slipped over Luke's features. His game face.

"Nate," he said a few seconds later. "We had an accident at the beach, and we're wondering if you'd like us to bring Connor home or meet us at the hospital."

Hannah turned away from Luke as he continued to explain what had happened. She couldn't imagine getting a call like that. How would she react? Would she go numb the way she had waiting for Luke to resurface?

She also had no idea what type of physical force it took to punch someone so hard they died. She pressed her eyes closed and felt the swaying of the Earth as it spun through space. How did someone do that? Had he felt bad about it at all?

For a minute there, Luke had sounded like he still thought he hadn't done anything wrong. Hannah wasn't sure, because he hadn't finished his explanation of how he felt. She'd kept her hand in his, but it had been harder than she'd anticipated. He'd killed another human being with those hands.

She definitely had to work through some things when it came to Luke, and she reminded herself that he wasn't the same person now as he'd been then. She had experience with the men who came from River Bay, and almost all of them that she'd interacted with had been repentant, changed, and sorrowful about their behavior.

Nate, Ted, Dallas, and Slate had gone on to face their own problems and rebuild their lives one square at a time. Luke was doing the same thing.

She drew in a breath as the warm sun painted gold on the backs of her eyelids. So much had changed today, and Hannah felt so insignificant. At the same time, she felt perfectly sure that God had been aware of what was happening on the beach. He'd sent the older gentleman to her.

He'd sent her to Missy.

He'd sent Luke to Connor. Then Tamara and Gill Weeks. He'd definitely been aware of the situation, and Hannah believed with her whole mind, body, and spirit that Connor would be one hundred percent fine.

"Okay," Luke said. "Yes, we're going now. We'll meet you there."

She turned back to him, already knowing their day was about to get longer. "The hospital?" she asked anyway.

He nodded and handed her phone back. "I hear hospital food is pretty decent these days." He tossed her a small smile that didn't contain nearly any wattage. "Gotta be better than what I had in prison, right?"

Hannah smiled too, glad he wasn't going to beat himself up over the incident. At the same time, she suspected he would—in private. He'd paint over everything with that mask until he was alone, and then he'd crack and break.

It was what she would likely do too, and she sent up another prayer that she could find a way to be present when Luke needed a soft place to fall.

CHAPTER ELEVEN

L uke gripped Nate in a hug the moment he walked through the door. He'd already told Connor his dad was here, as he'd been stationed by the window for the past ten minutes. He found it incredible that he and Hannah had arrived at the hospital before Ginger and Nate, but apparently, Ginger had been asleep.

"He's okay," Luke whispered, working hard to keep the lump from overtaking his whole soul. "The nurse said he's fine and can go home any time."

Nate pulled away and took Luke's face in both of his hands. His skin felt rough and calloused, and he wore fire in his gaze. "This is not your fault."

Luke closed his eyes. "I was watching him." He opened them and looked at Nate, pleading with him to understand.

"I know you were." Nate flashed him a small smile. "Of course you were. That's how you got to him so fast. It's how you knew he was gone in a second. It's how you got him out of that current before he was too far out."

Luke nodded, encouraged by Nate's faith in him.

Nate dropped his hands and stepped around Luke. He turned and watched as Nate approached the hospital bed where Connor lay. Nate climbed right into bed with him, curling his big, tall frame around the small boy. He said something to him, and Connor looked up at him with pure hope in his eyes.

Ginger entered the room and paused, looking from the bed to Luke and back. She nodded to Luke and said, "Thank you for rescuing him, Luke," going straight over to Connor and Nate. They both looked at her with pure love shining from their faces, and Ginger leaned down and hugged Connor tightly.

Luke enjoyed witnessing the love they shared as a family, and he wanted something just like it for himself. He didn't know what that looked like exactly, but Hannah came through the door next, and he found someone to hang onto.

He extended his hand toward her, keeping his arm low, and she stepped right to his side and secured her fingers in his. "How is he?"

"Good," Luke said. "He's going to be just fine."

"Are they going to do the CT scan?"

"The nurse hasn't come in yet." Luke squeezed her hand slightly. "I didn't have the guts to tell Nate that was an option."

"He spoke to the nurse's desk when he got here," she

said. "Ginger stopped there for several minutes too. I saw them when I left to take Missy down to Ted and Emma. And I stopped on the way back to get the cookies." She held up her other hand. "Which are right here, by the way."

Luke managed a smile and looked over to the bed as Nate got up. "You guys can go," he said. "Honestly. We're going to stay and have Connor do a CT scan, and you don't have to be here."

Luke didn't mind staying, but he knew he wanted to simply to punish himself. If he was uncomfortable, that was good. He deserved to feel that way. He'd felt that way in prison too, and the inmate counselor had helped him work through those confusing thoughts.

"Okay," Hannah said. "I think we'll go grab something to eat. Do you guys want us to bring you something?"

"I'd love a fish sandwich from Oscar's," Ginger said from across the small room. "I've been craving the vinegar and salt for days."

Luke could finally smile. "Okay," he said. "We can do that." It wasn't where they'd planned to go, but it didn't matter. He would do anything to make sure Ginger and Nate were happy with him and could trust him.

"No one but my beautiful wife likes Oscar's," Nate said as he rounded the bed and stood behind her. "Connor and I want those bacon and cheese fries from Western Grub."

Luke looked at Hannah, his eyebrows up.

She finally realized he was waiting for her to give her

opinion. "I agree with Nate," she said. "Sorry, Ginger. Oscar's is *not* good."

"It is too," Ginger said. "They're still in business."

"You must be eatin' more fish sandwiches than I know about, then," Nate teased. He chuckled and leaned down to kiss her forehead.

"Bacon and cheese fries," Luke repeated. "Fish sandwich at Oscar's. We'll be back in a little bit."

"Take your time," Ginger said. "They said it would be a while until they could get him in for the scan."

Guilt sliced through Luke's gut again, and he couldn't believe he was going to leave his friends here while he went on a date.

Foolishness and shame moved through him, and he only left the room because Hannah led the way. His phone chimed when they reached the elevator, and he pulled it from his swimming trunks. Everything felt crusted with salt, and he needed a hot shower.

The elevator car dinged, and Luke used it as a distraction from reading Slate's text. In his attempt to slide the phone in his pocket, he dropped his phone. It slid across the floor with a sharp crack, and Luke groaned.

Hannah bent to pick it up, and she dusted it off on her tank top. She glanced at it as she extended it back toward him, stalling before her arm had fully straightened. "This text has my name in it."

"I'm sure it does," Luke said coolly. "Did you or did you not hold my hand in front of Ginger and Nate?" He cocked one eyebrow at her, hoping she'd pick up on his flirtatious tone.

Hannah blinked rapidly, her eyes widening a little with each movement. "I think you asked me to hold your hand."

"That I did." He slowly reached out and took his phone from her, and without looking at it, slid it in his pocket. He used that same hand to take hers in his again. "Oh, look at that. *I* held *your* hand this time." He slid her a grin and found her shaking her head with a giggle slipping from her mouth.

When they reached the lobby, Luke asked, "Do you think we're doing the right thing?"

"Going to dinner in our swimwear? It's not my first choice for a first-date outfit, I'll admit."

Luke chuckled, but he appreciated her attempt at light-heartedness. "But seriously."

"I think...I think we should go. They don't want us hovering around. Nate doesn't want you to feel bad. What happened was an accident. It wasn't your fault."

"I know that in my head," he said. "My gut keeps flipping over in a strange way, and then my mind starts conjuring up some strange scenarios that *could've* happened."

"I'm sure that's true," she said. "We've all gone over and over things that might have been."

Luke frowned, but he turned his face away from her so she couldn't see. They reached his truck, and he helped her up and in. He'd have to drive her back to her car in the parking lot at the beach, as they'd all piled into his truck to bring Connor to the hospital.

He got behind the wheel and sighed. "Maybe we should just go back to the ranch and fill everyone in. Take a shower. Eat something out of the fridge."

"If you'd like," Emma said, her tone pitching up a little.

Luke hadn't had a super serious girlfriend in the past, but he knew enough about women to know she wanted to go to dinner. What he wanted—well, Luke didn't know what he wanted.

He adjusted the air conditioning so it would blow cooler air, and he took his phone out. "Let's see what Slate said."

"Thank goodness," Hannah said. "I've been formulating a plan for how I could get that phone out of your pocket without a fight." She grinned at him, and Luke looked up from the text to meet her eyes.

"What were you thinking?"

"Oh, I was going to use my impressive hips to pin you against the wall at Grub and then use a one-handed approach to pin your arms above your head while I snatched the phone from your pocket." She burst out laughing, and Luke did too.

It felt good to laugh. Really good. The laughter cleansed his soul, and he let his voice out of the cage he sometimes kept it in.

"One-handed approach," he said. "I'd *really* like to see you try that."

"Please," she said, still giggling. "I can't even get my fingers around one of your wrists, let alone both of them."

"Come on," he said, looking at his phone again. "My muscles are up in my biceps and shoulders. No one has muscular wrists."

"Mm, you keep telling yourself that."

Luke switched his gaze to his wrists. They looked normal to him. He could see the bones and everything. "Well, now I'm all self-conscious about my overweight wrists."

Hannah pealed out another round of laughter, and a measure of powerful satisfaction filled Luke. He really liked making this woman laugh.

"Okay, so Slate said, Is it true that you're seeing Hannah now?"

"How would he know that?" Hannah asked.

Luke's thumbs flew across the screen, but a picture popped up. "Oh, he sent a picture. I just got it. Must have some bad reception in the hospital." He peered at it, trying to make out—"Oh." He started laughing and handed his phone to Hannah.

She took it, curiosity burning through her dark eyes. "You're laughing. That's a good sign." She looked down, and Luke saw the moment she understood what she was looking at.

"Nate took a picture of us." She looked up and out the windshield. Her chest rose and then fell. "Well, it's not like we need to keep it a secret." She handed the phone back to him. "Now, I brought all this food to the beach, because I was going to soothe myself with snacks for hours, and I've yet to eat anything. Let's get this show on the road, cowboy."

Luke put the truck in reverse. "Your wish is my command," he said, and he navigated to the parking lot exit. He paused, looking left and right. "I have no idea where... whatever that place Nate said is. Left or right?"

"You're going to need to learn your way around town again," she said.

"From Beeville, we used to go up to Vicksburg for groceries and stuff."

"Really? It's closer?"

"It was a thirty-minute drive instead of forty-five. Trust me, when I was fifteen, that was a big deal."

"I don't mind driving around the winding Texas roads," she said. "I find it kind of soothing."

"Is that right?" He waved left and right. "Which way?"

"Left," she said, and Luke flipped on his signal. "Once, when I was thirteen or fourteen, my sister had a miscarriage."

Luke swung his attention back to Hannah, and she gave him a warm smile. "I'm a caboose baby. My next oldest sister is eleven years older than I am. She was married and had a two-year-old already." She paused, almost like she was sifting through the memories for the rest of the story.

"How many sisters do you have?" he asked.

"Two," she said. "Bethany is forty-six, and Ruth is forty-eight. I have three nieces and one nephew. Eleven, twelve, thirteen, and fifteen."

"Wow," Luke said.

"You?"

"One brother and one sister. I'm right in the middle. Brynn is the oldest, and she's married but doesn't have kids. Joey's the youngest, and he works with my uncle in Beeville and the surrounding area." He shifted in his seat, wishing he knew where he was going. "Remember I said we had some property up there?"

"Resorts, I think you said," Hannah said.

"Right. Resorts." Luke scanned the street on both sides, trying to remember the name of the place Nate had mentioned. "What's the name of this place where we're going?"

"Western Grub," Hannah said. "Take a left at the light up there."

"A left." He put his blinker on to change lanes. "Keep going with your story."

"My sister was really upset, naturally," Hannah said. "I remember my mama telling her she already had a child, and that she'd have other chances to get pregnant." Hannah emitted a nearly-silent scoff and Luke caught her shaking her head. "I just remember Ruth being so angry. The only time I've ever heard her yell back at my mother. She stormed out of the house, and her last words were, you have no idea what I did."

Hannah fell silent again, but Luke didn't prompt her

again. He made the turn, and the sign for Western Grub appeared up ahead, also on his left.

"My mother tried and tried to get Ruth to explain, and she never would. A month or two later, when I went over there to watch her daughter, she told me she needed me to come over after school on Wednesdays, because she was going to start attending therapy. I was young, and honestly really scared, and I asked her why she needed to go to therapy. She said she couldn't stop thinking about all the things she'd done when she didn't know she was pregnant. Everything from eating a lot of fish one weekend to continuing her jogging schedule. She was *certain* she'd done something to jeopardize the viability of her pregnancy."

Luke could see where Hannah was headed with the story. He eased into the turn lane as she said, "She had to go see a counselor to move past the what-if stage. What if she'd done that? What if she *hadn't* done this other thing? Why hadn't she known? It was very hard for her, but she got some help, and she healed. Within six months, she was pregnant again, and you know. Happily-ever-after."

Luke made the turn and pulled into a parking space. "Do you think everyone gets their happily-ever-after?" Luke asked, putting the truck in park but leaving the engine running.

Hannah's gaze landed on him, but he resisted the urge to look at her. "You know what, Mister Holt? I do. I believe in the happily-ever-after."

He swung his attention toward her, giving her the same goofy smile she had on her face. "For everyone?"

"I think for everyone who wants one, who looks for it, and who works to keep it once they have it."

Luke nodded a few times, suddenly so tired. He'd swallowed at least a gallon of seawater while trying to get to Connor, and when he closed his eyes, all he could see was dark, gray-blue water everywhere. He was surrounded by it, the same way he'd been encircled by the red-hot rage during his last fight. He hadn't been able to stop then, because if he just kept hitting, hitting, hitting, he'd be able to work the fury out of his body.

Today had been so similar. The color surrounding him had been different, but the drive to get to Connor had been the same. He'd seen him there, his eyes wide and his mouth open, his hand reaching toward Luke. The fear on his face had struck Luke full in the chest, and it still hadn't left him completely.

Connor hadn't been able to get out of the clutches of the current, though, and the next time Luke had gone under, Connor's eyes had been closed.

He shook his head to get the horrible image out. It didn't go far, but with a breath, Luke managed to get out of the truck. Hannah met him at the hood, and she reached up and ran her hand down the side of his face. Her eyes searched his, and softness entered her whole expression.

"You're a good man, Luke Holt. I can see it inside you."

"You think so?" he whispered, his pulse suddenly

pouncing through his body. Only his mother had assured him that he was still a good person after everything that had happened and everything he'd done.

"Mm hm." She dropped her eyes to his mouth, but they quickly rebounded. "My sister went over and over what might have been. I've dated pretty constantly for the past five years to find the right man for me. I keep thinking, maybe I'm doing something wrong." She dropped her hand and stepped back. "Maybe I won't get my happily-ever-after. Sometimes I lie awake at night and go over what went wrong with this man or that one. What could I have done different? It's impossible to know, and all it does is drive a person mad."

Luke understood her point, and he took her hand in his and lifted it to his lips. "Thank you, angel."

"Angel?"

"You know, I'm not super religious, but you feel like, I don't know." He ducked his head, a smile moving through his soul. "I feel like you're really good for me." He lifted his eyes to judge her reaction.

Hannah grinned at him and said, "All right. You can call me angel."

CHAPTER TWELVE

H annah lifted her head from the form she'd been filling out. Part of her ranch responsibilities included going over the budget at the end of every month, and while Emma ran paychecks, Hannah had to authorize the funds to be released.

She had to balance the expenses for the maintenance supplies they ordered every month, something Dallas did almost all the time for her. She had to calculate the amount spent on feed, supplies, human resources, everything.

She loved numbers, because they didn't lie. They told the truth, and they lined up. She could understand them, and she enjoyed balancing the books every month. The ranch was thriving right now, and they had some concerning accounts, but that was due to the construction and expansion of their horseback riding program.

The air conditioning blew softly across the back of her

neck, causing a shiver to slide down her spine. The weather had definitely warmed in the past month, and her body temperature went wild whenever Luke Holt got close to her.

They'd been out several times in the past few weeks. He held her hand, and they'd taken some time to get to know each other. He hadn't scheduled formal appointments with a counselor, but she suspected he talked to his friends about how he felt. They met in the equipment shed at six-thirty every morning to lift weights, something Luke claimed he enjoyed doing even when he wasn't going to step inside the boxing ring.

He seemed better and better every day, and Hannah was glad he had friends he could rely on. She wrote down the number on the next receipt and looked up when she heard a cry from the office next door.

She rose to her feet, her chair scraping on the tile floor. "Ginger?" she asked. Ursula started barking, and the German shepherd ran down the hall past Hannah's office.

"Hannah," Ginger gasped, and Hannah flew around her desk and out the door. Three steps later, and she darted through the doorway of Ginger's office, where her friend had been working more and more often.

Ginger had one palm pressed firmly to her desktop and one holding the bottom of her belly. Her eyes were wide and filled with fear, and as she stared at Hannah, another wave of pain rolled across her face.

She blinked, and Hannah remembered the numbness that had assaulted her on the beach. She wasn't going to do that here. One of her best friends needed her, and she was going to help them.

"I'll call Nate," Hannah said, striding forward. "Sit down, Ginger." She helped Ginger ease into the chair, and Ginger panted and groaned. Ursula came tearing back into the office, and Ginger reached for her, quieting her barks.

Hannah quickly dialed Nate, who picked up with, "Hey, Hannah."

"Ginger is having contractions," Hannah said in a brisk voice. "It's time to take her to the hospital."

"I'm on my way. Three minutes."

"I'll meet you in the driveway." Hannah hung up and shoved her phone in her back pocket. "Do you have an overnight bag, Ginger?" She crouched down in front of the tall, strong redhead. "Where is it, honey?"

"By the front door at the cabin," she said, her voice breathless. "Don't leave me here."

"Ursula is with you. She's not going anywhere." Hannah took both of Ginger's hands in hers. "I'm going to go get the bag for you and the baby. I'll be gone for less than sixty seconds. Then, we're going to meet Nate in the driveway. You're going to stay right here until I get back."

Ginger nodded, the movement almost frantic.

Hannah nodded in a more controlled manner, and then she stood and strode out of the office. She ran down the hall and through the kitchen. Hannah didn't do a lot of running, but her adrenaline fed her muscles to move quickly. She took the steps two at a time up to the front door of Ginger and Nate's cabin, and she grabbed the bag from just inside the front door. She had no idea what to put in a bag to take to the hospital to have a baby, but Ginger was always prepared for everything in every way.

She called Jill on her way back down the steps. She couldn't run back, because the most physical exercise Hannah did was some yoga on the weekends and her work around the ranch. She didn't race from task to task, and her chest heaved while her lungs burned.

"Ginger's gone into labor," Hannah said. "I'm helping her get out front to meet Nate."

"How exciting," Jill said, laughing. "I love babies so much."

Hannah grinned. "Me too." She hesitated. She wasn't going to the hospital. She could've easily texted Jill and Jess and anyone else she wanted once she got Ginger in the truck with Nate.

Her chest constricted. "Let's have dinner together tonight," she said. "Just me and you. Can you?"

"I—of course I can."

"I love Slate, but I just...miss you."

"Aw, Hannah," Jill said. "For the official record and all of that, you're the one hosting a very cute blond-haired man at the West Wing every evening."

Hannah hurried up the steps to the back door. "I know. I'll tell him he needs to find something to do with Slate tonight."

"Perfect," Jill said. "See you later."

"Yep." Hannah let her disconnect the call, and she shoved her phone in her pocket and dropped the bag on the edge of the living room carpet before heading down the hall to Ginger's office. She still sat in the chair behind her desk, Ursula's head resting on her knee, and Hannah put a smile on her face. "All right, honey. Time to get up."

Tears ran down Ginger's face, and Hannah's heart squeezed. "Come on, now. Your baby is coming."

"I'm so scared," she whispered.

"It's going to be fine," Hannah said, hoping to soothe her. "Nate is going to be right there with you the whole time, and he's not going to let anything bad happen to you." She put her hand under Ginger's arm and helped her stand. "It's just a few steps."

Ginger took a long breath and took the first step. Then another. And another. Ginger always faced hard things with strength and determination, and Hannah marveled at her calmness in the hurricane of fear.

"All right," Hannah said, stooping to get the bag as she passed. "Just a little further. Nate's going to be out there, and you're going to get to the hospital no problem."

Ursula trotted ahead of them, as if she could open the door with her paws. She got to the door and looked back, panting.

"Connor's done with school at three-fifteen."

"I know what time Connor's done with school," Hannah said. "Emma's picking the kids up today anyway, remember?"

"Yes," Ginger said. "That's right. Emma's getting him."

"Jill and I will keep him here at the West Wing. I have those fruit ropes he loves right in the cupboard. He's going to be fine."

"Emma said—"

"It's all fine," Hannah said, reaching past Ginger to open the front door. "Back up, Ursula. Get out of the way."

The dog went outside instead of behind her, but it didn't matter. She'd moved, and Hannah guided Ginger out onto the porch.

Nate jogged down the sidewalk, looking up as he practically flew up the steps. "Hey, hon." He nodded gratefully at Hannah and took Ginger's arm. "Just down the steps, and we'll be to the truck."

A sidewalk stretched toward the classic farm fence that separated the grass from the gravel, but Hannah didn't say anything.

Hannah paused at the top of the steps and watched Nate get Ginger down them. Ursula barked from the fence line as if alerting the whole ranch that something was going on with her master.

When they were halfway down the sidewalk, Hannah remembered she still held the bag in her hand. "Your bag," she called, hurrying down the steps now. "I'll put it in the back."

She went past Nate and Ginger, who seemed to be moving backward. She opened the back door of Nate's truck and tossed the bag in, then stepped to open Ginger's door.

Nate finally got his wife there, and he helped her get up and into the seat.

"Good luck," Hannah said after Nate had closed the door. "Drive safe."

"Thank you, Hannah." He started around the front of the truck.

"Don't worry about Connor. I've got him." Hannah fell back as Nate pulled out, and she watched as dust kicked up beneath his tires in his haste to leave the ranch. "Come on, Ursula." The dog barked as she came to sit beside Hannah, who was clearly second-best.

She pressed one hand over her heart and said, "Please watch over them. She's so scared, and she just needs to be comforted." Ursula barked her contribution to the prayer, and the two of them turned and went back into the house.

———

"He's out," Jill said as she came down the hall. Hannah looked over to her from her position at the bar, pure exhaustion pulling through her. She picked up the second spoon and offered it to Jill.

"I thought I wanted kids right away," Jill said, taking the spoon and sitting down. She pulled the container of ice cream toward her. "But he wore me right out tonight."

"He's eight," Hannah said, smiling. "They don't come out that age."

"Thank goodness," she said, digging into the mint chocolate chip, and then adding a dab of plain chocolate.

"You're getting them all messy," Hannah said, frowning at the two containers.

"I've always eaten ice cream this way."

"No, you get that peanut butter kind and sit on the couch, your legs curled up underneath you while you emit a long sigh every few seconds."

Jill burst out laughing, the sound loud and beautiful in the nearly empty house. "Every few seconds," Jill said between giggles. "That's so not true." She took another bite of ice cream, ignoring Hannah's displeasure about the mixing. "So...you and Luke? Anything new going on there?"

"No," Hannah said, perhaps a little too casually. "Same old, same old."

"You haven't kissed him yet?"

Hannah acted shocked and scooped up another bite of mint chocolate chip from the opposite side of the container so she wouldn't get any chocolate with it. "I'm waiting for *him* to kiss *me*," she said.

"Mm." Jill nodded like that was the right thing to do. "When do you think that's going to happen?"

"I don't know," Hannah said. "Luke is...he's sort of enigma. He's super sweet almost all the time, and then sometimes, he's got this mask on, and I can't tell what's going on in his head."

"That's the Y-chromosome at work," Jill said.

Hannah giggled and licked her spoon clean. "We get along great. We're learning about each other."

"The chemistry is still hot, though, right?"

"Mm." Hannah didn't normally spill too many relationship details, especially physical things like kissing, but she'd told Jill all about the fireworks that cartwheeled through her body whenever Luke so much as walked in a room.

"Are you going to Beeville with him for his birthday?"

"Yes," Hannah said, looking up as sudden alarm ran through her. "Do you think it's too soon?"

"It's not until May," Jill said, meeting Hannah's eye. "It's like, six weeks from now."

"His parents will be there."

"You can meet his parents," Jill said.

"Then he'll want to meet mine," Hannah said, giving Jill a meaningful look.

"Hey, I took Slate home to meet my family," she said. "Haven was there and everything, and wow, it was almost a bloodbath." She trilled out another laugh, but Hannah's stomach pinched.

She put her spoon down. "Okay, I'm done with this. I'm not gaining back that ten pounds I lost with mint chocolate chip."

"Seriously," Jill said. "Save the calories for the butter pecan." She grinned at Hannah, who always ate her way through several cartons of butter pecan ice cream after a break-up. Except for Chuck...who hadn't even warranted a single spoonful of the stuff.

She wasn't sure what that said about him, or about their relationship. Maybe nothing. Maybe she hadn't liked him as much as she'd thought she had. Maybe everything about their relationship had been superficial.

"Your family isn't that bad," Jill said as she got up and put their spoons in the sink.

"Are you kidding? Remember that Thanksgiving you spent with us? You looked like you'd witnessed a horrific crime and couldn't wait to get away."

Jill laughed again, capping the ice cream containers and turning toward the freezer. "That was only because Bethany had called the wishbone, Hannah. The *wishbone*."

"She was thirty-eight years old," Hannah said, and they both burst out laughing again. With the ice cream put away, they migrated over to the couch in the living room. Jill sighed as she sat down, and Hannah did too, putting her feet up on the coffee table.

"Are you ready to get married?" Hannah asked.

"I'd go say I-do tomorrow," Jill said, tucking her feet under her body. "The dress will be done next week. We're doing a final walk-through with full color illustrations and even a 3-D rendition of the hall on the twelfth." She smiled at Hannah. "Yeah, I think we'll be ready."

"How's your mom?"

Jill's sadness descended on the room quickly, as if the sun had suddenly been snuffed out, leaving only darkness behind. "She's doing good, actually." She reached up and wiped her eyes quickly. "She just really wanted her hair to be back in time for the wedding."

"Oh, I'm so sorry," Hannah said, reaching over and taking Jill's hand in hers. "She'll be beautiful, no matter what."

"That's what I told her. I said, Mom, this is what you look like. This is where you are in your life. It's okay." She shook her head. "I just wish she'd go get a wig. She'd be so much happier."

"Why won't she?"

Jill shook her head again and slipped her hand away from Hannah to pick at something on the cuffs of her jeans.

"What is it?" Hannah pressed.

"Haven said she won't go get a wig, because they're expensive, and Mom and Dad have spent everything they have on the wedding."

"Oh, come on," Hannah said. "She did *not* make it your fault your mom can't get a wig."

Jill looked at her out of the corner of her eye before turning fully toward her. "You've met my sister, right?" Jill and Haven didn't see eye-to-eye on many things, and Jill claimed she was the perfect older sister who did everything right.

Haven's view of Jill was that of a spoiled kid who got what she wanted, because she was the favorite. Neither of them were exactly right, because the truth always lay somewhere in the middle. Truth could be gray sometimes.

"I've been saving up," Jill admitted. "I'm going to get her a wig for Mother's Day."

"That's a great idea," Hannah said with a smile.

"It won't be in time for the wedding, though." Jill leaned over and rested her head against Hannah's shoulder. "Thank you for tonight. I didn't even know how much I missed this until now."

"Yeah." Hannah looked out the big front windows and into the darkness. "Do you think she's had the baby yet?"

"If she has and Nate hasn't texted us, I'll seriously rip him apart when they get home."

Jill and Hannah laughed together again, and then both of their phones sounded in near harmony. "Has to be them," Hannah said, struggling to get her device out of her back pocket. The corner caught, and Jill sucked in a breath and squealed.

"Oh, it's a boy," she said, looking up with pure sunshine pouring from her. She'd definitely have a baby very soon after she and Slate got married if at all possible, and Hannah couldn't lie and say that wasn't what she wanted too.

She finally freed her phone and swiped on the text from Nate. It was a picture of him, Ginger, and a cute, tiny, red-faced baby wrapped in a soft, blue blanket. A sigh escaped Hannah's mouth. "He's perfect."

Another message came in. *Meet Ward Talbot Mulbury. 20-inches long. 9.2 pounds. He arrived at nine-sixteen this evening, and he can really cry.*

Hannah smiled at the message, so many feelings running through her.

Ginger did great, Nate said next. *She's fine and asleep already. I know a lot of you have been praying already, but we'll take any more you can give. She was so stressed and so scared, and I think she just crashed.*

Hannah's heart went out to Ginger, because she'd seen and tasted that fear on her. She'd experienced it when she stared at the gulf, begging the Lord to bring Luke and Connor up out of the water.

"Talbot is the perfect middle name," Jill said. "In fact, I really like it for a first name..."

"You can't be serious," Hannah said, though she knew very well that Jill meant it. She'd always liked strange or quirky names. Last names for first names. All of that. "You would too if you'd been named Jill," she always told Hannah.

"Yeah," Jill said. "Talbot Sanders...it's got a nice ring to it."

"Heaven help us all," Hannah said. Jill settled against her again, and they sat there, the two of them, in wonderful silence. Hannah loved her friends on the ranch, and in quiet moments like this, she knew and understood that she'd never truly be left alone, whether she got married or not.

It only felt like it sometimes.

"PINK OR YELLOW?" JILL ASKED A COUPLE OF WEEKS later. She turned from the full-length mirror in the bridal shop. The dress had been delayed, and she only had fifteen days until the wedding. Her gown had fit like a glove—finally—and now she needed help picking out her headgear.

Jill wasn't what anyone would describe as traditional, and she didn't want a veil. Right now, she held two flower crowns in her hands, holding them up for Hannah's vote.

"Put the woodsy one on again," Hannah said, moving to stand next to Jill. She wasn't the only person there, but perhaps everyone would like a second look at their choices. Jess came up beside them, and Emma crowded in with her baby in her arms.

Ginger hadn't come on the trip, because she'd only been home for a couple of weeks, and she didn't want to risk exposing baby Ward to anything dangerous.

Jill fitted the larger of the two crowns around her head, and this one had delicate pink flowers nestled among tan and nearly white sprays of what looked a lot like fur. They were really very thin and delicate pine needles that had been colored and secured in the band of the crown. Tiny twigs adorned the wreath as well, and it fit the country theme of Jill's wedding perfectly. She looked like a woodland elf, and that was definitely Hannah's favorite.

The other crown made her look more like a hippie, and it clashed with her blonde hair.

"Pink," Hannah said at the same time Emma and Jess said, "Yellow."

"I knew this would happen," Jill said with plenty of exasperation in her voice. "I'd choose pink too. It's a tie."

"It's your wedding," Emma said. "Pick the one you want." She bounced her baby and smiled at Jill in the mirror. "You know what? The yellow flowers aren't that great with your hair color."

Jill held the string of flowers up to her hair, and Hannah widened her eyes and nodded. "Okay," she said, meeting Hannah's eyes in the mirror. "I'm going with the pink one." She turned and handed it to the saleswoman. "This one, please."

"We'll put it in your file and have it ready when you come to pick up the flowers." She smiled in the most professional way possible, and Hannah was glad she didn't have a job in customer service. She wasn't sure she could keep the smile in place for hours on end.

The bell on the door chimed, and Hannah automatically turned that way. Jill's sister walked in, and she looked like a tornado about to touch down. "Incoming," Hannah muttered, and then she got out of the way.

Haven barely glanced at Hannah and Jess, her gaze going right back to Jill. "Jill," she said. "You're done already?"

"Yep," Jill said, signing something on the counter in front of her. "I told you it would be fast."

"Mom and I wanted to see the crowns."

Jill turned toward her sister. "How did it go with the announcements?"

"Fine." Haven waved behind her. "Mom's putting them in the car."

"You left her to put three hundred announcements, plus envelopes, in the car?" Jill asked. "By herself? There has to be several boxes."

Hannah's attention swung back to Haven, and she felt like she was watching a really bad game of tennis. "You said you'd be a few minutes."

"No," Jill said. "I said it would only *take* a few minutes." Jill shook her head and practically slammed the pen down on the counter. "You know what, Haven? This is *my* wedding, not yours. It's annoying and a little pathetic that you have to make everything about you." She marched away from her sister, and Hannah silently cheered for her friend.

"So...lunch?" Jess said brightly, stepping over to Haven. "I hear you make an amazing pot of chicken and dumplings. Is that true?"

Haven blinked a couple of times and then softened completely. "It is true."

"My husband *adores* chicken and dumplings, and I need a really good recipe," Jess said, starting toward the door and somehow working some sort of Pied Piper magic to get Haven to go with her. "I'd love to try yours."

Hannah met Emma's eyes, and the two of them dissolved into giggles before following everyone out of the florist shop and onto the quaint Main Street in Sweet Water Falls.

CHAPTER THIRTEEN

Luke stood at the window and gazed out across the field beyond. It wasn't a hay field, or corn, but more like a pasture. A pasture where animals didn't graze. Right now, rows and rows of chairs sat in the field, and a couple of people moved around, setting up the arch in front of the altar.

Slate was getting married today, and Luke had been looking forward to and dreading the day all at the same time. Tonight, Slate wouldn't be on the ranch. He and Jill would be gone on a honeymoon for a couple of weeks, courtesy of Nate and Ginger, who'd given them a huge trip to an all-inclusive resort in Cozumel.

When they returned, they'd both live in the cabin where Slate had been for a couple of months now. Luke told himself he'd see him all the time. They worked the same ranch. He literally lived a couple hundred yards away.

For some reason, though, Luke existed under a thunder-cloud that refused to drop its rain and then move on.

Someone came to stand next him, and Luke glanced over at Ted. He extended a single rose toward Luke, and said, "This goes on your lapel."

Luke nodded and took it, turning and holding it against his lapel. Ted used the large straight pin to attach it to the fabric, and Luke marveled that his thick fingers had been able to do something so delicate.

"How are you feeling?" Ted asked, turning his attention back out the window.

"Okay," Luke said. "I think I'm just ready for it to be over."

"I think everyone feels like that by the time the wedding actually arrives." Ted laughed, but it wasn't one of his big, booming ones that filled the whole universe with joy.

Luke still grinned and chuckled, glad Ted had chased away some of the melancholy feelings inside him.

"I think they're almost ready," he said. "We have to go line up in a different room."

"The smaller waiting room," Luke joked, because the wedding wasn't set to start for another thirty minutes. The very first guests had just started to arrive out in the field, and Luke watched the workers finish with everything and get out of the way.

"Guys," Slate called, and Luke turned from the window. "We're moving over to the stable house."

Luke didn't know what that meant, but he followed

everyone else. Slate had several groomsmen in the wedding party, including his own brother, the four men he'd spent time in prison with, and Jill's brother. His grandparents lived nearby, and Luke had gone out to Short Tail a couple of times with Slate on a couple of Sunday afternoons.

His parents and siblings and their families had come from Austin, and Jill had her two sisters and their significant others and children here too.

Other than that, family friends and then Slate's and Jill's friends from around Sweet Water Falls would make up the audience.

Slate had asked Luke to be in the wedding party, and he'd be escorting Hannah down the aisle ahead of Jill.

He glanced to his left when he heard his name in somewhat of a hiss. He found Hannah poking her head around the corner, and she gestured for him to go down the short hall and join her. Luke's heart leapt at the thought of finding a private spot on this piece of beautiful land and kissing her.

He hadn't done that yet, and he really needed to get the job done soon. He'd been moving pretty slow with Hannah, mostly because he wanted to make sure the sizzling attraction between them had more of a foundation than just the physical.

They worked together, but that didn't provide a lot of time or opportunity for meaningful, personal conversations. It did show him her hardworking side. She was firm and kind to the cowboys and cowgirls who worked on the stable. She was detailed and organized in her accounting work for the ranch, and she loved to eat at out-of-the-way restaurants with unique and eclectic menus.

She knew the people at those restaurants and Luke hadn't taken her to one yet where they didn't love her to bits and pieces. Everyone had good things to say about Hannah, and Luke did too.

He glanced at the backs of the men still moving away from him, and he ducked down the hall. He rounded the corner and found Hannah with her back pressed into the brick there. "What's going on?" he asked in a low voice. He could kiss her right now and be very happy. Just put one hand on her hip and the other along her face and hold her in place while he pressed his lips to hers.

His throat almost closed at the very thought.

"Jill wanted to see you."

"Why?" He glanced down the hall to the only visible door.

"I told her about the wig."

Luke leaned away from Hannah. "I thought we weren't going to do that until after the wedding. After they got home from Mexico."

"Her mother is wearing it," Hannah said. "It was this huge uproar, and everyone wanted to know where she'd gotten it. Sabrina tried to play it off as a gift, but then Jill and McKenna started accusing Haven of buying it for her and trying to make this wedding about her again, and I had to say something." Hannah pressed one palm to her forehead, obviously stressed. "I'm so dang hot. You have no idea how stressful it is in that room."

She pushed away from the wall and started down the hall. Luke did not follow her.

Pausing, she said, "Come on."

"I'm not going in there," he said. "The room full of stress?" And women. Luke shook his head.

Hannah turned fully, which was a feat in that dress. It was the color of fresh butter and hugged her ample curves to the waist, where it flowed in beautiful waves down to the ground. "You made her cry."

"*I'm* not the one who told her we bought her mother a wig."

Hannah smiled at him, and Luke knew he was about to lose. He even took a step toward her. She extended her hand toward him. "Come on. She just wants to say thank you."

"Sabrina already told us thank you." Luke took Hannah's hand. "You owe me big for this."

"Is that right?" Hannah teased.

"Yes," Luke said. "We're going to a regular steakhouse for dinner tomorrow night. You have to get a steak and baked potato—no special toppings."

"You have got to be kidding." Hannah looked at him like he'd just told her she'd have to eat roadkill.

Luke laughed, his sad mood completely gone with Hannah at his side. "Yeah, I won't punish you with food. I'll think of something else."

"What else is there?"

"No ice cream after dinner?" he guessed.

"You're taking all the fun out of life," she said.

"That's the point of a punishment," he said.

"You said I owed you something, not that I needed to be punished." She opened the door and led him inside. "Jill, I have Luke."

Everyone turned toward him, and Luke froze as if with stage fright. He'd been in the ring in front of thousands of people. Shirtless, no less. Now, he felt like he wasn't wearing anything as he stood in front of all these women.

There seemed to be dozens of them, though there couldn't be.

Sabrina approached, and she looked beautiful and bright in a silver dress with plenty of sparkle on it. Her dark hair fell to her shoulders, and the wig looked absolutely real. It was made with real human hair, and she'd told him and Hannah all about how the consultant had worked with her to get the shade exactly right.

"Look at you," Luke said, smiling at her. "It's beautiful." He stepped into her as if she were his own mother and hugged her tight. Her chest shook against his, and Luke wished she wouldn't cry. "Please don't," he whispered.

Sabrina stepped away and wiped quickly at her eyes. "I didn't mean to cause a big problem," she said.

"It wasn't your fault," Hannah said. "Sometimes a situation just gets out of control."

Jill stepped next to her mother, her eyes wide and searching. "You bought my mother a wig?"

Luke fell back to Hannah's side, hoping she could help him against Jill. He'd known Jill for a year now, and he liked her just fine. He'd even say they were good friends. She'd helped him with Hannah last year, and she'd encouraged him in every decision he made.

His chest tightened, and he looked at Hannah.

"We pooled our money," Hannah said. "Luke and I." She glanced at him, and he leaned over and pressed a kiss to her cheek.

"Hannah said it would mean a lot to your mother to have hair for your wedding, and the money was just sitting there." Luke shrugged, hoping that didn't make what they've done unimportant. "It was supposed to be a surprise."

Jill's bottom lip wobbled, and she stepped into Luke and wrapped her arms around him. "Thank you so much."

"You deserve the very best wedding," Luke said, and he meant it.

Jill hugged Hannah again, and Luke's phone rang. "I'm probably being summoned," he said when he saw Nate's name on the screen. "They probably think I ran away." He grinned and lifted the phone. "See you ladies soon."

He made his escape and answered the call.

"Where'd you go?" Nate asked.

"Jill summoned me to the bridal room," he said. "I'm on my way now. I might need someone to come get me, because I'm not sure how to get to the stable house."

"Slate nearly called in the National Guard," Nate said. "He's a bit on-edge."

"Sorry," Luke said. "I'm on my way." He made it back to the hallway he'd been in before and continued the way everyone else had been walking. A man came out of one of the doorways before Luke had to decide which one to go down, and relief filled him.

"Thanks," he said to him, and down another hall, he entered a room with one whole wall of windows. They looked out across the field, the rows facing the altar and arch, clearly visible down the middle of the aisle.

"You snuck off to kiss Hannah, didn't you?" Slate asked, not joking at all.

"I did not," Luke said, quite defensively.

"Where'd you go then?" he asked as Nate and Ted gathered around. Dallas edged closer too, questions in his eyes too.

"I told Nate: I had to go to the bride's room. Jill wanted to see me."

"Jill?" Slate asked, his voice full of disbelief. "Why in the *world* would *my* fiancée want to see *you?*"

The emphasis on every other word annoyed Luke to the point of frowning and scoffing. "Calm down," he said. He didn't want to tell them about the wig. He and Hannah had discussed it, and yes, he had some money in the bank. Enough for wig, at least. Enough for a little more too, because he'd won a lot of fights before his life had taken a drastic turn.

"Look who's telling someone to calm down." Nate

glanced at Ted, both of them smiling. That only irritated Luke further.

"Leave him alone," Dallas said. "Luke had lessons to learn, just like the rest of us. We don't go back to who we were over and over, do we?"

Emotion welled up in Luke's throat. He met Dallas's eyes and hoped he could communicate his thanks for sticking up for him with just a look.

"You're right," Ted said. "I'm sorry, Luke."

Nate remained stoic for a few moments while everyone looked at him or Luke. Or back and forth between them both. Luke would bend under the wrath of Nathaniel Mulbury. Even under just a hard look like this.

He closed his eyes and looked away, and Nate said, "I know you learned a lot in prison, Luke. No one's denying that. I just wonder if you learned enough."

"What does that even mean?" Luke asked. "I'm not back on steroids. I'm not fighting. I left Las Vegas, even though it was very hard to do." He felt his chest unraveling, one breath at a time, and they came quickly now.

"You're still fighting," Nate said quietly. "You're fighting yourself, and you're fighting the verdict. Still."

"It was involuntary," Luke bit out.

Slate stepped to his side and faced Nate too. "Are you saying he's not repentant? Because he doesn't think he did anything wrong?"

"I didn't say that," Nate said. "But I think it's interesting that *you* did."

"I did my time," Luke said. "I don't have to stand here and justify anything to anyone. Not even you, Nathaniel." He backed up a step and looked at Slate. "Jill wanted to see me because Hannah and I bought her mother a wig to wear today. Her mother has been upset and worried about coming to the wedding and having a whole bunch of pictures taken of her without hair."

He took a deep breath as someone opened the door and said, "The ladies will be here in five minutes. We'll open the glass doors then, and you guys can get lined up."

No one even acknowledged the woman who'd spoken.

"It wasn't anything bad. She found out, and she wanted to say thank you. Hannah pulled me down the hall and into the bride's room, where everyone stared at me like a freak." He glared at Slate, though he wasn't really angry with him. Luke didn't care. The anger was an old friend he actually liked. He switched his gaze to Ted, then Dallas, and last Nate. "Just like they are now. I've had quite enough of it, and I certainly didn't expect to have to take it from the men who should assume the best about me instead of the worst."

So he wouldn't form his fingers into fists, Luke reached up and adjusted the collar on his shirt and jacket. "Excuse me." He turned and left the room, though both Slate and Dallas said, "Luke," and then something else.

Something like, "Don't go," or "Stay here."

Luke couldn't stay at the moment. He just needed to find air that wasn't filled with accusations. He'd had no idea

Nate thought he hadn't accepted his verdict. It had been *years* since the verdict. Years.

How did he prove he'd accepted it? "Why do you even have to?" As far as he knew, no one else had to prove to their friends that they'd done something terrible, felt bad about it, and accepted their punishment.

Luke knew he'd done something terrible. He did feel bad about it. He'd accepted his punishment. He'd lived in a dormitory for forty months. Three and a half years.

He went out a door in a burst, pulling in a breath that felt so thick it wouldn't go down right. He bent over and braced himself with his arms against his knees, trying to find a proper amount of air.

"Dear Lord," he gasped. "Help me." He couldn't say more than that, and he hoped agony and embarrassment couldn't swallow a man whole.

The door opened behind him, but he barely heard it. "Luke," a woman said, and a ray of light burst through the darkness cascading through him. She touched his back, and even through his jacket and shirt, a zing started.

"Baby, what's wrong?" Hannah pressed in close to him and bent down too.

His angel. Luke got a breath to go into his lungs the right way, and he used it to stand up straight. Luke couldn't remember the last time he'd cried, and he had no tears today either. He also didn't have an answer for her.

He simply took her into his arms and held her tightly.

Thankfully, she didn't ask again, and she allowed him to hold her in silence until he felt like himself again.

"We should go," she said, still examining his face. "I just saw Slate go down to the altar, which means they're getting close."

Luke nodded, taking a look out toward the chairs, which had filled in the past several minutes. "One thing first," he said.

"What's that?" she asked.

He looked at her, wondering if this was a smart thing to do or not. A hint of distress still streamed through him, and maybe he just wanted to kiss her to make himself feel better.

No, he thought. "I want to kiss you," he said out loud. "Because I really like you, Hannah."

A smile bloomed on her face, and she ducked her hair, causing some curled tendrils of hair to fall forward. "I really like you too, Luke."

He reached up and curved his fingers along the side of her face and neck, the way he'd imagined several times in the past. Her skin rolled like silk along his, and he stepped right into her personal space. "It's been a while for me." His heartbeat crashed against his ribs for an entirely new reason now, and Luke prayed desperately that he remembered how to kiss a woman properly.

"You're good at everything," Hannah whispered.

Luke smiled at her gentle encouragement, and he let his eyes drift closed as he took a breath of her. She smelled sweet as sugar, and clean as fresh laundry, and decidedly feminine in a floral way that drove Luke mad.

He finally closed the distance between them and touched his lips to hers. A roar moved through his whole body, filling his ears as fire raced down his throat and through his veins.

His other hand slid along her waist as she put her hands on his shoulders and moved them up into his hair.

He'd planned to keep the kiss sweet and simple after such a long hiatus, but he found he couldn't stop. Everything with Hannah had been explosive, and Luke wasn't sure why he'd expected their first kiss to be any different.

CHAPTER FOURTEEN

Hannah had kissed a lot of cowboys in the past twenty years, and not one of them came close to Luke Holt. He existed on an entirely different planet. A whole new universe, probably.

She breathed in through her nose and enjoyed every stroke of his mouth against hers, sparks and popping sensations erupting in every skin cell he touched. Her internal temperature felt near to boiling, and it wasn't until she heard someone say, "We have to find them. Jill will be devastated if they're not in the wedding," that she thought she should pull away.

Luke actually broke the kiss, his breathing heavy and shallow at the same time. Hannah knew the feeling, because he'd stolen her breath with such an amazing kiss, and she couldn't breathe in deeply enough to replace the oxygen she needed.

"Come on, angel," he said quietly. "I don't need any more attention on me today, and I think they're looking for us."

Hannah opened her eyes and looked at the glorious handsomeness of Luke's face. They smiled shyly at one another, and Hannah went as far as giggling. Luke took her hand in his and stepped back inside. She hadn't known why she'd come toward this door, only that she'd arrived here to find someone bent over as if in distress.

One step outside and one breath in had identified the man as Luke. She'd know his cool, clean scent anywhere.

Luke rounded a corner and lifted his free hand to signal to Ted. Pure relief poured across the other man's face, and he waved at them to hurry up. They ducked into the stable house and took their place in the line. Hannah noticed that Luke didn't look at anyone, even when Dallas turned to look at him, and Ted bent forward to say something to Nate.

Nate also turned and looked behind him, but Luke stood still and straight, his eyes boring into something only he could see.

Something had definitely happened, as the tension between the four men rode on the air like a scent. In front of her, Jess shifted her feet and whispered to Dallas, who shook his head. So she didn't know what had gone on in the past twenty minutes either.

"Here we go," the wedding venue coordinator called from the front of the room. "All the way to the altar, wedding party. Circle around to the sides, where there's a row for you to sit. All the way to the end, even across the aisle, if you will."

The music started as she said the last few words, and the line moved forward. Hannah tried to shrug off the awkward-ness surrounding her, and she linked her arm through Luke's. He kept her close to his side, and they marched together to the beat of the music.

She noted the relief on Slate's face as Luke approached, and Slate even reached out to touch Luke's arm as they went by.

They had a bit of a struggle getting to their seats, as Nate and Ginger had to go all the way down two rows.

"She said across the aisle," Ted said in a not-so-whisper, and they finally all got where they needed to go. Hannah stayed standing, the heat of Luke's body behind her as they faced the stable house again.

A mechanical whirring sound filled the air, and Hannah watched in awe as the aisle got raised three feet into the air, grass and all. A murmur and a low "wow" ran through the crowd. Hannah stared, because Jill had not mentioned an elevated aisle. Not even one time.

She appeared at the end of the raised aisle and beamed at her father. They linked arms and came slowly down the aisle. Jill kept her gaze fixed on Slate, and Hannah looked back and forth between the two of them. They both wore identical looks of love and joy, and Hannah's emotions tightened in her chest. Tears popped into her eyes, and she decided not to hold back at this wedding the way she had the others.

Jill was her best friend, and she deserved every good thing in the whole world. That was the reason she'd told Luke about Sabrina Kyle's desire to have a wig for the wedding, as well as all the family pictures.

She'd been beyond surprised when he'd said, "Let's get her one, then. How much are they?"

Hannah had immediately contacted Sabrina and asked a lot of questions. She'd learned where Sabrina would buy from, and she had gone with Jill's mother to get the process started. Luke had told her he had some money in his bank account from his boxing winnings, and they'd been able to pay for a rush on the wig to get it done and in Sabrina's possession before the wedding.

Sabrina cried a few seats over in the row in front of Hannah, and she thought of her own mother. Hannah texted and called dutifully, but she hadn't been up to Honeyfield since Christmas.

She and Luke were going to Beeville to see his family for his birthday, and Honeyfield lay directly east of that. It might add fifteen minutes to their drive, and she determined she should mention it to him, and see if they could extend their trip by just one day to stop and see her family.

It was the right thing to do, and she might as well get it over with. She could text both Bethany and Ruth and ask them for help with their mother. Maybe she'd be on her best behavior then.

The pastor said beautiful things about love and forgiveness, Slate and Jill read their vows, and Hannah cheered and clapped after they'd said "I do," and as they kissed over the altar. Beside her, Luke whistled between his teeth, and Ted's bellow had to reach all the way into outer space.

He frightened his baby daughter, who started to cry in the arms of Fran, who'd come down from San Antonio to sit with Emma and Ted's kids so they could walk in the wedding.

He laughed as he took Frannie from her namesake and comforted her, and Hannah stole a look at Nate and Ginger on the end of the row. Ginger held Ward in her arms, her smile warm and genuine as she witnessed Jill and Slate lift their joined hands, their smiles as wide as the ocean.

"My grandmother lived in that house," Luke said as they drove by one of the biggest homes Hannah had ever seen. Beeville was an old, Texas town that didn't look like time had come in and run it over. The buildings sported their age well, like an old woman with plenty of money to keep her hair done and her clothes at the height of fashion.

"Your grandmother?" she asked.

"Mm." Luke nodded. "My uncle rents it to the mayor now. It's the mayoral house."

Hannah had no response to that. Luke had mentioned that he had some money in his bank account due to his prize fight winnings. He'd said his mother was a Bee, and that they owned a few resorts in this part of Texas.

She hadn't realized they owned half of the town, and that their bank accounts were probably padded to the hilt too.

As he continued driving down the main street in the town's center, he pointed out the building that said LIBRARY across the top of it in clearly old stones. Blocky capital letters that reminded Hannah of simpler times. "We own that building," he said. "The town rents it for the library."

"How much of this town do you own?" She must have carried something in her voice, because he looked at her out of the side of his eye.

"I told you my mother is a Bee."

"You mentioned that. I thought maybe they'd owned a big ranch or something, and then the resorts you mentioned. I didn't realize you owned the mayoral house."

Luke smiled and looked out his side window. "The Bees own a lot of Beeville," he said. "My mother has a sister and a brother. They both live here. My aunt Clementine has a real green thumb, and she runs all the yard care and landscaping for the properties we own here. My uncle manages the resorts and rentals. My brother works for him, and he'll take over when Uncle Tucker is ready to retire."

"Fascinating," Hannah said. "You're not interested in joining the family business?"

"I suppose," Luke said, lifting one shoulder in a shrug. "I was on a different path."

"But you're not now," she pressed. "Why are you at Hope Eternal, when you could be here, doing something for the family? Something to invest in yourself?"

The mask Luke sometimes wore slid right into place, and Hannah sighed.

"What?" he asked.

"You just shut down," she said, deciding not to hide how she felt. "I can see it on your face. You put this mask on, and it's like, that's it. I'm not going to get a real answer." She folded her arms and looked at the shops still passing by.

Restaurant, pet store, boutique. The town was charming, and she'd forgotten it. Her family went down to Sweet Water Falls to the discount stores to shop for food and clothing, and once she'd learned to drive and got a bit more freedom, she still didn't have money to spend in Beeville.

"I could come back here," he finally said, turning right and heading down a lovely little street that could've straight from a Hallmark movie. Flags in the shape of flowers hung from every pole on both sides of the street, varying in color from pink to yellow to purple.

The benches had flower boxes hanging off the backs of them, and petunias spilled over everywhere. If time stopped, and Hannah stood on this street, it could become a painting people would hang above their fireplaces for generations to come.

"What would you do?" she asked. "If you came back."

"I'd probably work with Aunt Clementine, honestly," he said. "She does a ton outdoors, and she's got crews with foremen and supervisors."

Hannah nodded, knowing Luke liked to work with his hands, and he had no problem working outside all day. "You don't want to?"

"It's not that I don't want to. It's...it's not something I've spent a lot of time thinking about," he said. "Ever. It's taking me some time to even come to it as something I could do with my life."

"Would you have a house to live in here?"

"Yeah, sure," he said. "There's a couple we own out on the west side of town. I grew up out there. Joey lives in that one, but it's pretty big. I could easily move in there. The one next door is ours too, and my sister lived there with her husband for a while as he finished college. Then he got a job in New Orleans, and they moved. That house is empty."

Hannah could not fathom owning an empty house. "You don't rent it?" Her voice pitched up for a reason she couldn't name. Shock, maybe. She felt a bit gobsmacked, like Luke should've told her all of this before they'd come to Beeville, as it was a lot to absorb and consider.

"Not that one," he said. "We do have a farm out there, and my mom is pretty particular about the houses out there."

"Yet she lets her bachelor son live in it," Hannah said dryly. "Sounds like a recipe for disaster."

Luke laughed, and Hannah basked in the sound of it. He hadn't done a lot of laughing recently, despite clearing the air with his friends. They'd done that right at the wedding, actually, in the few minutes between the end of the ceremony and the beginning of the dinner. Ted had grabbed Luke and everyone else—Slate included—and the five of them had huddled together out in the field for several minutes.

When Hannah had asked Luke about it, he'd explained quickly. Hannah had been thinking a lot about Nate's assessment that Luke hadn't accepted his verdict, but she'd said nothing to him about it.

The truth was, she could see both sides. Luke had been boxing for years before that fateful fight. He'd done exactly what he'd been trained to do. Most boxers also took steroids. On his side of the equation, she could see why he felt like he'd done nothing wrong.

On the other side, the fact remained that someone had died at his hand. Whether he'd kept punching when he should've stopped, Hannah didn't know. Whether he'd been in a steroid-induced rage, she also couldn't judge.

That was why lawyers and judges had jobs, and they'd decided that yes, Luke had unintentionally killed his opponent. He'd gotten a sentence, which he'd completed. Was more required of him? Did he have to believe that he'd done something wrong before he could be forgiven?

And who's job was it to forgive him? Hers? Nate's? His opponent's family?

Hannah always came back to the same conclusion: It wasn't her job to judge him, and it wasn't within her ability to declare him forgiven. Only the Lord could do both of those things, and Luke had to live his life according to his conscience.

She wished she could tell him all of that, but she didn't feel like she could. He had not come to church even once, and when everyone returned from the sermon, his truck was usually gone. He'd return around lunchtime, and he'd come over to the Annex and eat with everyone. He hadn't gone to the beach again, and Hannah felt like he had some dangerous things building behind a dam that would break eventually.

"Joey's pretty responsible," Luke said. "We worked in housekeeping in the resort growing up."

Hannah swung her attention back to him. "Like, you can make a bed with crisp, hospital corners?"

"Yes, ma'am," he drawled, and in that sexy cowboy hat and his golden-boy smile, Hannah fell a little bit more in love with him.

She laughed and shook her head, sobering as he made another turn, this time into a driveway.

"All right," he said. "Here we are."

Hannah peered out the windshield at the house, impressed by the pristine nature of it. The pink brick had seen a lot of days, but it looked proud and clean, and the house charmed Hannah with a single glance. The front flowerbeds contained rose bushes that someone loved very much, and the grass practically shone like an emerald.

"Wow," she said.

"My uncle lives here," he said. "My parents are already here."

"How can you tell?"

He nodded toward the huge, white SUV in front of him. "My father won't drive anything smaller than a tank, and that has a rental car license plate."

The front door opened, and a thin woman stepped outside.

"That's my momma," Luke said, though Hannah had never heard him say anything but mom when referencing his mother. She'd also never heard this tone of voice—one filled with happiness and love and laughter all at the same time. He got out of his truck, already laughing.

He jogged toward his mother and lifted her right up off her feet. She laughed, but when Hannah closed her door, the resulting slam drew his mother's attention. Luke put her down, and the two of them faced her.

Luke radiated joy, and Hannah's smile sprang to her face because of the one on his. She wiped her hands down the front of her slimming jeans, glad she'd chosen to wear them despite the length.

"Mom," Luke said. "This is Hannah Otto."

"Hello, Hannah," his mom said in a warm voice. She glanced at Luke and extended her hand toward Hannah.

Hannah quickly closed the last of the distance between them and secured her hand in his mother's.

"Hannah," he said. "My mom, Starr."

"Starr," Hannah repeated, pouring warmth into her tone. "So nice to meet you." After the handshake, she immediately slipped her hand into Luke's, and his mother watched it all.

Her eyebrows shot up, and Luke added, "We're dating. She's my girlfriend."

"Is that right?" Starr asked. "I see why you wanted to come back to Texas so badly."

Luke laughed, but he didn't deny it. "I hated selling houses in the desert," he said. "That had something to do with it too."

"Yeah, yeah," his mom said. "C'mon in, you two. I hope you're ready for the circus. The twins are here, and they brought all of their kids."

"Perfect," Luke said, but his tone of voice suggested it was the opposite of perfect. He let his mother lead the way inside, and he kept a grip on Hannah's hand as he went second. The house was deceptively quiet, and Hannah's nerves started to settle as she drank in the magnificent wood on the floor, the bannister right in front of her that went up to the second floor, and the lower half of the walls. That had been painted a bright white, with the upper half of the walls a light gray. Combined with the dark wood on the floor, the house was modern and clean while also maintaining its 1800s charm.

"This is beautiful," Hannah said. "Oh, my word. Is that a Pollock?" She stepped over to a painting, sure it couldn't be.

"Good eye on this one," Starr said, smiling as she joined Hannah in front of the huge painting that took up the entire wall leading further into the house. "He came to Texas once, and my brother had the opportunity to house him in one of our places here in Beeville."

Hannah heard the words, but they really made no sense to her.

"He painted this while he was here, and he gifted it to Tucker."

"Amazing," Hannah said, tracing the thick blue line as it went flying across the canvas. "I love the movement in his art."

"Me too." Starr patted her on the shoulder blade and added, "We'll eat as soon as you come back."

"Okay, Mom," Luke said, but he stopped next to Hannah while his mother continued through a doorway into the back part of the house. "She likes you."

Hannah tore her eyes from the painting to look at Luke. "She does?"

"Mm hm." He smiled up at the painting. "I've never understood abstract art. Like, what is it?"

"It's energy and movement," she said, turning her gaze back to the painting. "How do you know she likes me?"

"I just do," he said. "Something in her eyes."

Hannah let the information wash through her, realizing

she wanted his parents to like her. "Luke," she said. "My parents...they're much older than yours."

"Okay," he said.

"My mother isn't the nicest person ever," she said. "Sometimes my sisters and I get tired of catering to her, and then there's some fighting. Then my dad starts to cry, and everyone leaves feeling worse than when they'd shown up. We don't get together for a while, then someone will feel the call of trying to renew the family bond—it's usually me, to be honest—and we try again."

Luke released her hand and slipped his along her waist, settling it on her opposite hip. "I can handle your family."

Hannah leaned into his body, so comfortable with him. She sighed, and he did too. "Hannah," he whispered, his lips right against her ear.

Shivers cascaded over her shoulder and down her arms. "Hmm?"

He didn't say anything, but gently indicated he wanted her to turn toward him. She did, and he kissed her, right there in his uncle's house, with the Jackson Pollock painting standing guard above them.

He'd kissed her lots of times since Jill's wedding, but this one felt a little bit different. He didn't go on too long, and when he pulled away, he said, "I am thinking about coming up here to work."

"Really?" she asked, tucking herself against his chest.

"Just recently," he said, his voice mostly down in his throat. "I don't know. It's an idea percolating in my head."

"You do that for a while," she said. "Percolate."

He chuckled, and she stepped out of his embrace. "I can admit to that."

Hannah grinned at him too. "Okay, we better go back. It sounds like they're waiting for us to serve dinner."

Luke faced the hallway and doorway his mother had gone through, drew in a breath, and nodded. "Let's do it."

CHAPTER FIFTEEN

Luke laughed and hugged his father. He turned to Hannah and introduced her to him. Then to Joey, his brother. Joey's girlfriend, Kara Mannon. His uncle Tucker, who had gained at least twenty pounds since Luke had seen him last.

He already stood six and a half feet tall, and Hannah looked like a child next to him. His sons—the twins—had shown up with their spouses and children, and even Luke didn't get all of their names right.

Hannah kept her beautiful smile on her face and shook hands. She asked the smallest children questions about what they were going to do with their summer vacation, and she talked to the teens about some band he'd never heard of.

While she did that, he migrated over to the cooler and pulled out a can of strawberry lemonade. Joey came to stand next to him, and he indicated Hannah with the oldest teenagers. "She's pretty amazing."

Luke looked at his younger brother, noting that he kept his light hair trimmed and neat. Very professional. He'd never gotten any tattoos, though he and Luke had talked about it many times. He probably wore a suit and tie to work, and Luke felt choked already.

What had he been thinking when he'd considered coming up here to work?

Joey's eyes were a shade lighter than Luke's, as was his hair. He smiled, and Luke decided he didn't have anything to hide. "Yeah," he said. "I think she's pretty amazing too."

"How long have you been together?"

"Couple of months," Luke said, popping the top on his can and lifting the lemonade to his lips.

"You've fallen fast."

"Don't I always?"

"Fair point."

"What about you and Kara?" He watched the blonde woman as she spoke to Uncle Tucker. "Does she work for you?"

"Technically, she works for Aunt Clementine. She's the scheduling secretary for the gardening."

"She grew up here," Luke said.

"Yep." The clipped tone told Luke to drop it. He wanted to ask his brother why he hadn't married her yet, but he kept his question to himself. He'd missed some of his brother's life, and he didn't spend a bunch of time talking to him now. Regret filled him with the realization, because he wanted to have strong relationships with his family.

The truth was, it took a lot of work to maintain a relationship, and he had four men back at Hope Eternal Ranch that meant a lot to him. He thought about Nate, Ted, Dallas, and Slate, glad they'd been able to talk through the issue at Slate's wedding.

It had only taken a few minutes too, and Luke had simply said he didn't appreciate his friends—or men who were supposed to be his friends—judging him when they had no idea what he really felt.

Ted had said that Luke should tell them how he really felt, and he'd promised he'd try. He didn't know how, though. The emotions inside him swirled and tangled, and he ended up frustrated and angry that he didn't know how he felt about specific events in his life.

It was easier not to think about them at all. Just get up and go to work, day after day. Couldn't he just do that?

"Let's eat," Mom called, and relief rushed through Luke. Once they ate, everyone would leave, and he'd get to visit with his core family. He wouldn't have to be so guarded, and he wouldn't have to worry about someone saying something to Hannah that would annoy or upset her.

He walked over to her and touched her lower back. "You ready, angel?" He smiled at the girl she was talking to. "Hey, Portia."

"Luke." She nodded and walked away, and Luke rolled his eyes. He told himself he didn't need the approval of a fourteen-year-old and managed to wipe the irritation from his face before Hannah turned toward him.

"Wow, she doesn't like you, does she?" Hannah asked. She never missed much, and Luke had forgotten that for a moment.

"No," Luke said.

"Why not? What's the story there?"

"She doesn't believe in redemption, I suppose." He surveyed the lot of them gathering around the long tables where his mother had placed the food. "She'll grow up and realize people can change. People can change a lot."

"Do you feel like you've changed a lot?" Hannah asked.

"Sometimes," Luke said, not quite sure why she needed to know.

"Luke, come on," Mom called, and he had no choice but to join the fray. A pretty terrible rendition of *Happy Birthday* started up, led by his father, and Luke chuckled through the last half.

"Thank you," he said. "Thanks, everyone." He stepped over to the three-tiered cake Mom had likely ordered from the bakery and blew out the candles with one big lungful of air. Everyone cheered, and then Uncle Tucker raised both hands to quiet everyone down.

"Miranda's gonna tell us what we have."

His wife detailed the food, and Luke thought it was just

a way to rile up the lions before turning them loose on fresh meat. By the time she finished, he'd tuned out her girlish voice to the point that he didn't even know she'd said everyone could come eat. The only way he knew was the surging forward of Uncle Tucker's twins.

The grown men pushed their kids back, claiming they should let the adults go first, and good-natured arguments and ribbing broke out. Luke found the whole affair nearly insufferable, and he wasn't even sure why.

Last year, he'd gone to dinner with his parents for his birthday, and he much preferred that.

"Cake?" Hannah asked, lifting a small dessert plate toward him.

He looked at her as she put a forkful in her mouth. A bit of chocolate clung to her bottom lip, and he wanted to take care of that for her. She got the crumb as she smiled. "I just figured we'd want to stay out of that fray, and I'm starving."

He took the plate of cake and held it for her while she took another bite onto her fork. He sure did like this woman, and Luke understood that feeling as it deepened and grew, getting dangerously close to love.

He cleared his throat and reached for his own fork. "Guess I better get a bite before you eat the whole thing."

"You better," she teased. They polished off the cake in no time, and Luke took her fork and threw everything in the trashcan that had been placed out of the way near the corner of the house. He looked up and saw a car parked at the curb.

His heart seized, and Luke blinked, trying to make out the driver. The dark sedan had tinted windows in the back, but the front ones were clear. He simply couldn't see well enough to identify the person behind the wheel.

They were clearly watching him, though, and Luke glanced to the party behind him. When he looked back at the car, a man finished getting out of it, closed the door, and leaned against the driver's door.

It was Tick Stein.

Luke's muscles seized, then started to vibrate violently. His fingers automatically curled into fists, and Luke took a breath to puff out his chest.

"Who's that," Hannah asked, coming up behind him and pressing into his back as she took his left hand in both of hers and worked his fingers out of the tight fist.

"Atticus Stein," Luke said, his mouth barely moving. "He was my trainer here in Beeville, back when I was boxing."

"He doesn't look like he's got a birthday present," Hannah said.

No, he didn't. But he'd shown up for a reason. Luke didn't think it was because his family had been too loud, as this neighborhood was far above the likes of Tick. "I'm going to go talk to him," Luke said.

"Luke," Hannah said, her voice full of fear. "I don't think that's a good idea."

"I'll be fine," he said, twisting to look at her. "I'm just going to tell him to leave."

"Be careful," she said, releasing his hand. Luke started toward Tick, coaching himself to release the tension in his shoulders. Then his biceps. His forearms. His fingers.

The fists had fled by the time he was close enough to talk to Tick without calling too loudly. "What are you doing here?"

"Heard you were in town," Tick said. "Wanted to see for myself."

Luke had been in Beeville a couple of times since he'd been released. Tick had never sought him out before. "We're having a family birthday party," he said. "You really don't need to be here, and I'd appreciate it if you'd leave."

Tick laughed, his face tipped up toward the sky. He looked utterly relaxed against the car, his arms folded and one ankle crossed over the other. He'd parked in the shade of a tree, which cast his blue shirt in even darker shades of the same color. He wore jeans and sneakers, and he seemed so normal.

Luke knew better. He'd been young when boxing, and he'd let Tick manage his career. If he didn't know about something, he couldn't take the heat, but somehow, it had still been him who'd ended up in jail.

Tick had first brought him steroids and said everyone was using them. If Luke wanted to win, he'd need to take them too.

Tick had arranged fights under the radar that allowed Luke to fight more often than the rules allowed.

Tick had managed Luke's winnings, and he'd have lost

all that money when he went to prison if not for his father's intervention. Tick couldn't be happy about that, but Luke should've never allowed his manager to put his name on the bank account.

Tick quieted, his eyes practically shooting bullets at Luke. "I've been watching that cousin of yours." He nodded past Luke, and he spun around.

"Who? One of the twins?"

Tick scoffed, and Luke turned back to him. "As if. They're older than you."

Luke knew it would be one of the teens. Probably Daniel, the sixteen-year-old, Uncle Tucker's eldest grandchild. "He's not a fighter," Luke said.

"He's got the right disposition," Tick said. "Heard he got in a fistfight in school last week."

Luke hadn't heard that, but that wasn't a surprise. "You need to leave."

Tick didn't so much as blink. Another car rolled up to the curb, this one a dark, shiny SUV. Luke had a very bad feeling about the situation, and he fell back a step. "I don't want any trouble."

"That's the first thing that's changed about you."

"That's right," Luke shot back, his anger rising. He worked to tame it, to keep it way down deep in his stomach. "I have changed."

"What's going on here?"

Luke couldn't look at two people at once, but he needed to, because he didn't trust the man in front of him, and an icy hand gripped his throat when he turned his eyes to the man who'd just arrived.

Stephen Whitechapel, otherwise known as The White Devil, at least in the ring. He wore a mean, pinched look in his eyes and his biceps were as big around as Luke's thighs.

"I don't want any trouble here," he said, lifting both hands up in surrender. His mother was in the yard behind him. His aunt. Hannah.

He backed up one step at a time, praying that the Lord would protect him and his loved ones. He thought of Slate, and how he and Dallas had gone to Austin with him so he wouldn't have to go alone.

He thought of Nate, and the first time he'd met him. They'd been on the same team since. Luke needed his team right now, and he realized that in the ring, it was just him. It didn't matter who sat in the corner on the other side of the ropes. It was only him.

He didn't want to live like that anymore.

Stephen moved to a position a few feet in front of Tick, and Luke kept putting distance between them and him.

"Luke," his dad said, and Luke spun and strode toward his dad. He went right behind him while the two men on the street started to laugh. The sound of a police siren met his ears, and Tick and Stephen both looked to their left.

They seemed to be moving as a unit, and they looked back at Luke as if he'd called the cops. He hadn't; he'd been standing right in front of them the whole time.

"This is over," Dad called, and Stephen headed for his

SUV while Tick got behind the wheel of his car. They made plenty of noise by revving their engines and squealing away from the curb in plenty of time to be long gone by the time the cops arrived.

CHAPTER SIXTEEN

Hannah's nerves would not settle, even though the cops had left hours ago, and the party had continued undisturbed. Everyone just acted like nothing had happened, and she didn't understand that.

She didn't want that kind of relationship with anyone. She already had to tiptoe around her mother, and after a disastrous visit, it was always Hannah who broke the silence and texted her sisters. Then they'd all reach out to their mother after they'd all vented their true feelings.

She hated the tension in the silence, and she just wanted to talk through everything.

She stood from the bed where she'd been reading for the past hour. She couldn't remember a single sentence she'd read, and she'd have to go back several chapters and start again. Otherwise, she'd never be able to solve the mystery in her book before the heiress.

Luke's uncle had been kind enough to let her and Luke stay in his house that evening, and Luke's parents were here tonight too. Tomorrow, they planned to spend the day with just his parents, and Hannah was actually looking forward to going to Wolf Mountain. She'd only been once, and she remembered feeling like she'd arrived in a magical place.

She had many more years behind her now, of course, but she still liked shopping, eating good food in a good restaurant, and lying beside a swimming pool in the warm sun.

They'd stay at the resort tomorrow night, and the following day, Hannah had arranged for an early dinner at her parents' house in the woods. Both of her sisters would be there, along with her nieces and her nephew. She and Luke would then make the forty-five minute drive back to Sweet Water Falls.

As she stepped out into the hall, Hannah didn't want to continue the trip if she had to deal with anxiety every time she even thought about being with Luke, This trip was supposed to bring them closer together, not pull them apart or reveal to her something that could kill their relationship completely.

Watching him stride toward that man had terrified her, and she'd only hesitated for a few moments before hurrying over to his parents and telling them he'd gone to talk to someone named Atticus Stein. They'd obviously known who he was, and Luke's father had called the police within the next two minutes.

After the party, Luke had claimed he needed to shower,

and then he'd texted Hannah that he was tired and going to bed.

His room was at the very end of the hall, with his parents between his and Hannah's. She didn't care. She was thirty-five years old, and she wasn't going to bed without talking about this. She stepped right up to Luke's door, her ear practically pressing against it. She rapped lightly, and said, "Luke? It's Hannah, and I just want to talk to you for a minute."

The house was old, and the floorboards up on the second level echoed with every step. She heard them behind Luke's door, and she backed up just as he opened the door. Their eyes met, and Luke definitely hadn't been asleep—or even close to it. He did wear a pair of gym shorts and a bright blue T-shirt that was a snug fit across his broad shoulders and chest.

"I can't go to bed like this," she said. "Can we please talk?"

He stepped back and opened the door even further, a clear invitation for her to come in. She did, her nervousness increasing and coming out in the trembling of her hands. She went all the way across the room to the window and looked out. The street lamps came from a century ago, and they had bright, white lights shining into the night.

She drew strength from the way the poles stood so straight and tall, and she pulled in a breath and turned around. Luke had stayed by the door, and he leaned against a desk, looking very much like the thug who'd shown up and almost crashed his birthday party.

He seemed to realize it, and he straightened and unfolded his arms.

"I'm not sorry I told your parents about Atticus Stein," she said, cinching her strength tight. She'd broken up with several men. She'd been on the receiving end of a hard break-up. She could have this conversation.

"I was worried about you, and when that other man pulled up, I blinked, and I could see things spiraling out of control." She lifted her chin. "So I'm not sorry about that."

"I'm not upset by that," he said quietly.

"What are you upset about?"

"That I'm even in this situation in the first place," Luke said. "That you had to be afraid at my blasted birthday party." His gray-blue eyes practically spit fire. "That a potentially dangerous situation manifested itself in my uncle's backyard, in front of everyone. That I had to be rescued by my father and my girlfriend." He stopped, his chest rising and falling rapidly. "That suddenly, Beeville—a place I love and have always loved—suddenly doesn't feel safe for me."

Hannah's heart broke listening to him. She hurried across the room and wrapped him in her arms. He stood still and rigid for a moment, then two, and when he finally softened and hugged her back, Hannah's tension broke.

"Nowhere feels safe but you," Luke whispered. "Things are even different with Nate now, and Ted. Slate and Dallas are about the same, but they're busy with new wives and new babies on the way." His voice cracked slightly, and she felt him swallow.

She wanted to bind up his broken heart and tell him everything would be okay. She didn't, because sometimes things broke, and sometimes they didn't end up okay.

"I feel safe with you," he said again. "And I'm scared about that, because it's unreasonable to be with you all the time. It's unreasonable to think I can protect you when I know I can't, and it's terrifying to think you might be in any sort of danger because of me."

Hannah stepped back, letting her hands drop to his. "Why would I be in danger?"

"I don't know." He looked down at their joined hands. "I just keep thinking about Slate, and how his drug guy followed him to the ranch."

Hannah's heart skipped a beat, then two, then stalled completely. "Do you think Tick or whoever that other guy was would go there?"

"I don't see why they would," he said. "It's not the same situation at all. Tick didn't earn money from selling me drugs. He knows I can't fight again." Luke looked into her eyes. "I'm falling in love with you, Hannah, and what happened today is embarrassing for me."

Her eyes widened, and she searched his face for any tell of a lie. While she sure did like what he'd just said, she also needed to get one more point across. "It is extremely impor-tant to me that you don't shut down on me," she said, her throat so dry. "Because, Mister Holt, I'm falling pretty fast for you too, and it's not fair to wall off and keep me out of the hard things you're thinking about and worried about. That's not the kind of relationship I want, and I'm just not going to live like my parents for my whole life."

There. She'd said it.

Luke studied her now "Your parents?"

"They don't talk about anything important," she said. "There are three safe topics at their house: the weather, work, and food. But only sometimes on the food. My dad has made fun of me for not liking mushrooms before, and my mother gets her feelings hurt if you say you don't want a glass of iced tea but you wish she had some ginger ale." She shook her head. "You can't get it until you meet them. Trust me, it's not healthy. I'm not going to tiptoe around you, and I'm not going to tiptoe around hard conversations. I *want* to have them. It's important to me. It's how we make sure we're on the same page, and how we strengthen the bond between us."

Luke pressed his lips together and nodded. "I don't mean to wall off. I think it's a defense mechanism that happens to protect myself from saying something hurtful or doing something I can't take back."

"Like what?" she asked.

"Like punching something or someone," he said, and that made Hannah take another step back.

He sighed and dropped her hands, as they stood far enough apart to make it awkward. "I'm a fighter, Hannah.

That's our solution to everything. Hit it. Hit something. I thought for a long time that if I just hit hard enough, I could find a way through some of the darkness inside of me."

She swallowed, a new kind of buzz moving through her veins. "Darkness?" she managed to ask.

"It's mostly gone now," he said quietly. "I learned to deal with a lot of it in prison." He looked up at her again, the beginnings of a coy look on his face. "They make you talk to a counselor, you know."

Hannah was glad for that. She swallowed again, wishing she had a bottle of water. "Do you think you need to see a counselor now?"

He shrugged and pulled the chair out from the desk. He sank into it with a sigh. "Sometimes? Maybe? I don't know. I think I deal with things fairly well."

"If you need help, that's not a weakness," she said. "I'd rather you get the help than lie to me about it."

He nodded, though his eyes had that blazing edge in them again. "I'm not lying to you. I haven't lied to you."

"Okay." Hannah stayed very still for a moment, trying to find a new way to shatter this tension between them. She took a tentative step toward him, and then another. He opened his arms and she settled onto his lap, though women who carried the extra weight she did probably shouldn't sit on their boyfriends' laps.

"Thank you for being brave tonight," he whispered. He pressed his lips to her collarbone. "Thank you for acting. For having my back." He tilted his head and looked up at her. "I need someone watching out for me, and I especially like that it's you." He graced her with a small smile. "That's why you're my angel."

Hannah returned his smile, leaned down, and kissed him. She'd initiated kisses before, but this one was once again different than the one they'd shared in front of the painting. This one held more depth. This one held more of who she was, and more of who Luke was, and more of who they could be together.

Her doubts quieted, but she'd inspect them later, just to make sure she'd gotten all of her questions answered and that she could operate from a place of full knowledge. She hated it when she didn't have all of the facts to consider, and she was willing to have the conversations necessary to get the facts.

"I should go back to my room," she whispered against his lips.

"Mm, in a minute," he murmured, claiming her mouth again.

———

"Okay," Hannah said a couple of days later. "It's that road right there." She indicated the slip of a dirt road up ahead on the right.

"That dirt road?" Luke asked, clearly confused.

"I told you they lived just outside of town."

"Yeah, but I didn't think that meant..." He didn't finish

as he made the turn. He'd showed her the house where he'd grown up, and it took had been coated in some sort of magical spell that made her fall in love with it upon first sight. That house sat just outside of town, but the road was still paved, with plenty of land surrounding the home, which was also well maintained.

Her parents hadn't mown their lawn in a couple of years, she was sure. Maybe longer. Every so often, the youth group from the church would come, each of them bringing tools and weed whackers, lawn mowers and wheelbarrows. They'd work for a few hours on a Saturday morning and clean up the yard as much as they could, haul everything away, and attribute their time and energy to the service project.

As Luke rumbled down the road, Hannah prayed that the youth pastor had been inspired to come do a spring clean-up in the recent past.

The house sat under a huge canopy of trees, so the grass didn't grow very fast anyway. If her father would even mow it once a month, it would probably be enough. Hannah strained forward to see once Luke had passed the last tree on the right. She and her sisters had once called it the bron-tosaurus tree, because it had a long limb that arched over the road like the neck on a huge dinosaur.

She told Luke that, and he smiled as the house came into view. "It's not bad, Hannah."

"You don't have to be nice," she said. "At least when we're alone." She knew the house existed in various stages of disrepair. Ruth had called to get the roof fixed a year ago, and Hannah had helped her pay for it. Before that, Bethany had united the girls and pooled their money to get their parents a swamp cooler that would at least keep the living room and kitchen temperature bearable.

The front porch sagged, and Hannah felt it pulling down her soul. "I really don't like coming here."

"You grew up here?" he asked, peering at the house.

"Yes."

"Your sisters still live nearby?" He turned and looked at her.

"Nearer than me," she said. "Ruth's in Blossom, and Bethany's on the other side of Honeyfield."

"Are they...?" He didn't finish, but Hannah heard the rest of the question.

"They're very normal," Hannah said. "Sometimes Bethany can act a lot like my mom and get her feelings hurt at the littlest of things. She doesn't hold her tongue, either, and she's usually the cause of the blow-ups."

"How old is she?"

Hannah smiled at him. "She's forty-eight."

"Wow."

"I told you," Hannah said quietly. She'd only brought one other man home to meet her family, and it had started about like this. They thought they understood what she meant when she said her family didn't really get along. They thought they knew that feelings would and could get hurt easily. They thought they could fathom what a house looked like when no one took care of it.

Until they came face-to-face with the reality of it, they couldn't understand. Hannah had lived it and knew it deeply, and sometimes she was still shocked by what she found at her parents' house.

Another car appeared behind them, and Hannah said, "That's Bethany. She's got—"

"Two kids," Luke said. "Jolene is almost sixteen and about to get her license. That's why she's driving the car." He grinned at her. "And Thad, who's thirteen."

"You're sexy when you're showing off," she teased, and he burst out laughing. That was exactly what she needed to get herself out of the truck, and she reached for the handle while he continued to chuckle.

"Aunt Hannah," Thad said, busting from the car almost before Jolene had stopped it completely. The boy ran to her and hugged her tight.

Hannah returned the hug and asked him which Harry Potter book he was on.

"I started over, so I'm on number three again."

"My favorite one," she said with a smile. Her niece got out of the car, and Hannah called, "Jolene, look at you driving, girl. You did great."

"Thanks, Aunt Hannah." Her eyes darted to Luke, who grinned at her.

He reached up and touched the brim of his cowboy hat and said, "Howdy," and Jolene swooned against the car.

Hannah giggled and went around the tailgate to his side. "Thad, Jolene, this is my boyfriend, Luke." She beamed up into his face. "My niece and nephew."

"Hello," Thad said. "Do you like the Marvel movies?"

Luke blinked, then looked at Hannah with a blank look on his face. "Marvel movies?"

"You know, like Antman, Spiderman, Thor." Thad went on naming characters, overwhelming poor Luke by the end of the first sentence.

"Where's your mom?" Hannah asked.

"She's coming with Aunt Ruth," Jolene said. "Daddy's in Savannah."

"Oh, that's right. Beth told me that." She'd just forgotten. "How far out are they?"

"No idea." Jolene stepped toward the nearly dilapidated front porch. "But we can't eat until they get here, because they're picking up the food."

"I hope it's fast," Thad said, running up the steps. "I'm starving."

Hannah hoped her sisters would arrive quickly too, but it had nothing to do with eating and everything to do with when she could leave.

CHAPTER SEVENTEEN

L uke let Hannah grip his hand hard as they walked through the front door of the house in the middle of the woods. He knew it wasn't quite in the middle of the woods, but the whole place felt way out in the center of nowhere.

Her parents exclaimed over the kids, and Luke wasn't sure why, but he was expecting the inside of the house to mirror the outside. He'd expected shoddy furniture, with well-worn dirty carpet and run-down appliances. He wasn't sure what kind of people her parents were, but he didn't expect to find a tall man with dark hair wearing a pair of slacks, a white shirt, and an undone tie looped around his neck.

He wasn't expecting a woman in a pretty blue dress, her hair the exact same shade as Hannah's, and the d, brown eyes and high cheekbones.

"Hey, Momma." Hannah smiled and stepped past sensible, but clean furniture in the living room which the door opened into. "Daddy." She released Luke's hand to hug her parents, and then the three of them faced him, a trio of smiling people that made him tired instantly.

"Luke, this is my daddy, Lester Otto." She linked her arm through her father's. "And my momma, Shirley." She beamed at her mother.

Luke stepped forward and shook both of their hands, wondering if she'd hired clones. The way she'd spoken of her parents, he'd envisioned someone much different. "So great to meet you."

"You too," her mom said. "You two are dating?" She looked at Luke with sparking diamonds in her eyes, and Luke knew that look. His mother had often worn it when trying to get Joey to propose to his girlfriend. It was like they already had the perfect wedding planned, yet no one wore an engagement ring yet.

"Yes, Momma," Hannah said with plenty of warning in her voice. "Just for a few months now, so don't make a big deal out of it."

"Too late," Lester said. "She made the cowboy caviar." He chuckled and turned back to the kitchen. There was no island, but a long table had been set up to delineate the space from the living room and the kitchen. "The kids have found it."

"Hey," Shirley snapped as she spun around. "You monsters. Stop it. Step away. Your mother is bringing food for you." She turned back to Luke while Lester said, "You're not really monsters. Gramma's teasing. She made that for Aunt Hannah and her new boyfriend."

"Are you hungry?" Shirley asked while Luke was still trying to figure out what was going on.

"Uh," he said, glancing at the man who'd brought the kids in the first place. He hadn't him yet.

"My sister's husband," Hannah said quickly, seeing his look. "James is married to Bethany, and those are his kids. Connor is married to Ruth, but he's out of town. She's not here and neither are their kids."

"Great to meet you." Luke shook James's hand too, trying to remember all the names. He told himself just to remember her parents and work on everyone else over time.

"Come have some caviar," Hannah said, meeting his eye. "It's really good, and my mom's recipe is the best in the county."

Luke stepped over to her, and they faced the makeshift island together. Several bowls of dips sat there, and Hannah indicated the special one. It had a lot of corn, black beans, tomatoes, and avocados. It looked creamier than the other cowboy caviar Luke had eaten in the past—he was Texan, after all—but certainly delicious.

"Looks amazing," he said brightly. "And you have the big Frito scoops. I *love* those." He gave her mother a smile, and she swelled under the compliment and grin. Hannah handed him a paper plate and Luke started piling chips onto it. He took plenty of the cowboy caviar, as well as what

Shirley quickly explained was cheese and chili dip, and then a scoop of the fresh guacamole.

"Don't fill up," Shirley chirped. "Hannah's sisters are bringing a bag of tacos."

"Tacos?" Hannah asked with some measure of surprise and horror in her voice. "Mom, no. Tacos? Tell me they didn't go to Taco Cat."

"What's wrong with Taco Cat?" Lester asked. "You can get fifteen tacos for ten dollars."

"Dad, come on," Hannah said. "We've been over what's appropriate for certain meals." She put a scoop of cowboy caviar on her plate, and then another one. "If I have to eat one of those greasy tacos, I'm having two spoonfuls of this." She said the last sentence in a voice barely loud enough for him to hear.

"It's not a birthday," Lester said. "Or Christmas. Or any other major holiday."

"I brought my boyfriend to meet everyone," Hannah said. "I suppose I didn't specifically specify that such an event warrants more than the bargain tacos that Elias sells out of the back of his van, but I can't believe it's not implied."

She met Luke's eyes, and he tried to communicate to her that he didn't care what they ate for dinner. He was interested in knowing more about this Elias and his van.

"The kids like the tacos," Shirley said. "You used to too, if I remember right."

"I'm thirty-five," Hannah said. "Not twelve." She rolled

her eyes and didn't take any other dips. She sat down at the table with built in benches on two sides, and Luke sat beside her. "Sorry," she hissed. "If you're still hungry later, we can stop somewhere in Sweet Water Falls to eat."

"Will I still be hungry later?" Luke asked. "I like tacos."

"These are—" Before she could finished, a girl burst into the house and let loose a piercing, high-pitched, operatic note. Luke choked on the corn chip and dip he'd just put in his mouth, surprised when another girl entered behind the first, doing a beat box with her mouth.

The pair continued the odd mashup of opera and rap, even doing a little dance with it. When they finished, Hannah's parents burst into catcalls and applause, as did a pair of women who'd come onto the porch behind the girls.

Hannah left her plate on the table and crossed the room to the girls, taking them both into a hug at the same time. They clearly loved her, and Luke liked watching her fit right in with these people. She seemed to fit wherever she was and whoever she was with, and Luke envied that.

"She's pretty special," Shirley said, coming to stand next to Luke.

He glanced at her and then back to Hannah, who finished exclaiming over the girls and then stepped over to embrace her sisters. "Yes," he said. "She is."

"Do you think you're the one for her?"

Luke looked at Shirley fully now, not sure how to answer her. If he had to truly examine himself and Hannah, the answer was obviously no. He wasn't good enough for her. She deserved someone who could make the fancy, off-the-wall food she loved. Someone who wanted to take her to those places, and many more, just to see her smile. Someone who had more to offer than a criminal record and dangerous people at his birthday party.

Hannah turned back to face Luke, and she gestured for him to get over there and meet her sisters.

"Excuse me," he said to her mother, the weight of the woman's eyes on his back as he maneuvered through the cramped living room. It wasn't a huge space, and they'd filled it with things. In Luke's new state of mind, he nearly tripped on a stack of magazines next to the recliner.

When he reached Hannah, she took his hand in hers and inclined her head toward the two other dark-haired women. They all belonged to each other as evidenced by the shape of their faces, and the slope of their noses.

Bethany was the oldest, and she definitely had a few more wrinkles around her eyes. They shone at him as Hannah introduced him, and she took him right into a hug. "Oh, okay," he said with a chuckle.

"He's gorgeous," Ruth said in a voice that hissed like a whisper but that she clearly hadn't tried to keep quiet.

"Shh," Hannah said with a giggle. Bethany stepped back, and Hannah added, "And Ruth. She's eleven years older than me, and those were her girls who did that performance when they arrived." She indicated the two tweens. "Maisey and Diane. They're Irish twins, and only eleven months apart."

"One in February and one in December," Ruth said. "Same year."

"Wow," Luke said, looking at the girls. They had some lighter features from their father, whose name he couldn't remember. "You're very good singers," he said. "Do you take lessons?"

"Maisey does," one girl said. "I take gymnastics."

"You did the beat box, though," he said.

"I learned it from videos online," she said, beaming.

"That's amazing."

"Don't encourage her," Ruth said. "I'm trying to get her *off* the videos."

"Oh, uh—"

"Tacos!" Bethany bellowed, holding up two brown paper bags. "Come get them while they're still nice and hot."

Luke blinked as everyone flowed further into the house. Thankfully, Hannah stayed at his side and put her hand back in his, further grounding him. "They're a special bunch," she said.

Luke watched as Bethany unceremoniously tossed the two bags on the table and one of the men dove for them as if he needed to get one in his mouth right now or he'd starve to death. The rest of them similarly attacked, like lions on fresh meat, and Luke suddenly knew why he'd be hungry later.

"You're not missing anything,' Hannah muttered. "It's called Taco Cat, because Elias's van is dressed like a cat."

Luke squinted at the scene in front of him, and then at her. "What?"

"His van is dressed like a cat," Hannah said, staring at the crowd too as the noise increased. "Like, legit. The vehicle has a furry suit on it, with a tail that pokes straight up in the back. It's got eyes on the front and whiskers and the whole nine yards. Or nine lives. Whatever. He sells tacos out of the side of it. Fifteen for ten dollars. It looks like they got thirty, and we'll be lucky if we get one."

Luke tore his eyes from the fray. "Yeah, I'm afraid to go over there."

She giggled and tugged on his hand. "Come on. Let's try to get one, at least. When can you say you've eaten a taco that came out of a van-cat?"

Luke laughed, because he'd never said that, and he hoped he never would again.

LUKE BENT AND FIRED THE NAIL GUN INTO THE JOINT. *Ka-chink. Ka-chink.* He loved the high-pressured sound of things getting nailed together. He could work quickly with the nail gun in his hand, almost like it was an extension of his arm.

He stepped over the gap in the beams, following Sarah as she moved to hold the pre-cut wood in place. They'd spent all day yesterday on the ground, working the saws and getting the pieces cut. Today, they'd hopefully go through a large majority of them and get them nailed in place.

After that, the huge, flat pieces of plywood needed to be attached to the studs, and finally, the stable would start to take shape. They'd been laying the foundation of the skeleton for a while now, and Luke actually really loved that part of construction the best.

He didn't care about the outside structure once it was complete. He found beauty on the inner workings of something, which most people didn't get to see. How everything came together to house wires for electricity, and ducting for heating and air conditioning. Water lines, and heat-proofing liners. It all had a spot to belong, and if pipes got installed in the wrong place, the building could have problems for years and years.

He had to maintain enough concentration to put the nails where they belonged and make sure he didn't fall between the slats in the floor. Other than that, his mind wandered where it wanted to go, and it liked lingering on Hannah. He'd had a decent visit with her parents and family, though they were definitely unlike anyone else he'd ever met.

They'd been kind, and no one had fought. The tacos had nearly been gone when he and Hannah had arrived at the table, but they'd each gotten two. Considering that Luke could eat one in only three bites, he and Hannah had stopped in Sweet Water Falls for more to eat before they'd returned to the ranch.

Another week had passed since then, and then another, and Luke liked Hannah more and more with every conversation they shared, every touch of her hand against his, and every kiss he snuck behind the existing stable.

At the same time, her mother's question burned through his veins at night, especially after they'd separated and he lay in his room all alone, trying to fall asleep. Her words twined with the doubts which already existed inside Luke, and he couldn't root them out no matter how hard he pulled on them.

A dangerous fire simmered in his mind, and he couldn't get it to go out. He'd asked Uncle Tucker and Joey about Atticus Stein and Stephen Whitechapel, and neither of them had seen either of the men again. Neither of them seemed all that concerned about having problems with the manager or the boxer, and Uncle Tucker said they usually just stuck to their gym on the south side of Beeville.

Luke wondered why they'd shown up at his birthday party then. He couldn't get them out of his mind. They went with him all the time, and he couldn't shake them. If he wasn't thinking about them, Nate's words about him still not accepting the truth haunted him.

He honestly felt like he should be farther along in his recovery and healing than he was. The other guys had gotten out of prison and moved right on with their lives, even Slate, who'd worried so much about going back to the drugs. Even Dallas, who'd lost his entire support system when his wife had filed for divorce.

Ka-chink. Ka-chink. The nail gun fired again and again, and Luke's mind went round and round with it. He wiped the sweat from his forehead with his elbow, took a breath, and followed Sarah to the next row over.

"Luke," she said, and he looked up from where he'd just put two nails. Something beeped, and he realized his phone alarm was going off.

"Sorry," he said. "Are we close to done? I'm supposed to head down for the horseback riding lessons."

"Me too," she said. "We just need to notate where we are, so when Marc and Jack come up, they don't have to search for it."

"Right."

She held the board, and Luke nailed the last beam in place. "Rooftop, section four."

Luke usually knew stuff like that, but his brain held too much information at the moment. All he could do was nod at her and flash a tight smile.

Back on the ground, Luke took a couple bottles of water from the cooler and drank one before reaching the entrance to the stable. Ginger harped on everyone to drink enough in the summer heat, and Luke knew better than to let himself get dehydrated.

"Do you teach the horseback riding lessons?" he asked Sarah.

"No," she said with a smile. "But this year, with all the new sign-ups, Ginger wanted everyone there."

Luke nodded. He hadn't helped that much with the

lessons last year, because he'd been building cabins. He didn't remember it being that big of a deal, but the moment he stepped out of the stable and heard the noise of children's voices, he knew this was going to be a bigger deal than last year.

The moment he and Sarah rounded the corner, Ginger grabbed them. "You two are on the front rows. One, Sarah. Two, Luke. You're helping with mounting today." With that, she turned to someone else, baby Ward strapped to her chest and along for the ride.

Luke smiled at how seamlessly she'd integrated motherhood into the ranch, and once he was in place, he had a moment to watch as Nate approached his wife, kissed her and then the little baby, and then went to the front of the crowd.

He raised both hands and whistled between his teeth in an ear-splitting sound that got everyone to settle down. "All right," he called, his voice loud and authoritative. He started explaining the rules for the lessons, and the first rule was "There will be no crying here at Hope Eternal Ranch."

Luke chuckled, as did a couple of kids, but Nate wasn't kidding. By the end of the day, Luke felt like crying a little bit, if only because he'd never been so tired in his life. He'd been taking care of horses his whole life, though he'd taken a break during his boxing career. It didn't matter how long he'd been away from horses. They spoke to his soul in a way nothing else did.

He spent the next week riding after the kids did, talking

to a particularly gentle silver roan named Whitewashed. He was a good horse, tall and proud and very obedient.

He didn't have any answers for Luke, but Luke was starting to get a clearer picture of what he needed to do in order to find the closure he needed.

He had to accept and admit that what he'd done in the boxing ring over five years ago had been wrong. Unintentional or not, he'd done something terrible, and it was time to face what that was, deal with it, and find a way to move forward.

CHAPTER EIGHTEEN

Hannah wasn't surprised when Luke's truck was gone on Sunday when she returned from church. He always went somewhere after they'd all gone to church. She hadn't asked him to attend with her, though she wanted to.

She didn't think he'd come, number one. Number two, she didn't want to make things awkward between them.

A month had passed since their trip up to Beeville and her hometown of Honeyfield. All things considered, Hannah thought the meetings had gone really well. Her parents had been personable. Bethany and Ruth had been on their best behavior. Despite the tacos—which had earned her an extra dinner at The Blue Cowbell, one of her favorite all-beef restaurants—the visit to her parents had gone as well as Hannah could've expected.

She and Luke got along well; she saw him every day as

they worked together on the ranch. They usually spent time together in the evening, even if it was him simply sitting on the couch in the West Wing. She didn't go to the Annex, because it felt awkward with all the other men there, and she lived in the West Wing by herself now.

"Emma's cooking," Ginger said as she followed Hannah inside. "Lunch in about an hour?"

"I'll be there," Hannah said. "Are you working in the office?" She paused to take off her heels, as Ginger didn't usually come to the house with her.

"Yep."

"I'll take Ward, if you'd like," Hannah said, bending to pick up her shoes. She'd change really fast, because no one wanted to wear a body shaper if they didn't have to, and then she'd get a bag of chips and hold the precious baby.

"That would be great," Ginger said, smiling.

"Let me change real quick." Hannah went down the hall to her bedroom and peeled off all of the elastic and stretchy fabrics that kept her looking ten pounds lighter than she was. She didn't know who she was trying to impress at church, but she couldn't quite bring herself to leave the shaper in her drawer.

Once she had a pair of loose-leg pants on, as well as one of her favorite tank tops, she returned to Ginger's office. Ward babbled in his swing, and Hannah paused it to get him out. Ursula got to her feet, clearly interested in what Hannah was going to do with the baby.

The German shepherd had been fairly protective of

Ward since Ginger and Nate had brought him home three months ago. "Come on," Hannah said to the dog. "You can come too." She took them both out into the living room, and while balancing the baby in her arms, she got a bag of chips out of the cupboard and headed over to the couch.

Ursula jumped up onto the cushions next to her, and she settled her head on Hannah's leg. She positioned Ward in the crook of her arm and gazed down at him. "You're so perfect," she whispered to him, a smile filling her whole soul.

The baby had beautiful, pearly white skin, and the biggest pair of dark green eyes Hannah had ever seen. He had dark hair with a sheen of auburn in it from his mother, and he was simply the cutest human alive.

Hannah sighed and closed her eyes, leaning her head back and relaxing into the couch. "You're such a good baby, Ward." She patted his bottom and his eyes started to drift closed. Before she knew it, the three-month-old was asleep, and Hannah watched as Ursula's eyes drifted shut as well.

Hannah yawned, but her mind ran too fast for her to truly fall asleep. She needed to, because she hadn't been sleeping well at night either.

She was simply feeling unsure about, well, pretty much everything. Beth and Ruth had both texted her for a solid week after meeting Luke. They'd really liked him, and they wanted all the details they could get.

Hannah had admitted to how much she liked Luke, and she'd told her sisters that they got along really well. All of that was true. Hannah had started to fall in love with him, and she looked down at Ward.

"If he breaks up with me, baby, I'm going to eat so much butter pecan ice cream." She half-laughed and half-sobbed, though she had no reason to believe Luke would break up with her. He'd gone pretty quiet in the past few weeks, though, and while she'd asked him a few times if he had anything bothering him, he'd just smiled each time and said he was thinking about a few things.

When she'd asked what things, he'd asked her for more time before he could tell her. She had to respect that, and she'd tried not to press him.

"Should I ask him again, Ward? What do you think? Do you think he's thinking about us?" Hannah looked up and out the windows that showed a blue sky and a hint of the fence out front. "Do you think he's trying to figure out what to do with his life? I know he's not super happy here on the ranch."

She wasn't sure why, though. He was so good with animals, and everyone loved him, from the parents to the kids to the other cowboys. He worked hard from sunup to sundown, and Hannah didn't want him to leave. He did have a lot of family property up in Beeville, though, and he had mentioned talking to his uncle again in the past couple of weeks.

Ward didn't know what Luke was thinking, and Hannah didn't either.

"Maybe I want too much," she whispered to the infant,

and then she reached over and stroked Ursula. She wanted this life so badly. She wanted this baby to be hers, and she wanted a house of her own. She could handle a dog too. Maybe not one as big as Ursula, though she was an excellent ranch and guard dog.

A thread of guilt stitched through her for not being satisfied and content with the life she already had. It was a really good life, and Hannah had always had people surrounding her who'd supported and loved her.

On the couch beside her, her phone buzzed, and she reached over to pick it up with the hand she'd been using to pat Ursula.

Luke had texted with, *I'm going to Beeville for the day so I won't be back at the ranch for lunch. Just wanted you to know.*

She balanced her phone on Ward and typed with one finger. *Okay. Hope you're okay. Drive safe.*

I'm okay, he said. *Miss you already.*

Hannah smiled at that and laid her head back again. "Maybe I'm just too far inside my own head," she whispered as she closed her eyes.

LUKE DIDN'T RETURN THAT EVENING, OR THE NEXT DAY. He didn't text her to say why at first, either, but Ginger. That made sense, as Ginger was technically his boss.

By Tuesday when she arrived at the construction site,

Hannah had only slept for a few hours at a time, and she'd put in an order at the grocery store for four quarts of butter pecan.

She'd texted Luke a half-dozen times, and he hadn't responded to her yet. Ginger had told her that he'd asked for a few days off so he could "take care of some things" in Beeville. When Hannah had asked to know what things, Ginger had met her eyes with an even gaze.

"I don't know, Hannah," she'd said. "I didn't ask him those types of personal questions. I expect he'll tell you if he wants you to know."

Hannah had nearly fled from Ginger's front porch, where her friend and boss had been sipping coffee with her husband while their baby lay on a blanket on the ground.

Ginger had texted to apologize for what she'd said, and Hannah had apologized too. She hadn't really asked what Luke was doing in Beeville. She'd demanded that Ginger tell her.

Her words still cut through Hannah, though. Luke hadn't told her, which meant he didn't want her to know what he was doing in Beeville.

A horrible thought hit her, and she pulled her phone from her pocket. She hadn't called Luke yet, preferring to give him the space he so seemed to want.

The line rang and rang, Hannah's heartbeat picking up steam with every second that passed. "Hello, Hannah," he said, his voice even and pleasant.

"You're alive," she said breathlessly. "Are you alive? Have you been taken captive?"

Luke let a few seconds of silence go by, and then he started laughing. Instant foolishness filled her, and Hannah stared off at the horizon as she fought back her tears.

"I am alive," he said through chuckles. "Since I answered the phone, I thought you'd know that."

Hannah reached up and wiped her eyes. His voice held a definite teasing quality, but Hannah wasn't in the mood. "I've texted you a bunch of times," she said carefully. "And I had this sudden, terrible thought that maybe you hadn't answered me because you couldn't. I was worried."

"I'm sorry to make you worry," he said calmly. "I'm okay. I'm just...facing some things, and it's taking longer than I thought it would."

"When will you be back?" Hannah pulled the phone from her ear so she could sniffle without him hearing her.

"...not sure," he was saying when she got the phone back to her ear. "I'm staying with Uncle Tucker, and I'm doing fine."

"Okay," she said, nodding. What else was she supposed to do? Demand he call her every night and check in?

"Wild about Slate and Jill, right?" he asked, and Hannah seized onto his words.

"What do you mean?"

"Haven't you heard? They're expecting already."

"I hadn't heard that," she said, turning back toward the

row of cabins she'd left behind when she'd nearly run from Ginger's porch earlier that morning.

"Shoot," Luke said. "Maybe I wasn't supposed to say anything. Pretend like you don't know, okay?"

"Okay," Hannah said, but she was terrible at pretending. It also stung that Jill hadn't told her the moment she'd found out about her pregnancy. If Luke knew already, why couldn't she?

"I have to go," he said. "I'll call you later, okay?"

"Okay," she said again, hating that she'd said it so much during this conversation.

"Bye, angel." The call ended, and Hannah let her hand fall back to her side. She turned in a full circle, surveying the ranch in all its glory. She saw a tractor moving out in the field, and plenty of activity surrounding the stables. Horses got led out in a steady stream, and Jess organized everything with a clipboard resting on her very pregnant belly.

She still had a month until her baby was due, and Hannah turned away from her, sudden bitterness coating her tongue.

She put her head down and worked, the sun baking everything that day. She showered that evening and stayed in her room though she lived alone now. She didn't want to run the risk of bumping into Ginger and her beautiful baby.

She thought of Emma and Ted, and their perfect little family. Dallas and Jess seemed to have the All-American life too. Now Slate and Jill were already on their way to achieving all of the dreams Hannah had kept close to her heart for so long.

Luke didn't return by the weekend, and he didn't come back to Hope Eternal the next week either. He called here and there, but not as much as Hannah expected from a man she considered her boyfriend.

Jill and Slate announced their pregnancy at the following Sunday's luncheon, this one being held on the back deck of the Annex, as Spencer had put together lunch that day. Hannah sat by herself, removed from everyone, until the tall, dark-haired cowboy she'd been out with once or twice came to sit beside her.

"Hey," Spencer said, plunking his plate filled with only potato salad onto the table and then sitting in front of it. "You look miserable."

"Just what every woman wants to hear," she said dryly.

Spencer didn't chuckle or even smile. "Sorry," he said with a sigh. "You look how I feel."

"How's that?" she asked, perking up at the unrest she heard in his voice. It streamed through her in waves.

"Discouraged?" he asked. "Ready to move on? Desperate to find that one person I can spend my life with?" He scooped up a huge bite of his salad and put it in his mouth. "Like that."

He'd summed everything up quite nicely, in fact. "I've eaten four quarts of butter pecan in two weeks," she admitted. "Luke left the ranch."

"Permanently?" Spencer looked at her with those dark eyes firing with curiosity. "I thought he was coming back."

"Do you see him here?" she asked, gesturing around the deck. She shook her head, the desperation she'd spoken with choking her now. She swallowed and reached for her can of soda. After drinking enough to get her throat open, she shook her head. "No, I think he left. I don't think he's coming back."

"He hasn't told you? Weren't you two dating?"

"Thus, the butter pecan." Hannah ran both hands through her hair. "He's hardly called or texted at all."

"Do you know where he is?"

"Yeah, he's up in Beeville."

"Maybe you should go up there and find out what he's doing." Spencer ate more of his salad.

Hannah considered what he said, but she knew she'd never do it. Luke had a phone, and he knew how to use it. He hadn't called her because he didn't want to talk to her. She wished he'd been more of a man and said so, but Hannah was well-versed with the hints and messages men gave.

"What are you going to do?" she asked. "Dating app?"

"You know what?" Spencer looked thoughtful, and Hannah realized they'd been friends for a very long time. "I think I'm going to look around for another job at another ranch. Hope Eternal isn't the only one around here."

Hannah nodded, though his statement surprised her. "Sometimes we just have to find a way to move on."

"Yep." Spencer sounded as miserable as Hannah was about that prospect, and she reached over and covered his hand with hers. He squeezed, and Hannah finally felt like someone understood the pure agony she'd been in since Luke had left the ranch.

CHAPTER NINETEEN

L uke arrived at Wolf Mountain Resort before his uncle, as he had been for the past couple of weeks. The woman standing behind the reception desk smiled at him, her red-painted lips curving up way too much.

He barely raised his hand in her direction and kept moving fast. He wasn't interested in Laura, and she'd made it abundantly clear she'd go out with him if he even gave her more than three seconds of attention.

He should've called Hannah last night. Or the night before that. Or at all. Misery laced through him, along with a healthy dose of regret, guilt, and self-loathing. He'd meant to come to Beeville for a day. Two, tops. He just needed to find closure to his past life as a boxer, and he hadn't antici-pated all that would entail.

"You should call Ginger too," he muttered to himself as

he went down a hallway guests overlooked and into his uncle's office. Uncle Tucker didn't make it out to the resort very often, and his manager had quit three weeks ago.

It felt serendipitous to Luke, and though he wasn't sure how to manage a resort, he'd felt strongly that his family needed him, and he'd stayed.

Uncle Tucker kept saying he'd been doing interviews for a new manager, as Luke didn't particularly like desk work, more managing budgets and employee schedules from a spreadsheet. But for the time being, Luke liked helping his uncle, and he needed to be in Beeville for some reason.

He'd been avoiding everything and everyone, even the second family he'd found in prison. He wouldn't be surprised if Slate or Dallas showed up at the resort at any time, and then Luke would have to explain everything.

If only he could explain it to himself. "That would be a start," he told himself as he sat down behind the desktop computer. He jiggled the mouse and waited for the dark screen to brighten, wondering what he needed to do first. A new week had just begun, so the schedule was set. Paychecks had gone out on Friday, and thank all the stars above, the resort had a full-time bookkeeper who took care of that kind of stuff.

Luke managed guest services, housekeeping, activities, and all the behind-the-scenes items. Luke thrived on the activity end of things, and he stood from the computer without doing anything on it.

The resort had morning yoga classes that coincided with

a children's horseback riding adventure, and if he hurried, he'd have time to help saddle the horses. The animals soothed him, and honestly, they reminded him of Hope Eternal Ranch. And every time he thought of the ranch, Hannah wasn't far behind.

He shoved the feelings way down deep as he crossed the back lawn behind the resort. He knew he was making a mistake, but he didn't know how to fix it. His phone rang, and he honestly couldn't bring himself to check it.

At the same time, he couldn't just let it go. On the third ring, he looked at it and saw Hannah's name. His heart leapt, and his feelings for her wouldn't be ignored. "Hey," he said, trying to make his voice as light and as casual as he could. "What's going on?"

"What's going on?" she repeated, and Luke slowed his steps.

"I keep meaning to call," he started.

"I'm calling to tell you not to bother," Hannah said. "I mean, not that you have concerned yourself with me, or how I might feel after you left town for what was supposed to be a day and haven't come back."

"Hannah—"

"You left the crew high and dry, Luke. You left Ginger without someone to handle the horses and the lessons. She's been hiring in a day laborer, and he's terrible. *Terrible*, Luke."

"I'm sorry," he said.

Hannah laughed, and it sounded cruel. "You are not

sorry, Luke. I'm not even sure you know how to feel sorry for the things you do."

"That's why I'm here," he said, practically yelling the words. "I'm trying to find a way to make peace with what happened five years ago. I'm trying to find closure to what landed me in prison so I can move forward with my life. With you." He exhaled heavily and ran his hand up his face. "Don't you feel like we're stuck?"

Hannah didn't answer right away, but he could still hear her breathing on the other end of the line. "It does feel that way, a little," she finally said.

"We *are* stuck," he said. "And it's because of me. I'm not ready to move forward, because I'm still stuck in the past. Nate was right—I haven't truly accepted the verdict, and I'm trying to find a way to do that. I *know* that's the way forward, and I'm struggling to do it."

Desperation clogged his throat, and he swallowed to try to get his emotions back in check. Hannah said nothing, and that was like her saying a whole lot.

"I am sorry," he said, his thoughts jumbling into a giant ball of yarn. "Besides, I'm no good for you, Hannah. You deserve a man who knows how to dress well for a fun dinner at places like The Blue Cowbell or Madam Croque. You deserve a man who can figure out where those kind of places are and plans a big surprise at your favorite one for your birthday or just because. I'm not that man. I'm never going to be that man."

"Who told you you're not good enough for me?"

"No one," he said, though her mother had insinuated as much. "I just already know I'm not."

"I get to decide those things for myself."

Luke shook his head, his teeth pressing together in a painful way. He didn't have room in his life for this kind of hurt, and it seemed to go on and on. "I have to go," he said, grinding the words through his throat. "I need to help get the horses saddled."

"Horses?" she asked. "Where are you?"

"I'm really sorry, Hannah," he said. "If we can just maybe pause for a while, I think I'll be able to get to a place where I can be the man you deserve."

"Luke," she said, but he honestly couldn't hear her say anything else.

"Please," he begged. "I just need a break."

Silence poured through the line for several long seconds. Hannah finally said, "Okay," and Luke sighed.

"Thank you," he said.

"Good luck, Luke," she said. "I honestly mean that. I hope you can find what you're looking for." With that, the call ended.

Luke put his phone back in his pocket and faced the corral. He suddenly didn't care about helping with the horses. The resort employed three full-time groomsmen to run the riding programs and take care of the horses. He only helped because it helped *him*.

Everything he did came down to how it made *him* feel.

Perhaps it was time to think about how someone else felt.

Luke turned on his heel and headed away from the horses. Away from the stables. Away from this resort out here in the western wilds of Beeville. He didn't need to be here today, and he had plenty of other places he could go to try to understand the gravity of what he'd done.

FORTY MINUTES LATER, LUKE PULLED INTO THE cemetery. He'd been driving for a while, trying to figure out where to go and what to do. His opponent had been Robert Houser, and he'd thought about going to the Houser's house and apologizing for his actions.

In the end, he hadn't been brave enough to do that. He wasn't even sure where they lived, though they had to be in the surrounding area, as the fighting district didn't extend that far.

He didn't know where Robert was buried, but he stepped over to the caretaker's office. He knocked on the door and twisted the knob at the same time, and when he entered, a woman came through a door in the back.

"Good morning," she said, clearly surprised to find him there.

"Good morning," he replied. "I'm looking for someone I know is buried here. Is there a map or anything like that?"

"Sure," she said, settling in front of her computer. "Name?"

"Uh, Robert Houser."

"Robert...Houser," she said as she typed his name into her machine. "He's in plot F-twenty-seven." She turned in her chair and picked up a paper map. "It starts with A in the center." She circled the middle of the paper. "Goes out in concentric circles from there. F is over here, on the side of the hill. Twenty-seven will be down on the terrace."

She smiled at him and handed him the paper. He looked at the scribbles she'd put on it and turned to leave. He remembered to say, "Thanks," over his shoulder as he left, but his mind could barely think past that.

Time slowed down as he searched for the grave, but he eventually found it. He'd only taken two wrong turns, and no one else was in the cemetery that morning.

He looked down at the headstone with Robert's name on it, and everything from the fight rushed at him. He could smell the sweat that always came with a boxing match. The jeers and yells from the crowd echoed in his ear.

Tick's mint gum usually rode the air between them, as he sat and yelled instructions at Luke between every round. *Watch the right hook. He's creeping around on your left, because he knows you're hurt over there.*

Keep your gloves up, Holt. You can't afford to take another hit like that.

Hit him hard, Luke. So hard, he won't get up again.

You've got the strength, and if you can just get in that one hit, his speed won't beat you.

On and on, and Luke had loved every minute of it.

Luke had hit Robert as hard as he could. He hadn't been able to get up again, though he'd tried.

Luke had hit him again. And again. And again.

It had taken the referee and three more men to get Luke off of Robert.

His eyes filled with tears, and he knelt down in front of the dark brown stone. He reached out toward the letters, but he didn't touch them. "I'm so sorry," he said, pure agony and regret flowing through him. "Your family was right. I was on steroids, and I'm not making an excuse, but there was some definite rage in that fight."

So much anger, and back then, Luke hadn't learned how to deal with it. He wasn't sure he knew how to manage it now, but he felt much more in control now than he'd been then.

"I deserved my time in prison," Luke said, the last of his resistance to the involuntary part of his sentence fading into nothing. "I probably deserved a whole lot more."

He bowed his head and let his tears drip down his face. He'd never cried over what he'd done, but faced with the headstone, the full weight of what Luke had done was simply too much to handle.

Where do I go from here?

He'd felt like this in the nine months leading up to his trial, and every day since the conviction.

"What do I do?" he whispered. He tipped his head back and looked up into the clear, blue Texas sky. "Help me." He'd never been terribly religious, but he really needed the help of the Lord right now.

He needed to believe he could find his second chance at a real life.

He needed to believe he still had worth, despite what he'd done.

He simply needed someone to tell him how much he meant to them.

His phone chimed, and Luke sniffled as he straightened. Slate had texted to say, *I'm thinking about you right now. Are you okay?*

Luke's throat closed again, and he quickly tapped out, *Not really. At the cemetery right now. I'll call you later.*

Cemetery? Slate said anyway, and the phone rang.

Luke needed more time to stuff his emotions away before he spoke to Slate. He didn't want to admit he'd been crying, and embarrassment squirreled through him. He swiped the call away, telling himself he really would call his best friend later.

The silence in the cemetery brought peace to his soul, and Luke seized onto it. The breeze kicked up, and Luke took a deep breath of it. The pathways in his mind opened, and Luke could see some things with exactness.

He wanted to be here in Texas, but not at Wolf Mountain Resort.

He wanted to be at Hope Eternal Ranch with his friends—and with Hannah.

He was in love with Hannah Otto, and while he couldn't fathom how she could possibly love him, he had high hopes that if he could get past this roadblock, he could work on becoming the type of man she needed and wanted.

He thought about what else he needed to accept and face. Probably the men at the gym he'd had to walk away from. He had to make peace with Atticus and anyone else who had been affected by his behavior from that time of his life.

Taking a deep breath, he looked down at the headstone again. "I really am sorry," he said, unable to find more adequate words.

"What are you doing here?"

Luke turned around to find a man and a woman standing on the bottom step of the natural staircase that led back up to the main level of the cemetery. Robert had been buried down on a terrace, and Luke was surprised he hadn't heard their footsteps on the rock stairs.

The woman held a bouquet of flowers, and the man kept his hand on her arm, almost like he had to hold her back from flying at Luke and clawing his eyes out. They both stared at him, their frowns deepening the longer he stayed silent.

Cold fear gripped his heart when he realized who he was looking at.

Robert's parents.

CHAPTER TWENTY

Hannah reached to move her red piece, saying, "I made it into the home. Finally." She grinned at Remmy, who watched every move Hannah made carefully. As if *Sorry!* was the most important life-or-death game in the world.

She reached for a card and said, "Good job, Hannah. I hope I get an eight."

Hannah hoped she did too. Then the seven-year-old would win the game and they could be done. Hannah loved the little girl to bits and pieces, because she had a very positive outlook on life, and she always had a big smile and a great story from school.

Her older brother sat at the table too, but Thomas clearly didn't care about the game, and he looked like he'd rather be anywhere but here.

"Should I get out the ice cream?" Hannah asked, and the boy perked up.

"Can we have hot fudge?" he asked.

"I don't see why not." Hannah smiled at him. "It feels like a hot fudge night, right?" She got up as Remmy moved her piece—she hadn't gotten an eight—and got the half-gallon containers out that she'd brought over to Jess's and Dallas's earlier.

She'd been thrilled to be asked to babysit while they went to the hospital. Their baby was coming early, but neither Jess nor Dallas had seemed too freaked out by it. They'd called, and they'd been gone by the time Hannah had made the drive from the ranch.

She was just glad she didn't have to sit around the West Wing by herself. Worse, Jill would come over with a pan of brownies, and Hannah would war with herself for hours as they watched a movie, laughed, and ate far too much sugar.

The extra weight Jill had put on was due to her pregnancy, and no one would say a word to her about it. But Hannah's extra five pounds were starting to make her body-shapers really uncomfortable, and she'd worked so hard to lose the weight in the first place.

She didn't want to give Luke that kind of power over her, but as she got out three bowls, he had it anyway. She'd fallen in love with him, and she couldn't change that now.

"Does anyone want bananas?" Hannah asked.

"I do," Remmy chirped. "It's your turn, Hannah."

"Turn my card over for me," she said over her shoulder.

"You got a four."

"That one moves me backward, right?" Hannah turned back to the game board, a bunch of bananas in her hand. She surveyed her red pieces and pointed to the one clear over by Thomas. "Will you move that one back?"

Remmy knelt up and reached across the board to move it. She counted four backward and then said, "Oh, you get to slide. Good idea."

Hannah's piece ended up in the same place it had been in before, and she turned back to the bowls. "Thomas? Bananas?"

"No, thanks," he said.

Hannah sliced bananas for Remmy and herself, scooped in the vanilla ice cream, and set the jar of hot fudge in the microwave to heat slightly.

Thomas said he wanted the chocolate ice cream with hot fudge, so she scooped that for him and turned back to the table. "Nuts, Thomas?"

"What kind?" He looked up, hopeful.

"Almonds or peanuts." Hannah held up the little bags of chopped nuts.

"Peanuts," he said. "Please."

Hannah smiled and nodded, fixed up his bowl with hot fudge and peanuts, and placed it in front of him. She opened a couple of drawers before finding the silverware and got out spoons.

She took her bowl back to the table, along with Remmy's, and sat down to finish the game.

Remmy won a few minutes later, and Hannah looked at Thomas. "Okay, bud. Your turn. What do you want to do?"

"Anything I want?"

Hannah smiled and took another bite of her ice cream. "Within reason, but yes. School hasn't started yet, and the sun doesn't set for a couple of hours. Miniature golf? Go-karts? Movie and popcorn?"

She probably shouldn't have suggested the last one, as the kids hadn't eaten a single real food since Hannah had arrived a few hours ago.

"What about dinner?" she suggested next. "I know a great place with these amazing chicken fingers." She looked at Thomas and then Remmy. "And burgers. You like burgers?"

"I do," Thomas said.

"Let's go," Hannah said. They might not be broccoli-filled, but a hamburger would be better than a dinner of ice cream, hot fudge, and popcorn.

"Can we go fishing?" Remmy asked.

Horror struck Hannah right in the back of the throat. "Fishing?"

"There's a new pond on the south side of town," Thomas said. "Dad keeps saying he's going to take us, but he hasn't yet."

"Is it stocked?" Hannah asked. She couldn't remember the last time she'd gone fishing.

"Yep."

Remmy looked at her with wide eyes. "Please, Hannah?"

Hannah took a moment to think. "Will your daddy be mad he can't take you?"

Remmy's face scrunched up for a second. "I don't think so."

"He'll be really busy with the new baby anyway," Thomas said. "At least that's what he keeps saying."

Hannah detected a hint of teen attitude in his words, but she didn't say anything. "All right." She stood and picked up their bowls. "Get your shoes on. We're going fishing."

———

A FEW HOURS LATER, HANNAH WORE HER PRIDE RIGHT on her sleeve. She'd fed the two kids a real meal and then taken them for an hour of fishing at the new pond. There had been several children there with their parents, and it was clearly the hot spot to be. Hannah hadn't heard of it, but she had no reason to be going to a stocked fishing pond by herself.

"I'll get the freezer bags," Thomas said, who'd really perked up with a cheeseburger and then a fishing pole in his hand.

He'd listened intently to the man who'd told them how to store their fish, and Hannah had decided the moment he'd started speaking to let Thomas handle it all.

She could supervise and not have to touch any scaly skin, and since she didn't live here, she wouldn't have to deal with any fishy aftermath.

Once Thomas had the fish wrapped in heavy-duty aluminum foil, and then tucked into a freezer bag, he put them in the freezer.

"Time for baths and bed," Hannah said, and Remmy skipped happily down the hall to do what Hannah asked, and Thomas washed up in the kitchen sink.

"Can I go read in my room while Remmy's in the bathroom?"

"Yes," Hannah said easily. She hugged the dark-haired boy before he could escape from her, and he seemed surprised by the embrace. "You're a good boy, Thomas. You did so great with the fishing too, and with helping Remmy." She stepped back and pushed his hair back off his forehead. "Thank you for helping me with her today."

Thomas smiled in a quiet way and nodded. "Do you think they've had the baby yet?"

"I don't think so," Hannah said. "If they had, I think your dad would've called you." She nodded to his pockets. "Have you checked your phone?"

"No." He dug it out and pressed the power button. "I still forget I have it sometimes."

"Is that right?" Hannah giggled. "Most kids your age can't wait to get a phone."

"I don't see why," he said. "It's just a pain. This girl put me in a group chat, and now I get like, a thousand texts every day." He rolled his eyes, and Hannah really wanted to see his phone to find out what kind of messages he was getting. "It's all annoying."

"What kind of messages?" she asked.

"Stupid stuff like what the geography teacher will be like, or that someone wants to go to the skate park on Friday. They never go. It's just all this talk."

"Can you remove yourself from the group?"

"I have no idea." He focused on his phone and said, "Nothing from Dad." He walked away from Hannah, and she let him go.

She sent a quick text to Ginger, inquiring about Jess, and settled onto the couch.

Nothing yet, Ginger said. *Are you staying in town tonight?*

Yes, Hannah said. *I'll make sure I get the monthly reports done. I have my laptop, and I'll bring the kids out tomorrow morning to get the files I need.*

Thank you, Hannah.

She looked up from her phone, her thoughts moving through who else might need a text. It took all of her willpower not to text Luke every morning to let him know to have a good day. And every night to find out how his day had been.

She didn't though, her thoughts landing on Spencer. He wasn't happy at Hope Eternal either, and she wondered if he'd found another job.

Any luck on the job hunt? she sent to him.

She sent a quick message to Jill too, asking her how she felt. Hannah just needed to feel connected to someone, and she really hated evenings alone.

I have a job interview this weekend, Spencer said. *I still haven't said anything to Ginger, so please don't mention it.*

I won't, Hannah promised. *Where's the interview?*

Cooper & Co, Spencer said.

I'm good, Jill said. *How are Remmy and Thomas?*

Getting cleaned up, Hannah said to Jill. *And guess what? I went fishing tonight and didn't gag.*

So proud! Jill sent with a winking face.

Hannah smiled, her mood lifted as her friends continued to text.

Before she knew it, she had to put her phone down to tuck the kids into bed, and then she went down the hall to the guest bedroom. The only escape she got from Luke came when she finally fell asleep.

Tonight, she lay in bed, wondering if she should make the drive to Beeville to see him. Maybe if they just stood face-to-face, he would remember how he felt about her. Maybe she could apologize, and he'd feel worthy of her attention. He *was* worthy of her attention. Maybe she could just text him and ask how things were going in Beeville, and if he was any closer to a solution to his situation.

She forced herself to roll away from her phone, but when it went off again, she had to reach for it.

Dallas had texted, and she sat up, her heartbeat throbbing through her veins again. *Jonas Casey Dreyer has arrived finally. It was quite the struggle to make him come out, and Jess ended up having a C-section. She's resting now while they monitor her blood loss. They're bathing the baby, and then I'll send pictures.*

Hannah read the message once more, her stomach clenching at the thought of Jess having a C-section. She'd need a lot of help, and she wouldn't be back on a horse any time soon. She'd be devastated about that, and Hannah sent her a quick text though she wouldn't see it for a while.

Love you, Jess. I'm here for whatever you need.

She stayed sitting up in bed, because she didn't want to miss the first picture of Jonas.

Her phone buzzed in her palm, and she looked down to see Nate's message back to Dallas. She's been put in a group chat just like Thomas, and more messages started to pile up.

When Luke's name popped upon her screen, Hannah actually cried out audibly.

Congrats, Dallas and Jess! Can't wait to see him.

Hannah's pulse pounded now, and all thoughts of sleep fled.

Thankfully, a few minutes later, Dallas sent a picture of a cute, chubby baby with olive skin and lots and lots of dark hair, just like Jess.

Everyone on the string covered up Luke's text, and he didn't say anything else.

"Just like usual," she muttered as she silenced her phone and replaced it on the nightstand.

CHAPTER TWENTY-ONE

L uke bent over the toilet and retched. "I can't do this," he said as part of the groan. He didn't have anything in his stomach to get rid of, because he'd been sick for the past ten minutes.

The stench of the gym filled his nose, something like sweaty plastic, burnt rubber, and too many energy drinks. Perhaps that was the scent of testosterone, and there was plenty of that here too.

He had to do this though, and Luke raised his head.

He'd run into Benjamin and Tammy Houser at the cemetery a few days ago, and that conversation had started him down the path he was currently on. At first, he'd thought he wouldn't be able to get past the couple—Robert's parents—to get up the steps, back to his truck, and out of the cemetery.

Ben Houser had been angrier than his wife, but Tammy had allowed him to explain that he was trying to make things right. He was trying to accept responsibility for what he'd done. Acknowledge it and accept it.

Tammy had said he'd already accepted responsibility. He'd fulfilled his sentence, and he'd paid the price as set forth by the state of Texas. They couldn't ask for more than that.

She'd asked him if he was still fighting, and he'd said, "Of course not. I can't do that."

She and Ben had seemed puzzled, and Ben said, "You were very talented in the ring."

The door to the gym had been standing slightly ajar for five years, and Luke needed to close it once and for all.

He stood up and moved over to the sink. It bore a grayness that wouldn't come off with the strongest cleaners, but he turned on the cold water and splashed it across his face. He'd had to do this the first time he'd been in a championship fight too, and the chill from the water brought clarity to his mind.

"It's one match," he told himself. "To prove to yourself that you don't need this. That you've dealt with it, accepted things, and are ready to move on."

He blinked, his reflection morphing into Hannah's lovely face.

Just as quickly, it became Slate's, then Dallas's. He'd texted his friends off the string that included everyone at the ranch to let them know what he was doing, and they'd all encouraged him to do whatever he had to in order to find the closure he needed. Slate and Nate had each texted him individually, and Luke had promised to call Nate by five o'clock tonight.

He hadn't told anyone but his mother that Tammy Houser had invited him to dinner. Or that he'd said yes. He was going out with them that evening, and Luke realized what a horrible mistake he'd made by scheduling everything in the same day.

"You ready?"

Luke turned from the mirror and looked at Tick. The man had been nothing but surprised when Luke had walked into the gym and then his office three days ago.

"I don't know," Luke said, and a familiar smile crossed Tick's face.

"You've done a thousand fights like this." Tick walked toward him, his trademark clipboard in his hand. If anything, the man had grown a couple of inches and lost even more weight, making him more crane-like than before. He still exuded power, though, and he could intimidate anyone.

Luke had certainly been afraid at his birthday party.

"This is different," Luke said, but he couldn't explain how.

"It's two minutes. Winner stays in the ring. Whoever is still standing once the whole thing is over, wins."

Luke nodded. He knew the rules. He had done games and matches like this before. The prize for this one was five hundred dollars, which was nothing. If Luke had still been fighting, he wouldn't have bothered to enter something like this.

But everyone started at the bottom, and he'd done matches like this early in his career. It was how he was going to end it too.

"I haven't been working out," Luke said, though he had been lifting weights with his friends in the morning, and he'd done a little boxing in Vegas. *Four months ago*, he thought. He couldn't believe that much time had passed since he'd left Las Vegas, but it definitely had.

"You've still got plenty of power in your shoulder," Tick said. "I can see it. Now come on. You're the one who wanted me to set this up, and I've been working on it non-stop since you dragged your sorry self into my office." He didn't smile. Instead, he turned and walked out of the bathroom, leaving Luke alone once again.

"Just go," he told himself, and he did exactly that. He walked out into the gym, where a single boxing ring had been set up. Bleachers and chairs surrounded it, and the jeering started the moment Luke stepped onto the black mats covering the floor.

He held his head high, because he'd been the underdog in many previous matches. He'd also been the hated defending champion. A new kind of mask slipped into place, and he wondered what Hannah would say if she could see it.

You're doing this for Hannah, he thought. He reached the man Tick had appointed to be his corner, and he held out his hands so they could get gloved and taped. He bounced on the balls of his feet as his opponent ducked beneath the ropes to get into the ring.

Luke didn't know anyone's name anymore, but the guy had sandy blond hair and a chest that easily spanned a meter. He looked like he worked out morning, noon, and night, and Luke had a very real feeling he'd be done in less than sixty seconds.

Old boxing thoughts began to run through his head.

Keep your gloves up.

Move your feet. Don't stand still.

Watch for the open attack. Strike fast when you see it.

Be on the defensive, not the offensive.

That last one had been the hardest for him over the years. He always wanted to be the one in control, but prison had taught him to be more submissive. To accept what he couldn't control and make the best of what he could.

"Ready," his corner said, and Luke opened his mouth for the guard. It went in, and he hated it as much now as he had five years ago. He also valued chewing food with his teeth, so he wore the mouthguard in the ring without fail.

Someone plunked sparring headgear on his head, tightening the straps in the back. Luke felt a whole new energy come over him, and he tapped his gloves together. Their weight was familiar, and welcome, and his adrenaline ran through his body now, setting his cells vibrating.

At the same time, he couldn't believe he was going to fight today.

He'd never felt this level of control, though, and he knew that was because he wasn't on steroids. They'd definitely amplified him in every way—physically, mentally, emotionally. He rather liked himself without them, and he climbed into the ring and started the shuffle-step he'd done as a fighter.

The crowd jeered louder, but Luke tuned them all out. His focus existed on the edge of a knife, and when he looked across the ring, all he saw was the blond-haired man.

The bell rang, and Luke shuffled forward to tap gloves. Then his flew in front of his face and he hunched down into them, dancing backward as his opponent tried to get in an early swing.

It met dead air, and Luke saw the gap where he could've hit the other guy on the right cheekbone. A jab, straight out and back, and he'd been reeling backward.

Luke didn't make the punch. He skirted around the ring, the noise almost deafening as men yelled at him to do something. His opponent clearly wanted him to come closer and stop shying away, but Luke knew how the early rounds of this went.

He only had to last two minutes, and he only had to get one punch in. It didn't matter if it happened in the first ten seconds or the last ten. He blocked, and he danced, watching as his opponent grew tired.

Tired, in only two minutes. Luke remembered feeling like that, but today, he didn't.

The other guy came at him again, and this time, Luke held his ground. The other guy swung, leaving his whole right side open, and Luke dodged left, striking out with that quick left jab he'd been known for.

The other man's head snapped back and he stumbled away from Luke.

Horrified, Luke watched as a trickle of blood came from the man's nose. His gloves lowered. His feet stopped moving.

Before, the sight of blood would've thrilled him. It spurred him to hit harder next time, to go right for that same spot.

Gloves up! shouted in his mind, and he barely got them back in place in time before the other guy was on top of him. He took many little, tiny steps to get away from him, and his momentum took him right into the ropes.

Luke lashed out with a right uppercut, catching his opponent right in the kidney.

Two hits, and Luke felt like throwing up again.

His head pounded in time with the screaming on the outside of the ring, and Luke didn't need anything else to win this round. So he stayed away from his angry opponent, kept his gloves up, and waited for the bell.

When it sounded, he stopped and lowered his gloves.

His opponent rushed him, swinging for all he had. Luke went down in a wave of pain, trying desperately to cover his face again. Someone pulled the other guy off, and Luke looked up into the bright, white florescent lights above him in the ceiling.

Everything was so clear now.

He'd kept hitting after the bell. What he'd done was *wrong*, and not just because he'd broken the rules of the sport.

He honestly had no recollection of how many times or how hard he'd hit his opponent. The steroids did induce a rage inside him he hadn't even realized until that very moment.

You were wrong, he thought. *You did something wrong.*

"I was wrong," he said out loud as Tick's face appeared above him. "I did something wrong."

"Come on," Tick said, reaching out and hauling Luke to his feet. He raised his right hand in victory, but Luke felt like crying. The tears wouldn't be sad, and they didn't come from the pain in his lower jaw. They wouldn't be happy, either, but relieved.

He was simply *relieved*.

"I'm done," he yelled to Tick, who looked like he'd murder him if Luke walked out now. "Give the victory to that guy. I'm done." He lifted his glove to his mouth and ripped off a piece of tape.

He didn't care what Tick thought or did. He hadn't

come here for him. He'd come to find something for himself, and he'd found it.

"AND THEN I WALKED OUT," LUKE SAID, HIS VOICE rushing over itself. "It was incredible, Nate, and I've never felt like that before."

"I'm glad," Nate said, his voice low and slow but oh, so powerful. When he praised Luke, Luke felt like he'd finally done something right. "You faced it, and you figured it out."

"I was wrong," Luke said, calming now that the whole story was out. "I did do something wrong, and the punishment I got for it was warranted."

Nate didn't say anything for a few seconds. "I didn't mean to get on your case, Luke."

"No," Luke said. "I needed it. You were right." He looked out the windshield of his truck. He hadn't even left the parking lot at the gym yet. "How's...I mean... Is Hannah...? Never mind."

"You'll be ready for anything now," Nate said, a distinct wail starting on his end of the line. "I better go. I'm on duty with Ward, and he is not happy with me."

Luke laughed as the call ended. He was still getting used to Nate using the name Ward and not referencing his brother. His older brother had come to visit so often at River Bay that even Luke had started to worship him.

A few hours later, Luke found himself bent over the toilet again. This time because Benjamin and Tammy Houser would be here at any moment to take him to dinner. As Luke stood up, the doorbell rang. He quickly washed his hands and swished out his mouth before calling, "Just a second!"

He couldn't believe he was going to dinner with them.

He opened the door and looked into Ben's eyes first. "Hello," he said, working hard not to clear his throat.

"Good to see you, Luke," Tammy said. She actually stepped into him and gave him an awkward hug. "You look nice."

He looked down to make sure he was actually wearing pants, and he had on jeans. Thankfully. "Thank you," he said. "You do too."

"Have you ever been to Legacy?" she asked as she turned to go down the steps. Her husband followed her, and Luke brought up the rear.

"Uh, not for a long time," he said. "I haven't been in Beeville much in the past five years."

"What are you doing these days?" Ben asked, his voice still plenty sharp.

"I'm working for my uncle right now," Luke said. "But I came from a ranch down in Sweet Water Falls. I need to get back down there."

"Doing what?"

"Construction mostly," he said. "Some horse care. That type of thing. I like working outside, and I'm good with my... hands." He cleared his throat then, realizing what he'd said.

He paused before getting in the SUV. "Listen, I'm really sorry," he said. "I know that's not going to bring Robert back, and I want you to know I accept the verdict and all the responsibility for hurting Robert." The clarity from that day in the gym had really helped him. It had *cleansed* him from the tarnished thoughts of the past five years.

Ben stared at him, as did Tammy. "We know that, Luke," she finally said. "We're not here tonight to torture you, and you should stop torturing yourself."

"Why are we going to dinner?" he asked.

"Because," she said simply. "You're the same age as Robert, and no one talks to us about him. You did, a few days ago at the cemetery, and our therapist thought continuing to talk to you would be good for both of us." She offered him a small smile that seemed almost apologetic.

Luke didn't know what to say to that. "Okay," seemed appropriate, and he got in the back seat of the SUV as Ben walked around to the driver's seat.

"So," he said with a sigh. "Is Legacy all right? We like it there, but there are other good places in Beeville."

"Legacy is great," Luke said.

The restaurant had twinkling tea lights strung along the railing leading up to the front entrance, with aged barrels wrapped in more lights. Hannah would've loved it, and he wanted to take a picture of the perfectly Texas wreath on the front door and text it to her.

He did snap the picture, but he didn't send it to her. The only reason he hadn't returned to Sweet Water Falls yet was because of this dinner, and he needed to get on the road tomorrow.

Dallas and Jess had had their baby a couple of weeks early, and they were set to go home in the morning. He could stop and get breakfast and meet them at home to visit them and see their new baby.

Then he'd have to figure out how to get Hannah back into his life.

"Are you seeing anyone?" Tammy asked after they'd been shown to a table.

Luke looked up, surprised by the question. "Uh...I don't know."

"You don't know?" she asked, glancing up at the waitress as she set a glass of water on the table.

"It's complicated," Luke said.

"So many things in this world are," Ben said. "Tell us about her."

Luke looked back and forth between the Housers, sure this situation wasn't happening. But if there was one thing he could talk about, it was Hannah Otto.

"She's great," Luke said with a smile. He proceeded to tell them about her, about how they'd met, and how he'd left Texas to go to Vegas.

Their appetizers came, and then their food, and the whole dinner passed while Luke laid out the complicated situation. "So there it is," he said, waving away another cup of coffee. "Sorry, I've dominated this whole night with talk of her." It felt nice too, though, and Luke really liked having a neutral party to talk to.

His mother had clearly been on Hannah's side when he'd told her about their quasi-break-up. She had supported Luke's endeavor to find closure, though, and he had appreciated that.

"It's been nice," Tammy said. "Every situation in life is just as complicated. Listening to you talk has helped me understand you better, Luke."

"You're a better man than you think you are," Ben said, exchanging a glance with his wife. "Luke, I won't lie and say I didn't blame you for a long time. A really long time. But holding that blame inside my heart doesn't hurt anyone but me. You got a sentence, and you fulfilled it. It's not up to me what to do from there. Only the Lord can do that, and I believe He allows people to have a clean slate."

"You do?" Luke's eyebrows shot sky-high.

"I do," he said. "I'm not perfect, and Tammy and I have been through some rough times since Robert's death. I've said and done unkind things. I need the saving grace of God just as much as you do."

Luke had been migrating closer and closer to the Lord in the past couple of weeks, but he'd never thought about things the way Ben had just laid them out.

Everyone needed the saving power of the Lord. His misdeed might have been bigger—big enough to warrant intervention from the laws of the land. That didn't mean he needed more punishment from anyone, and it didn't mean the Lord would never forgive him.

"Dessert tonight?" the waitress asked, and Luke shook his head. He paid the bill, and he remained fairly quiet on the way back to his uncle's house.

Tammy and Ben both got out of the SUV and stood side-by-side on the sidewalk. "Luke," Tammy said. "You deserve that woman as much as she deserves you. You should forgive yourself and go see if she'll forgive you too."

He could only nod, because he wanted to do exactly that. Tammy stepped into him again and hugged him. He was ready this time, and he held onto her tightly for several long moments.

"Thank you," he whispered. He shook Ben's hand, and he stood on the sidewalk and watched them drive away. They'd forgiven him. He'd paid his price for what he'd done. Now, he just needed to figure out how to forgive himself—and how to get Hannah back.

THE NEXT DAY, LUKE DIDN'T DRIVE STRAIGHT TO Dallas's, though his texts told him that they'd left the hospital about the same time he'd left Beeville. As they only lived ten minutes from the hospital, and he had a good hour-long drive to their place, they'd definitely be there already.

Still, he found himself making the turn that would take him back to the ranch, not to Dallas's house in town.

He pulled up to the fence at the familiar ranch, feeling like he'd come home. "Home," he said to himself. The word meant so much to him, and he knew it had more to do with the people he surrounded himself with, and not the place where those people existed.

Hannah's car wasn't anywhere to be found, and Luke stayed in his truck, trying to decide what to do. He hadn't stopped for pastries or flowers. He had nothing to offer Hannah but himself, and as he got out of the truck and walked toward the West Wing, he decided that had to be enough.

He had to be enough.

He knocked on the front door, but no one came to answer it. Turning, he took up a spot on the top step, determined to talk to Hannah before he did anything else.

"I'm ready," he told himself again and again, whispering it when it felt like many minutes had passed and she still hadn't returned to the ranch.

He felt like throwing up again, and then the sound of tires crunching over gravel met his ears. He froze, but his stomach roiled violently.

Hannah's dark sedan came into view, and she pulled past the parking area out front and down the driveway. She parked in the open garage, and he heard the slamming of her door once she'd gotten out.

She must not have seen him sitting there, because she didn't come out of the garage, and he heard her voice on the air.

"...too much spice. I'm not into the spicy stuff, Emma." Her voice ebbed away, and then it disappeared as she went inside the house.

Luke's heart pounded as he stood. He could ring the doorbell again.

He could.

He stood in front of the door, his hands at his sides. "Come on," he muttered, but he still didn't lift his hand to press the button.

A moment later, the door opened, and Hannah stood there, her phone at her ear. "You're right," she said. "He's here. I have to go." She lowered the phone from her ear, but Luke couldn't say anything.

She was everything he wanted, and he couldn't look away from her wide, surprised eyes, her pink-painted lips, and all of that hope and desperation pouring from her.

"I love you," he blurted. "So much has happened, and the only person I need to tell is you. The only person I think about when I think about coming home, is you."

He drew in a breath. "I'm sorry I left like I did. I wasn't anticipating the way everything overcame me, and I'm sure I handled it all wrong."

He swallowed, unsure of what else it would take to win over Hannah Otto. She wasn't terribly dramatic, but she knew what she liked and what she didn't.

"Do you think...is there any way you might be able to forgive me?" he asked. "Do I even have a shot at a second chance with you?"

Hannah blinked, her shock gone from her expression now. She tucked her phone in her back pocket and settled her weight on one foot. She studied him, letting her gaze slide down to his feet and then back to his face.

"You have a very good shot," she said.

Just like that, Luke's whole world became brighter. He started to smile, noticing the way her lips curved upward too.

"Do you really love me?" she asked.

"With everything I have," he said, taking a step toward her. "I know it might not be much right now, but I'm getting better every single day. I'd boxed away so many emotions, but I've been slowly pulling them out and forcing myself to deal with them."

"I see," she said, falling back a step.

He closed the distance between them again. "Where were you?"

"I've been over at Jess's for a few days," she said. "Helping with the kids while she and Dallas have been in the hospital."

He nodded. "I need to go see them, but I wanted to talk to you first." He stepped into her personal space, hesitating as his hand lingered only inches from her waist.

"Go on," she whispered. "You've been torturing me for weeks. You're here now. Kiss me."

"I didn't mean to torture you."

"Luke, you've been in my head since the day I met you." Hannah touched his chest, breaking the barrier between them. His hand landed on her waist, and he drew her into his arms.

"I love you," he whispered again.

"And I love you, Luke Holt." Her eyes drifted closed, and Luke lowered his head to kiss her.

The same explosive chemistry that had existed between them since the first day they'd met flowed through him, and just like the first time he'd kissed her, he found he never wanted to stop.

CHAPTER TWENTY-TWO

H annah slopped through the mud, glad she'd worn the rubber boots that covered her jeans all the way to her knees. Rain had hit the Coastal Bend hard the past few days, as it sometimes did in the winter, and she kept her head bent as she hurried into the stable.

Jill would not be happy about the weather, as she'd been setting up for the first week of the Howdy Holiday Festival she'd started last year. The straw bales were soaking wet, as was the back drop Jill had dragged out literally the morning of the first rainstorm.

She hadn't been back out to put any of it away yet, because she was six months pregnant, and she'd told Hannah she didn't do anything she didn't want to do. "What's the point of being pregnant if I can't use it to get out of unsavory tasks?" she'd asked Hannah with a devilish glint in her eyes.

Hannah had laughed with her and agreed. Of course, now that Luke had returned to Hope Eternal Ranch, everything made Hannah happy. They'd been back together for a little over three months, and they'd been talking about getting married in the past few weeks.

He hadn't asked her to marry him yet, though, and Hannah tamped down her impatience as she bent to get a bottle of water from the fridge just inside the door. The rain seemed relentless, but it would calm down in a few minutes, and she'd be able to get back to the house without getting soaked to the bone.

Her phone rang, and Luke's name sat on the screen. "Hey," she said, her voice bright.

"Where are you? You're not out in this, are you?"

"I'm hunkered down in the stables," she said. "I just finished with the goats and chickens."

"Angel, it's getting worse. I'll come get you."

"There's no sense in both of us being soaked," she said. "It'll let up in a few minutes. It always does."

"The weatherman is saying it's going to rain for hours, and that the storm out in the gulf has just officially become a tropical storm."

Hannah's heart pounded. She'd lived through storms and hurricanes in the past, but they weren't fun—especially with animals to tend to. "Maybe you should come get me."

"I'll be right there." He hung up, and Hannah wished

she'd made it out earlier to get her chores done. She moved over to the door and peered into the weather. It was raining harder now, and the pounding on the roof increased.

She couldn't see more than a few feet, and she prayed for Luke to hurry. "And that goes for proposing too, Lord," she muttered.

A few minutes later, his headlights cut through the rain and mist, and Hannah ran the moment she left the stables. He somehow got her door open, and she rounded it and climbed into his truck, soaking wet. "Whew," she said, reaching up to push her wet hair out of her eyes. "It's crazy out there."

He grinned at her. "You look great."

She gaped at him. "I'm dripping wet."

"Yeah," he said, licking his lips. She laughed, and he did too, and she sure did like this happier, more whole version of Luke Holt.

He'd told her about all he'd done in Beeville, and they'd discussed moving up there so he could work for his uncle. In the end, he'd come out and said he didn't want to do that. He loved Hope Eternal Ranch, and if she was okay with him being a cowboy, that was what he wanted to keep doing.

"Of course it's okay with me," she said. "I just want you to be happy." She'd grinned at him. "And keep wearing that sexy hat."

He'd laughed, and he'd swept that hat off as he'd kissed her.

"I'm a little bit of a dreamer," he said. "A wisher on stars."

"That's fine with me," she'd said as they'd swayed together in the kitchen at the West Wing. "Just take me with you wherever you go."

Now, she looked at him, as he hadn't moved the truck yet. "Are we going back?" She reached over and turned up the heater. "I'm freezing. I want a hot shower and someone to make me a good cup of coffee." She slid him a smile, the wetness of her clothes starting to seep into her skin.

"I can do that," he said, but he still didn't move. "Listen, I wanted to talk to you about something."

"All right." Hannah quieted her nerves, because she and Luke had had a lot of important conversations over the months.

"This wasn't exactly how I wanted to do this, but I promised my mother I'd do this by today, and I'm afraid of what might happen if I don't."

Hannah sat very still, not sure what he was talking about. She had the quick thought that perhaps he was breaking up with her. Why else would his mother be involved?

"Will you open that glove box for me?" he asked.

"Okay." Hannah did, peering inside. A single red rose sat there, and she sucked in a tight breath. "Luke." She reached for it and let her eyes drift closed as she inhaled the scent of the rose. "It's beautiful."

She glanced over at him, and he now held up a little

black box, already open, with a glinting diamond nearly blinding her.

"I love you, Hannah Otto," he said. "I'd be down on both knees right now if we weren't in the truck, and I had this whole thing planned where I'd propose to you up on the roof of the stable we've worked on together, but then all this rain happened."

Tears stung her eyes, but they were such good tears, Hannah didn't mind them. She was already beyond wet as it was. What was a little more water?

"Will you make me the happiest man in the world and become my wife?"

Hannah let her tears fall down her face as she nodded. "Yes," she said. "Yes, I love you and I'll marry you."

He grinned from ear to ear as he took the ring out of the box and slid it on her finger. They both admired it, and then Luke lifted his eyes to hers. He kissed her, and Hannah had never been kissed by her fiancé before.

She sure did like it.

ONE YEAR LATER:

"Over here?" she called to Jill. Hannah's best friend turned from the bales of straw she and Emma were stacking into the throne where Cowboy Claus would sit once the Howdy Holiday Festival began.

"No," Jill said. "Mom, will you help her?" Her nine-month-old baby sat in a stroller, carefully picking up Cheerios while her mother worked.

Sabrina Kyle turned from where she and her husband were setting up a fifteen-foot Christmas tree. She left him hanging the cowboy boots and saddle-shaped ornaments to come help Hannah with the location of her sweet shop for this year.

The landscape of the festival changed every year, as Jill wanted every event to be different from the one before. This year, Hannah was getting her very own sweet shop, where she'd be teaching free classes for people as part of their entrance ticket to the festival, and special, paid classes that required an extra fee.

She'd been perfecting her sugar cookie recipe for weeks now, and she let Sabrina take the padded stool and move it where it should go. "I think she wants it over here," she said, beaming at Hannah. "There's going to be a tent here for you. I know that's coming this afternoon, because I heard Jill talking to the party supply store this morning."

"Okay," Hannah said. "Thanks."

"How are you feeling, dear?" Sabrina reached out and brushed Hannah's hair off her face. "How long until the baby comes?"

"Oh, he's due on Christmas Eve," Hannah said with a tired smile. "I'm going to make it."

"Of course you are." Sabrina stepped into her and hugged her, Hannah's big belly between them. "You and Luke are going to be great parents."

Hannah basked in the love and comfort of Sabrina's arms. Since she and Luke had bought a wig for Sabrina, they'd had a special relationship. Jill had even brought back the most delicious triple fudge brownies when Hannah had been pining over Luke last fall.

Nothing beat the butter pecan ice cream for a broken heart, but Sabrina's brownies had come close.

"I'm scared," Hannah admitted, her voice pitching up.

"Of what?" Sabrina pulled back and bent to help Hannah extend the legs on the first table.

"Of just everything," Hannah said. "I've always wanted to be a mother, but what if it's harder than I thought it would be?" She shook her head, her thoughts jumbling with the motion. "I mean, Ginger makes it look so easy. She's carried Ward around with her throughout every season. If she has to do something, he just comes along."

She glanced around as if Ginger and Ward would be right there. She knew they weren't, as Ginger had taken him home to put him down for a nap about twenty minutes ago. The boy was almost two years old now, and he could say a few words. Hannah loved him to death, as did everyone around the ranch, but she didn't know how to train him the way Ginger and Nate had.

Emma was much more relaxed in her parenting, but Frannie was the picture of perfection everywhere they went. Emma always had her hair done right, and Frannie could sit and play with anything—literally, Hannah had walked into Emma's office once and found her baby playing with an empty cereal box—for hours.

"What if my baby is a monster and won't take naps?" Hannah asked. "What if he doesn't want to be strapped to me while I go around and feed goats and chickens? What if he's high-maintenance, and I can't get any work done?"

Sabrina smiled in a knowing way, but that only made Hannah's nerves fire with frustration instead of fear. Neither were very comforting, and she just wanted someone to reassure her that her baby would be an angel, and she'd be fine.

Jess and Dallas brought their boy to the ranch every day too, and more often than not, the four little children would end up in the West Wing together, napping while one of their mothers worked in an office nearby.

Hannah had been looking forward to adding her and Luke's baby to the mix for eight months now. But her pregnancy hormones felt out of control from time to time, and since she hadn't slept much last night, her worries had surged to the front of her mind.

"Hannah, your baby is going to be perfect," she said. "Have you and Luke thought of a name?"

"We're going to name him Robert," Hannah said, bending to lift the table up onto its legs. "Ben and Tammy text Luke every day to find out if we've had him yet. I think they're more excited than my own parents." Honestly, Hannah didn't think that was terribly hard to do, though her mother had cried when Hannah had called to tell her about her engagement.

Perhaps she'd cried about the fact that Hannah wanted the wedding to be planned and completed in less than three months. She'd wanted to get married before her next birthday, and that meant they had a deadline of February twentieth.

She and Luke had been married on the eighteenth, right there at Hope Eternal Ranch, with a few friends and their families. Luke definitely had more family than her, and it had grown to include the Housers.

"Robert is such a good name," Sabrina said.

Hannah nodded, perfectly happy with the choice. She knew it meant something to Luke—and more importantly Ben and Tammy—and she wanted to provide healing and relief to anyone she could.

"Mom," Jill called, and Sabrina turned toward her voice. "I need you over here to see if this is straight."

"I'm never coming here to help her set up for this thing again," Sabrina said with an edge in her eye. "She's so demanding. Is she always like this here?"

Hannah burst out laughing and shrugged. "She knows what she wants when it comes to the Howdy Holiday Festival, I suppose."

"I'm even baking mint brownies to sell every weekend," Sabrina grumbled as she walked away. Hannah would be sure to sneak a few of those from the tray before they went out, because Sabrina made the best mint brownies in the whole world.

She continued to set up her part of the festival, which included a small cabinet where she'd keep non-perishable items like Ziplock bags and mixing bowls. Once the tent arrived, she'd hang her sign and then she'd be ready for next weekend's guests to the ranch.

Hannah bent down to pat Ursula, then looked around. "Where's your mama, huh?"

Ursula whined and tipped her head up to look at Hannah. Her heartbeat bounced in her chest. "Is she okay?"

She pulled out her phone, because she was far too big to go running down the road toward the cabin where Ginger and Nate lived. Ginger answered on the first ring, perfectly pleasant. "What's up?"

"Did you know Ursula is out here? She's whining at me."

"I let her out a few minutes ago. She was pacing in front of the door."

"Okay, well I've got her."

"All right." Ginger hung up, and Hannah looked down at Ursula. "Should we go find Luke? I think he's out working on the front gate."

It had been damaged in a terrible wind storm that had blown across the Gulf and then the state, leaving plenty of debris in its wake. He'd been fixing things around the ranch since, and she started in her slow waddle toward the road that led onto the ranch.

The noise and chatter of those setting up for the festival died, and only the sound of her own labored breathing and Ursula's panting filled the November air.

On her next step, a pain sliced through Hannah's abdomen, sending her to her knees. She cried out and flung out her hands as if there would be something there she could grab onto.

There wasn't.

She fell forward, landing hard on her hands and knees in the dirt.

Ursula barked, and Hannah looked at her but couldn't make sense of the situation. Before she could get a proper breath, another pain tore through her. Tears sprang to her eyes, and she tried to contain the cry, but it flew from her throat in an almost primal way.

Ursula licked her face and whined, then stood straight and tall and barked. She barked and barked and barked, and Hannah tried to quiet her.

"It's okay," she panted, but she knew it wasn't. Something definitely wasn't okay.

She wasn't due for another month.

Babies come early, she thought, and that was the last thing in her mind before another horrible, wrenching pain that ripped her open from her belly button to her spine sent her into unconsciousness.

CHAPTER TWENTY-THREE

L uke looked up at the sound of barking. Down on the other side of the gate, Slate had stopped fiddling with the pins as well.

Axle took off, barking in return, and Slate laughed at his dog. "Stupid thing. Ursula's probably found that rabbit hole, and she'll growl Axle out of getting any."

Luke smiled and focused back on the board he'd been trying to get loose. The wind had taken the gate and twisted it in several different directions. In his opinion, it would've been easier to remove this one and rebuild a whole new one. He'd suggested as much to Ginger, but apparently, this gate had sentimental value, and she wanted to salvage as much of it as she could.

Axle's barking continued, fading for a moment and then coming closer again. He circled Slate, barking at him in a way Luke had never seen before.

"What's going on?" Slate asked, looking out toward the stables and barns. Axle paced toward it, looked over his shoulder, and came back to circle Slate.

Over and over, until Luke said, "He wants you to go with him."

"Ursula is still barking too." Slate wore a specific worry on his face then, and Luke remembered the last time the two dogs had been worked up like this.

A trespasser had come to Hope Eternal Ranch.

They both abandoned the gate at the same time, and they both strode toward the sound of Ursula barking.

Though it was November, and Nick was working on keeping the grasses mowed down, he hadn't done it along this stretch of road. Most people used the one that ran from the back of the homestead toward the barns and stables, and only tourists used this road when they came for summer camps, the wild boar hunt, or to stay in the cabins out in the wetlands.

Luke caught sight of Ursula, though she wasn't moving. She held very still, in fact, her bark continuous and very loud now that he and Slate were closer.

"There's someone on the ground," Luke said, breaking into a jog. "Do you see that?"

"No," Slate said, catching up to him. "Who is it?"

"I don't know." Luke's heart pounded in his chest. Could it be someone from the ranch? Or someone who'd stumbled onto the ranch and needed help?

A few more strides, and everything inside Luke screamed. "Dear Lord," he said. "It's Hannah." He sprinted now, moving as fast as he could. His wife. His dear, pregnant wife was lying on the ground, two dogs around her now, barking for everything they were worth.

"Hannah," he yelled. "Slate, call nine-one-one." Luke slid as if he was trying to get to second base before the ball and nearly ran into Hannah's body. "Hannah." He panted, his lungs working overtime to get the air he needed. "Angel, open your eyes."

He tried to see what was wrong with her, scanning down her face, across her neck, shoulders, and down to her hands. She didn't appear to be bleeding, but her body jerked as if someone had hooked her to a bolt of electricity.

He rested her head in his lap, tears dangerously close. Nearby, Slate's voice said something, and Luke seized onto it.

"Hannah," he said, inhaling some reason into his mind. "Baby, can you wake up?" He put his hand on her belly where she was carrying their baby, and that was when he noticed the blood stains on her pants.

Terror gripped him, but he still somehow knew what to do. "She's gone into labor," he called to Slate. "How far away are they?" He stood and bent to lift his wife into his arms. The hospital was only fifteen minutes from here. If the paramedics wouldn't be here that fast, he could get her to the hospital.

"They've sent an ambulance," Slate said. "Eleven minutes." He held Luke's gaze as he settled Hannah's head against his shoulder. "No, she's not awake...yes, she's bleeding." He swallowed and looked at Hannah's legs.

"Okay," he said. "We'll do that. I'll stay on the line until we can get her back to the house."

"The house?" Luke asked, near panic. "What are they saying?"

"They want us to get her into a bed or the back of a car. Somewhere she can lie down but potentially have the baby."

"Have the baby?" Luke shook his head, his steps heavy as he started back toward the gate. His truck was parked there, and it was the closest to the ambulance he could get. "Tell them to hurry. She's not having the baby here at the ranch."

She would kill him if he let that happen. He looked down at her face, noting how white it was. He hated that she wouldn't open her eyes. "I'm not going to let that happen, angel, okay? You're not having our son here."

SLATE FOLLOWED LUKE CLOSELY, READY TO JUMP forward and brace him if he should start to fall. Hannah was eight months pregnant, but Slate wasn't surprised Luke could lift her. He'd always been so strong, and he could do anything when it came to Hannah.

Slate needed to call Jill, and Ginger, and everyone. They'd all come running, because that was what they did for each other around here. He saw someone moving up ahead to his left, and he put his fingers in his mouth and whistled.

Ted turned toward him, and all four of his dogs started streaking toward Luke and Hannah. A moment later, Ted broke into a run too. He arrived out of breath, but able to ask, "What happened?'

"She went into labor," Luke said his voice right on the edge of panic.

"We're taking her to his truck," Slate said, holding up his phone. "The ambulance is on the way." He put the phone back to his ear in time to hear the woman say, "Six minutes away, sir."

"They're only six minutes away, Luke," he called up to his friend. He looked at Ted. "Call and text everyone. We just found her out in the field like that. Ursula was having a fit."

Slate had no idea what he'd do if he were in Luke's boots. Probably pick up his wife and get her to the hospital too. He loved Jill with his whole soul, especially after watching her go through childbirth.

She'd given him a daughter of his own, and Slate hadn't known how wide his heart could expand. He did now, as he felt more love for his wife and his baby girl every single day.

Jill's labor had been normal, with her first contraction almost like a gas pain, she'd said. He'd still taken her to the hospital, where they'd sent her home. Two weeks of that until her contractions became severe enough to have the baby.

They'd named her Savannah Sabrina after her mother, who had been the first to hold the baby after Jill and Slate.

Jill was already talking about having another baby, and Slate would do whatever she wanted, because he now knew his heart could simply grow bigger with each addition to his life.

That feeling manifested itself again as he took in Hannah's face. He loved her too, albeit on a non-romantic scale. She'd been a good friend to Jill and Slate, and she was always willing to babysit or help out with whatever they needed.

She'd been mothering everyone on the ranch for years, and Slate had no doubt she'd be an excellent mother to this baby.

"Nate and Ginger are on the way," Ted said. "Jill and Emma are coming in from the festival site. Sabrina and Harold are here. Basically, everyone's on their way."

Luke groaned and said, "Teddy, I need help."

Ted dashed forward to help Luke open the door, and together, they got Hannah into the back seat of his truck. Luke turned around, his eyes as wide as beach balls. He had blood on his shirt, and he looked like he might fall down too.

"Move over, Ursula," Ted said, and he stepped right in front of Luke and grabbed onto him. Slate crowded in close too, his own desperation growing and growing

"It's going to be fine," Ted said. "The ambulance is almost here, and she's breathing. She's just passed out. It's going to be okay."

"Should we try to wake her up?" Slate asked, both the emergency operator and his friends.

"If you want to," the operator said. "Don't shake her."

More footsteps came running, and Nate arrived, glancing around at everyone.

"They said we can try to wake her," Slate said. "But don't shake her."

Luke turned toward Nate and the two exchanged a nod. Nate went around to the other side of the truck and opened the door on that side. Luke turned back to his wife, and said, "Hannah, baby. Can you hear me? Can you open your eyes?"

"Come on, now, Hannah," Nate drawled. "You're going to have your baby today, and you won't want to miss seein' him for the first time."

Luke said something else, but Slate was distracted by Ginger's arrival as well as the operator saying, "Two minutes, sir."

"Two minutes," he parroted.

Ginger straightened and got in the front seat of the truck. "Hannah," she said. "It's Ginger. Remember how you helped me stay calm when I went into labor? Guess who was right there to help you today? Ursula. Can you wake up and tell her what a good job she did?"

Ursula barked, and Slate flinched away from the volume of it.

"How is she?" Dallas asked, stepping next to Slate. "Jess is freaking out," he added quietly. "She's on her way in right now, but she's at least ten minutes out."

The wail of a siren filled the air, but right below that came a groan.

Hannah's groan.

DALLAS FELT SO HELPLESS, AND HE HATED IT. JESS HAD gone into labor at home. Early, yes. Surprising, yes. But at home, where he'd promptly picked her up and taken her out to the car. They'd been at the hospital less than fifteen minutes later, and she'd been admitted on their first try.

"That's it, angel," Luke said. "Wake on up now." Across the truck, Nate said something, and Dallas just stayed out of the way.

Luke turned toward him and said, "Dallas, I need you."

He stepped through the dogs and past Ted, who seemed to have taken up a protective position just like the six canines. "The ambulance is almost here," Dallas said

"She's bleeding a lot," Luke said. "Is that normal?"

"I'm not an OBGYN," Dallas said, not daring to look at Hannah though the sight of blood didn't bother him. "I haven't practiced for years."

"Is it normal?" Nate asked.

Dallas looked at Hannah, whose entire lower body was soaked in blood. He shook his head, fear ripping through him. "No. This is bad. This is—" He didn't allow himself to say what it could be.

A ruptured placenta. A tear in the uterine wall.

Hannah's skin looked like dry cement, and while her chest rose and fell, it was in quick, shallow breaths.

The siren came closer, growing louder, and Dallas quickly circled to Nate's side of the truck. He climbed onto the seat and leaned over Hannah, pulling up her sweater to just under her chest. No blood on her belly, which meant she hadn't fallen and injured herself there.

"She's hemorrhaging," he said. "I don't know how to stop the bleeding." He looked across her body to Luke, his thoughts growing clearer and clearer. "She's going to need a C-section to take the baby as fast as possible," he said. "Luke, listen to me. They're going to have to take her from you. They'll take the baby, and they'll bring him out to you. Then they're going to focus on saving her life."

Luke's face crumbled, and Ted took a step closer to him.

"It's going to be okay," Dallas said. "We got to her quickly, and the human body has a lot of blood. She's going to be okay." He shouted the last words as the ambulance pulled up.

He jumped from the truck and started briefing the man as he got out of the passenger seat. "She's going to need a blood clotting agent. I think she's got a ruptured placenta, and she's bleeding a lot. You should take the baby C-section. Call it in right now so they're ready. She's been down for fifteen minutes, and you have to save her."

The man asked Dallas question after question as they got Hannah onto a gurney and hooked up to an IV. Her breathing actually settled, and Dallas told Luke that was a good sign. "You ride with them, Luke. Go."

Luke climbed in the back of the ambulance and said, "You're all coming, right?" just before the door closed.

"You heard him," Ted said. "We're all going."

Everyone scrambled to get into a truck or car, and Dallas ended up alone, waiting for Jess to get back from her ride. She came running up to him five minutes after everyone had pulled out, and Dallas was still standing there, watching the dust settle.

"What's going on?" Jess asked, a sob coming from her throat. "Where is she? Where is everyone?"

Dallas looked at her and put his arm around her and their son in her arms. The boy was fifteen months now and squirmed under the weight of Dallas's arm. "She's going to have the baby early," he said, his voice almost numb. "Let's go. I'll explain on the way there."

"WE'LL BE BACK TONIGHT," HE SAID INTO THE PHONE. "You really don't need to make the drive. Missy is almost fourteen years old." He glanced at Emma, who couldn't stop crying. The desperation in the truck was the highest Ted had ever felt, and he'd seen Emma handcuffed to a chair before.

"We're already heading out to the car," Fran said. "I know Missy can handle it, but we haven't seen Frannie in a few months, and I have a gift for both girls."

Ted knew she didn't have a gift for his girls. Or maybe she did. He knew he didn't want to argue with her. "Thank you, Fran," he said as he made the turn into the emergency room parking lot. The ambulance had beat them there, of course, but they'd only pulled in maybe a minute ago.

"Of course," Fran said. "We'll pray for Hannah too."

"I'm sure she'll appreciate that." Ted pulled up to the circle drive as he hung up the call. "Go on," he said. "I'll park and come find everyone."

Emma slid from the truck, as did Slate, Jill, and Jill's mother, Sabrina. Nate and Ginger had her father with them, and Dallas had stayed behind to wait for his wife.

"I love you," Ted called to Emma, suddenly needing to tell her at least once an hour. That way, if something happened, she'd know how he felt.

She gave him a quick smile and wiped her face. "I love you too, Teddy." She closed the door and leaned into Sabrina, who seemed to have the most strength out of all of them.

Ted pulled back into the lot and began looking for an available space. He couldn't believe what was happening, though he'd faced some very hard things in his life. He'd sat through a trial at the defendant's table. He'd listened to a guilty verdict. He'd gone to a low-security federal prison, where he'd stayed for years.

He'd lost his career and his friends from his previous life.

In the past couple of years, Ted had learned that all he'd lost had been inconsequential compared to what he'd gained.

His friendships with Nate, Dallas, Slate, and Luke meant more to him than any of his lawyer friends had. His marriage and relationship with Emma was worth more to him than anything, and his little girl had captured his whole heart the moment he'd met her.

Emma had told him three days ago that she was pregnant again and due in mid-July. The same thrill he'd experienced then ran through him now, and he couldn't wait to have another little human in his life. He even loved that silly teacup piglet he'd bought for Emma a few years ago.

He loved everything about his life now, and he couldn't imagine it without Hannah in it. She'd always been kind to him, and she made coming to dinner at the West Wing fun and inviting. She genuinely cared about people—Ted included—and he simply couldn't imagine not seeing her every day and asking her how she was doing.

"Luke," he murmured, spotting a parking space and swinging his truck wide to be able to fit into it. "Lord, please bless Luke. He's already been through so much, and he loves Hannah with his whole heart. He can't lose her."

Ted parked and jumped from the truck, barely remembering to grab the keys. He jogged away from the vehicle, locking it with the fob over his shoulder as he went. "Bless that baby, too," he said right out loud.

Inside, he found everyone grouped together in a huddle in the corner, and he looked around for Nate. The man stood at the desk, talking to a woman, and Ted gestured to Emma that he was going to go find out what was happening too.

He approached Nate as the woman said, "...anything. She's here, and they're working on her."

"But where's her husband?" Nate asked. "Is he allowed back there? If so, one of us needs to be with him."

"Sir," the nurse said firmly. "We don't allow visitors in the ER."

"We're not visitors," Ted said. "We're family."

She looked from Ted to Nate, and they didn't look anything alike. She cocked an eyebrow and folded her arms.

"Gina," Nate said in a different kind of voice. "You know who I am. You know how much my men mean to me, especially this one. This is his wife, and she was bleeding heavily."

"Dallas said something about a ruptured placenta," Ted added. "They can fix that, right?"

Nate glanced at Ted, and they both knew the answer to that. Dallas had been pale and in complete shock—and he was a doctor. He'd dealt with people in pain all the time. Lots of blood. He knew how to act in an emergency, and he'd completely frozen.

It had been Slate who'd acted, and Luke, as Ted hadn't come upon them until they were almost back to the truck, Hannah hanging limply in her husband's arms. Ted closed his eyes, and all he could see was Luke's stricken face and Slate's panicked eyes.

He hadn't known what to do either, that was for sure.

"Let me see what I can find out," Gina said. "But Nate, I really don't think any of you are going to be able to come back. If she has a placenta abruption, she'll go immediately into surgery."

"What about the baby?" Ted asked.

"The surgery is to save the baby," Gina said. "And the mother. We have very good doctors here, Ted. In fact, Doctor Midgarf is here today, and he studied for a year in obstetrics. He's going to take good care of her."

"Midgarf?" Nate asked, frowning. "I don't trust that name."

"Would you like me to go check on her?" Gina asked. "Or stand here and argue with you about a name?"

"Go," Ted said, stepping in front of Nate, who's fingers had started to curl into a fist. "Come on, Nate. Back up a little."

Nate did, exhaling slowly out of his nose. Gina turned and went through the door that led back into the ER, and Ted could tell Nate wanted to follow her, rules or not.

"She's going to find out for us," Ted said. "We have to be the strong ones. Look at your wife." Ted glanced over Nate's shoulder to where Ginger stood with Emma and Jill. "She was scared to death of dying during childbirth. She has got to be freaked out."

Nate's eyes softened, and he nodded. "You're right."

"They're going to send Luke out, and he's going to need us." Ted turned Nate around. "Let's go sit down and not act like monsters."

Thankfully, the waiting room was mostly empty, and Ted got Nate back over to the group, where he took Ginger into his arms and held her tightly for several long seconds. Ted did the same with Emma, letting her cry against his chest.

"Come on now, sweetheart," he said quietly. "When Luke comes out, you're not going to want him to see you breaking down."

"You're right." She took a deep breath and held it. Her exhale was slow and shaky, but she inhaled again, fusing some strength into her expression. She wiped her face, and Ted looked at her.

"You're wonderful," he said. "I love you so much, and I admire so much about you."

"She's back," Slate said, and Ted turned around to find Gina walking toward them. Her strawberry blonde hair flapped as she strode toward them, and she looked as fierce and as determined as ever.

She paused a few feet from them, taking in the group of

them. "She's undergoing a Cesarian-section right now. Luke is with her, and he's going to stay back there with her and the baby."

"She's alive?" Nate asked.

"She is alive," Gina said. "They have the bleeding under control, and they're working to get everything back to normal."

"The baby?" Emma asked, her voice turning tinny again.

"We don't know yet." Gina gave her a kind smile and nodded. "I've asked Luke to come update you when he can."

"Thank you," Ted said as Gina turned to walk away. "Let's sit down, everyone. It sounds like we might be here for a while."

Thankfully, everyone listened, and they'd no sooner sat down when Dallas and Jess arrived with little Jonas. Emma and Ginger engulfed Jess in a hug, and Dallas migrated over to Ted and Nate to get an update.

After Nate had explained everything, Ted looked around at the group of them. They were his family, and he didn't care if he didn't look like any of them. These men and women meant a great deal to him, and he'd do anything and everything for them.

"Hey," Ted said quietly. "Will you—do you guys think we could pray together?"

"Good idea," Slate said quietly, and he reached up to remove his cowboy hat. All the other men did too, and then they looked at Ted again.

He cleared his throat and closed his eyes, waiting for the

right words to come into his mind. "Dear Lord," he finally said. "We thank Thee for our bounteous blessings, and we call on Thee for one more. Maybe two. Okay, three. One for our brother and friend, Luke Holt. If he is scared, help him to be strong. If he is worried, send him comfort. If he is sad, bless us with a way to cheer him up. We need a miracle for Hannah, our friend and Luke's wife." His voice broke, and Ted struggled to keep his sob contained.

He lost the battle, and the noise that came from his mouth sounded painful and anguished. Emma's hand in his tightened, and Ted drew from her strength.

Nate said, "I can finish," and Ted shook his head.

"Bless her with the best doctors," Ted said, his voice still a bit shaky but plenty loud. "Bless her body that it will be strong, and that she'll be able to deliver a healthy baby, and then recover fully."

He paused again, thinking of his perfect Frannie. "One last blessing for the baby boy being born right now. He is a gift from Thee, and we ask Thee to protect him and bless him with perfect health and both parents to raise him into adulthood."

His words ran out, and Ted simply added, "Amen," to his prayer.

"Amen," several others whispered, and Ted opened his eyes.

"Thank you, Ted," Nate said. "That was beautiful."

Ted nodded and wiped his hand down his face. He didn't cry very often, but everything in his head felt so hot right now. He sat back and looked at the door, praying silently that Luke would walk through it.

NATE WAS GOING TO GO CRAZY IN THAT WAITING ROOM. After twenty minutes, he got up and said, "I'm going outside for a minute."

"Nate," Ginger said.

"I'm fine, sweetheart," he said. "I just can't...breathe." He tried to encourage her with a single look before he walked away. Outside, the late November air went down crisply, and he leaned his back against the side of the building, trying to get more air on the next breath. Then more, and more, and more.

"Are you okay?" someone asked, and Nate opened his eyes. He hadn't even realized he'd closed them.

An elderly woman stood there, her concern for him plain. "Yes," he managed to say. "I'm okay."

She gave him a knowing smile and continued inside. Nate sighed and looked out over the parking lot. There were so many cars here, and he couldn't imagine having to come to this hospital for more than the couple of days it had taken for Ginger to deliver their son.

"I can't help him," Nate said, new misery filling him. "I've always been able to help them. All of them." He looked up, hoping to see sky but only seeing the roof above the overhang on the emergency room entrance. "How do I help Luke in this situation? Or Hannah?"

All he could do was pray, and he did that again and then again, as if prayer should be done as often as breathing.

He had to go back in, because if he didn't, Ted would come find him. Ted would worry, the way Ted did. Slate would too, and Nate appreciated his friends more and more.

He took a deep breath and went back inside. He hadn't quite reached the group yet when Dallas and Slate stood up. They looked beyond him, and Nate turned to find Luke coming toward them, a blue-wrapped bundle in his arms. A nurse accompanied him, as did a glowing halo around his whole countenance.

Luke had often called Hannah his angel, and he certainly seemed to have them standing watch over him right now.

"Here's Robert," he said in a whisper as he arrived. "They're giving me five minutes for you guys to see him, and then they have to take him again."

"How is he?" Emma asked, stepping right over to the baby and running her fingers along his hairless scalp.

"They want to do a lot of tests," Luke said, his eyes flitting away from Nate and landing on Slate. "Hannah's placenta tore away from the uterine wall, but only partially. But that's how the nutrients and oxygen get to the baby, and Robbie was compromised for over half an hour." He looked up, his eyes brighter than Nate had ever seen them. He looked simultaneously terrified and hopeful.

"So they're going to be running a lot of tests to see what, if any, impact that slower feed of oxygen had."

"He's so beautiful, Luke," Jill said, and that was the perfect thing to say.

"How's Hannah?" Dallas asked.

Luke looked up from his son again. "They were finishing up the removal of the placenta when I left to go with Robert. She hasn't woken up yet, but the doctors say as soon as they have the bleeding contained, she will."

His chin shook, and Nate wanted to take him into a tight, tight hug. Ted beat him to it, and he was bigger anyway, so his arms fit around Luke and the baby easily.

"Sir," the nurse said as the baby started to fuss, and Ted stepped back. Luke passed the baby to Ginger, and Nate grabbed onto him next.

"You're strong," he said. "You can do this." Nate took Luke's face in both of his hands and looked straight at him. "She has you for a reason, Luke. You're strong enough to be there for her through this."

Luke's tears streamed down his face, but he nodded. He hugged everyone, and actually thanked them for coming, before he took his baby and followed the nurse back into the emergency room.

People started to sit down, but Nate stayed on his feet, watching the door. Ginger stepped to his side and slid her fingers between his. He calmed, the way he always did with his wife's touch. She brought comfort to his soul, and he turned to place a kiss to her cheek.

"She's going to be okay," Ginger said. "I can just feel it."

Nate usually could too, but his emotions were so knotted right now, that he could barely think past the next moment. For now, he'd have to accept his wife's assurances, and he let her lead him over to his chair, where they sat down together.

CHAPTER TWENTY-FOUR

Hannah woke slowly, Luke's voice in her ears. He was reading out loud, a story she didn't know but seemed very simple. Something about a dinosaur and a baseball bat.

Her head hurt, and a groan came out of her mouth without explicit instructions from her brain.

Luke's voice stopped, and it came closer as he said, "Hannah? Angel, can you open your eyes?"

She could, and she did, the lights above her so bright. Too bright. She flinched away from them, and Luke said, "I'll turn them off." His footsteps hurried away from her and then came back.

Hannah opened her eyes before he'd fully returned, and it only took a moment for her to see the infant in his arms. Everything rushed at her then—the pain at the ranch. The fall forward. Ursula barking and barking and barking.

Flashes of other things moved through her head, including Luke's voice asking her to wake up over and over. Nate said something to her. She bumped around in the back of a van. Or something.

Her mind fuzzed, and she focused on the present situation. "Is that—?" Her voice scratched in her throat, and she couldn't continue, because the words got stuck in how parched she was.

"There's a drink right here, hon." Luke lifted a huge cup with a straw, and Hannah drank greedily. After several swallows, she looked at the baby in his arms.

"Luke," she said. "Is that our baby?"

"Yes." He grinned at her and then down at the tiny bundle in his arms. "Robbie, your momma is awake." He turned the baby toward her, and Hannah took the beautiful child from her husband.

Tears pricked her eyes as she took in his baldness and his perfectly round cheeks. "Oh, I love him," she whispered, looking up at Luke. He sat back down in the chair he'd dragged very near her bed and gazed at her.

"I love you," he said.

"What happened?" she asked.

A wave of exhaustion crossed his face, but he gave her a smile anyway. "Baby, your placenta ruptured. They call it a placenta abruption, and it means the placenta tears away from the uterine wall. You fell down, and you were unconscious when Slate and I found you."

Horror filled Hannah, but Luke kept talking. By the end of it, she wept.

She wept for herself, because she'd missed holding her son only moments after he was born.

She wept for Luke, who must've been so scared and so worried.

She wept for her friends, who'd been waiting to hear about her condition for hours.

She wept with gratitude for good doctors and nurses, for a dog who'd somehow known she wasn't well and had stayed with her, and for the mercy of the Lord in sparing her life so she could raise her son.

"You're okay," Luke whispered, taking one of her hands in his. "Don't cry, my angel. You're okay." He lifted her hand to his lips, but he was crying too. "I love you so much. I had no idea what I'd do without you, but you know what? That thought never stayed. It would stab at me, and then go, and I knew I wouldn't have to figure out what to do without you." He kissed her hand again, his smile gorgeous even if it was a bit wobbly.

"I love you," she whispered to him.

He nodded, his smile perfect. He drew in a long breath and wiped his face. "Now, dry your tears, baby. I want to get a picture of you to send to everyone, so they know you're awake and that you're holding your son."

Hannah really didn't want her picture taken right now. She felt like she'd been run over by a truck, and she was sure she looked like it too. But one look at her baby Robert, and a soft smile filled her whole face.

"Okay," Luke said, and Hannah glanced up, not realizing he'd taken the picture already. His thumbs flew across the screen, and once the text was sent, he tucked his phone away and focused on her again.

"Are you hungry?" he asked. "They say you can't have much, but I've got six to twelve people downstairs willing to bring you whatever you want." He grinned at her, and Hannah couldn't help but smile at him.

Before she could answer, the door opened and a nurse came in. "Dinnertime," she said as she carried a tray with plenty of food on it. "Look who's awake." She set the tray down on the rolling table and moved it over Hannah's lap.

"I'll get you sitting up more, and we'll need to start getting your vitals." She picked up a remote and pushed a button. The bed moved, and Hannah tried to push herself up. A pain cut through her, and she couldn't help the cry that came from her mouth.

"What's your pain on a scale of one to ten?" the nurse asked.

"That's was a ten," Hannah said, panting. "But normally, I'm okay. Four or five."

"I'll get you something. You'll be nursing?"

Hannah looked down at her son, and she wanted to connect to him in every way possible. "Yes," she said.

The nurse smiled at her and looked at something on the monitor behind her. "You can eat any time. If you'd like, I can bring in a lactation specialist to go over some things with you."

"Sure," Hannah said, glancing at Luke. "How long have I been out?"

"Oh, honey, just an hour or so. Maybe less," the nurse said. "Your husband here said you'd want to feed the baby first, and he's been such a perfect angel." She gazed at the baby with fondness. "But he should be fed soon."

"Okay," Hannah said, though she had no idea how to feed her baby. She knew, though, that she could figure it out.

"Let me check your bandage, and we'll give you some meds. You should have a few swallows of broth or gelatin, and then you'll be ready." The nurse smiled at her, and she took the baby from Hannah before she could even blink. "Here you go, Daddy."

Luke took Robbie, and Hannah marveled at how easily he settled the infant in his arms. She fell in love with him all over again as he did, and she held very still as the nurse pulled down her sheets and looked at the bandages that Hannah couldn't see.

"I had a C-section," she said, finally understanding the pain she'd felt.

"Yes," the nurse said, glancing at Luke. "You didn't tell her?"

"I sort of thought it was obvious." Luke glanced at Hannah. "Sorry, love."

Hannah tried to see her wound, but she couldn't. "How will I do the cooking classes now?" she asked.

Luke chuckled, but the nurse said, "Oh, honey, you're not doing cooking classes for at least three weeks."

EIGHT DAYS LATER, HANNAH STIRRED THE GRAVY WITH a whisk until it was perfectly smooth. She felt miles better with every passing day, despite her guilt at not being able to help Jill with the Howdy Holiday Festival this year.

She'd found someone else on the ranch to do the cooking classes, and Hannah had sat on the couch and gone over her plans with Sarah, the cowgirl who'd worked on the stable with her last year.

She glanced to the end of the island, where she and Luke had put Robbie's swing. The baby slept, his head practically sideways, and a rush of love moved through her.

Only Emma and Jill had arrived in the West Wing, and the three of them had been cooking for hours. Well, Jill and Emma had been. Hannah had taken care of the toddlers and babies, only getting up to help with the gravy, because she wanted to feel useful.

Plus, she was an excellent gravy-maker.

The back door opened, and a wave of chatter filled the house. Hannah smiled at it, because she loved having people in the West Wing. She and Luke had been living here since their wedding, because Ginger wanted someone to take care of the West Wing, and Luke would have to build another cabin for them as all the others were full.

"We've got the turkey," Nate said, and he and Ted lifted two roasted turkeys onto the counter.

"Good," Emma said. "Everyone take a name tag and go put it on a place at the table, please. No arguing about where you sit."

Luke came to Hannah's side, his hand slipping along her waist. "How are you, angel? You're not working too hard, are you?"

"The doctor said I can lift anything lighter than the baby," she said, lifting up the whisk. "I think this qualifies."

He grinned at her and pressed a quick kiss to her mouth. "Love you, baby. Should I get Robbie out?"

"Only if you want me to miss dinner." She glanced over to their baby. "Let him sleep. When he wakes up, he'll be hungry, and I can feed him then."

"Okay." He turned, and Emma immediately put him to work filling glasses with ice cubes. Emma moved from person to person, giving them each a task.

Five minutes later, Emma looked at Slate, who whistled. Everyone protested, Hannah too, her gaze flying to Robbie. The baby hadn't even flinched, and her heart swelled with love for the tiny boy.

"Time to eat," Emma said, gazing around at everyone. "Ginger?"

Ginger stepped forward, and Hannah loved her too. "We're so glad to have everyone at Hope Eternal Ranch for Thanksgiving this year. It's been such a good year, and none of us can do what we do and accomplish what we accomplish here without each other."

Her eyes welled with tears, and she glanced at Nate. He smiled at her and then around at everyone. "I love seeing my best friends every day," he said. "I love the men you were with me in prison, and I love the men you are now. I love the women who love my boys, and I love—" He cleared his throat. "I love this ranch that literally saved me and Connor." He looked back at Ginger, and she turned to Dallas.

"It'll be a quick prayer," Dallas said. "I know we're all hungry." He tucked his cowboy hat under his arm, and Hannah watched as all the other cowboys did too.

She watched them all as Dallas prayed, thanking the Lord for their blessings from the past year. Luke sidestepped over to her, and she looked at him. The perfect sense of love filled her, and Luke silently leaned down and kissed her.

"Amen," she said when everyone else did, and then she said, "I love you, and I love our life together here at Hope Eternal."

"I do too, angel," he said. "Can you believe this is where we are?"

Hannah grinned up at him. "You know what? Yes, I can." She looked at Jess and Dallas, who were helping their kids get food. She loved Jess so much, and she loved Thomas and Remmy and Jonas too. Dallas was the perfect compliment to all of them, and Hannah didn't know anyone who was more dedicated to his family and children.

She watched Nate bend down and pick up his son and start pointing to things on the counter. Anything Ward nodded at, Ginger put on a plate for him. Ginger had been the steady rock in Hannah's life for so many years, and it was a true blessing to see her bloom in new ways as she embraced her role as wife and mother.

Nathaniel Mulbury had changed everything at Hope Eternal Ranch, and a rush of gratitude filled her for the way he'd brought all of his friends here, kept them united, and pushed them to heal. Without Nate, Hannah wasn't sure she'd have Luke at her side right now.

She watched Ted and Emma inch through the line while Missy helped Frannie. Fran and Matt followed, as they attended almost every family function. How Ted had accepted Emma and all of her secrets, her past, and her friend warmed Hannah's heart, and she was so glad Emma had let down her guard and allowed herself to fall in love with the big, burly teddy bear of a man.

Hannah finally turned her attention to Jill, who currently knelt in front of her toddler and put a bib around Savannah's neck. She lifted the girl into her arms and passed her to Slate, who held a children's plate full of food already.

He took his daughter over to a highchair at the table and strapped her in. He put a sippy cup on the tray in front of her and then her plate of food. He bent down and pressed a kiss to her head, and it was really hard to believe that the man had been in prison at all.

Hannah looked at Luke, and the glow about him

warmed her soul. She snuggled deeper into his side, glad when he lifted his arm around her shoulders.

Yes, she loved him, and she loved this life she had at Hope Eternal Ranch.

———————

Keep reading for a sneak peek at your next great sweet romance read, **THE DAY HE DROVE BY**.

THE END

THE DAY HE DROVE BY, CHAPTER ONE

Ten years ago:

"Aaron, you have to stop the car. We're not going to make it." Gretchen Samuels hated the weakness and panic in her voice, but the pain ripping through her lower back made it difficult to speak any other way.

"We're in the middle of nowhere," her husband said. "I can't stop." In fact, he accelerated to a speed their twelve-year-old sedan certainly couldn't handle.

As another labor pain tore through her, tears spilled from Gretchen's eyes. She didn't want to have her first child on the side of the road, miles from nurses and antiseptic and baby warmers. And medication. She really needed a fast-acting painkiller.

"I'm sorry," she sobbed. Aaron hated living out on her granddad's lavender farm, but the housing was cheap and he was almost done with his online securities degree. Their plans for a future in Seattle while he led the data security team at a top technology firm were months from coming to fruition.

"Don't be sorry." He glanced at her, and she disliked the panic in his eyes too, and the white-knuckle grip he had on the steering wheel certainly wasn't comforting.

Her breath caught in her throat as it seemed like this baby was going to claw its way out of her no matter how much she willed the little girl to hold on a little longer.

"Call 911," she said. "Please." She must've infused the right amount of emotion into her voice, because Aaron slowed the car and eased it onto the gravel shoulder. He leapt from behind the wheel, left his door open, and sprinted around the front of the car.

"Let's get you into the back." He supported her—the way he'd been doing for the four years they'd been together —and helped her into the backseat before pulling out his phone and making the emergency call.

Gretchen's pain eased with the new position, but it didn't go away. She wondered if it ever would, or if this degree of agony would hover in her muscles like a ghost forever. "Hang on," she whispered as she put her hand on her very pregnant belly. "Just a little while longer."

"They're on their way." Aaron poked his head back inside the car. "They said to get any blankets, towels, napkins, anything we have. You're supposed to stay lying down and try to relax."

Gretchen couldn't help the snort that escaped. "Relax?" She let her head fall back as she focused on the car's ceiling. She hadn't been able to relax for months, not since her stomach had grown so large she couldn't see her toes. Simply getting up from the couch had grown increasingly difficult as the days had passed.

She hadn't minded, because she and Aaron had wanted this baby more than anything. The tears that heated her eyes this time were from desperation. A shiver ran over her body as the wind snaked its way into the car.

"Aaron, can you close the doors?" She lifted her head but couldn't see him anywhere. Fear flowed through her. "Aaron?"

The trunk slammed, and he came to the door closest to her head this time. "We don't have a blanket in the trunk. I found this jacket though." He balled it up and put it under her head before shrugging out of the one he was wearing too.

Gretchen steeled herself to deliver her baby and wrap it in her husband's polar fleece. Her range of emotions felt ridiculous as a wave of injustice slammed into her. "Close the doors, please," she said through tight teeth. "I'm cold." Should she be cold? What if she was going into shock or something?

Her jaw worked against the rising terror as he complied, going around the car—which had all four doors open—and shutting the wind out before sealing himself behind the wheel again. Gretchen thought the silence in the car might be worse than the wind, and she didn't want to bring her baby into the world under such a cloud of awkwardness.

"Remember when we first met?" she asked him, glad when his low, soft chuckle met her ears.

"You said my hair looked like a gorilla."

She giggled too, though the motion made her stomach muscles tighten uncomfortably. She hitched in a breath and held it. Aaron had been a freshman on campus though he was twenty-three years old. Gretchen had just finished her business management degree. His dark hair was swooped to the side, very much like the cartoon gorillas Gretchen had spent a lot of time watching while she nannied to pay for school.

He reached back and threaded his fingers through hers. "What if they don't make it?" he asked, his voice barely higher than a whisper. "I don't know how to deliver a baby."

And Gretchen knew there was more than just a baby that needed to come out. "They'll make it." She spoke with as much confidence as she could, the way she always did when Aaron confessed his worries to her.

You're the best in your class, she'd tell him. *You'll be able to find a good job.*

Don't worry about anything here, she said to him when he had to go to Seattle to take his tests, attend interviews, or deliver dissertations. *I'll be fine. Just watching the lavender grow.*

She closed her eyes and imagined herself in the fields of lavender now, the fragrant scent of the herbs wafting through the slow, blue sky. The same smile that had always accompanied her assurances when he left drifted across her face now.

Her next labor pain stole all the peace from her, and her eyes shot open and a moan ground through her whole body. Aaron's fingers on hers squeezed, and everything seemed clenched so tight, tight, tight.

The contraction seemed to last a long time before subsiding. Gretchen only got what felt like a moment's reprieve before the next one began. Time marched on, seemingly unaware of the pain she was in, the desperate way she cinched everything tight to keep the baby inside.

She wasn't sure how many labor pains she'd endured, or how much time had gone by, before Aaron said, "They're here," with a heavy dose of relief in his voice. He once again jumped from the car.

Moments later, the door by her feet opened and a gust of ocean air raced in. The scent of brine she normally loved only reminded her that this wasn't a hospital, there were no drugs, and she could do absolutely nothing about it.

"Ma'am, my name is Andrew Herrin, and I'm going to take good care of you."

She managed to look over her belly to a man who couldn't be older than twenty. A zing of alarm raced through her.

"Drew?" She couldn't believe she cared if the man whose family lived next door to her—who she'd walked with in lavender fields as a teen—delivered her baby. He had a bag of medical supplies. A faster ride to the hospital. And a kind face, with a calm smile.

"You're going to be fine, Gretchen." He snapped a pair of gloves on and touched her ankle. "So let's see what we've got."

THE DAY HE DROVE BY,
CHAPTER TWO

Drew Herrin felt the morning sun warm his back as he worked. He'd already fed the chickens, the horses, the cows, and the goats. His mother and step-father had quite the little farm just north of Hawthorne Harbor, down the Lavender Highway. He glanced up and took a moment to just breathe, something he hadn't been able to do in Medina, though the town sat right on the water too.

The air simply tasted different here, and while Drew had hoped to make something of himself in Medina—do more, be better, actually help someone—he'd only realized the job was the same there as it was here. Just more stressful. Less fun. No room to run with his German shepherds and experiment with his ice cream flavors.

The wind picked up, but Drew was used to being wind-blown. Everyone on Hawthorne Harbor was. The long-time joke was that if you didn't like the wind, you should leave. Because it was always windy.

He looked across the water to the body of land he could just make out in the distance. He'd grown up on the harbor, but it still gave him a snip of surprise to remember he was looking at another country when he looked at that land.

For a fleeting moment, the same restlessness that had driven him to Medina three years ago squirreled through him again.

Then he put his head down and got back to work. He finished fixing the tractor his step-dad used to get the lavender fields properly built up for watering. He sharpened a few tools and whistled for his shepherds to come with him as he headed back to the house.

With a single bark, Blue announced his arrival from the huge flower garden adjacent to the farm. He brought the scent of roses with him, and even a white petal from a flower Drew would never know.

"You rascal." Drew grinned at the dog and flicked the petal to the ground. "You can't go over there." He glanced at the expansive garden, bearing row after row of flowers in all colors, shapes, and sizes. His family owned the land, but he'd learned that his mother rented it to a local florist in town, who apparently hand-grew everything she sold in her shop on Main Street.

Drew had never met the woman. She tended to the flowers when he wasn't there, obviously. And he had no need for flowers, as he'd sworn off women and all common dating practices when his last girlfriend had carved out his heart and then left town.

A text. That was what he'd gotten after a fifteen-month relationship where diamonds and children had been discussed.

I can't do this.

Drew thought the words his ex had sent now, though he tried to stuff all memories with Yvonne in them back into the box where he kept them.

Can't hadn't been in Drew's vocabulary growing up. His father had taught him to fix cars, tractors, lawn mowers, all of it. He worked the farm, rode horses, raised goats, planted lavender, and played a major role in the Hawthorne Harbor Lavender Festival. There was nothing Drew couldn't do.

He'd taken that attitude into adulthood, first finishing his emergency medical technician training and then going on to be a certified firefighter. He'd gone on to take cardiac life support classes, pediatric training, and tactical emergency care.

No, *can't* didn't exist in Drew's world. At least until Yvonne.

Something wet met his palm, and Drew danced away from his second German shepherd, the much more silent and sneaky Chief. A chuckle came from his throat, and Drew crouched to let his dogs lick his neck and face. His laughter grew, and he was reminded why this remote farm on the edge of Hawthorne Harbor felt more like home than anywhere else.

"Morning chores are done," he announced as he entered the wide, white farmhouse, his dogs right behind him. Their claws scratched against the hardwood, and he pointed to the utility room where he kept their food and water. "Go on, guys. I'll come let you out in a minute."

"Thanks, Drew," Joel said. His step-dad didn't mind the farm and the equipment upkeep, but his true love was with the lavender, and Drew figured they could both do what they liked best if he came out and tended to the animals.

Joel had spent the first thirty years of his life in trade carpentry, and he'd improved the inside and outside of the farmhouse until Drew barely recognized it. He stepped into the kitchen with the high, honey-colored wood beams slanting up to the vaulted ceiling to find his dark-haired mother standing at the stove.

"Morning, Ma." He swept a kiss along her hairline as she scrambled eggs. The smell made his stomach turn, and he opted for turning away and pouring himself a glass of orange juice. Funny how his father had passed nine years ago, and Drew still couldn't handle the sight and smell of his dad's favorite breakfast. How his mother continued making it every morning was a mystery to him. Thankfully, the grief that hit at unexpected times only tapped his heart today. Sometimes it could punch, leaving him breathless and confused.

"Are you working today?" she asked, switching her attention to a pan of sizzling bacon.

"Yep. Gonna shower and head in." He wondered what

today would bring behind the wheel of the ambulance. Probably another cat stuck in another tree. Or a kid with a scrape or two. Drew chastised himself that he shouldn't *want* anyone in Hawthorne Harbor to need emergency medical care. But that seething need to *do something worthwhile* wouldn't seem to quiet today.

"Can I leave Blue and Chief here?"

"Yeah." Joel exhaled as he stood and refilled his coffee. "I'll take 'em out to the lavender fields and then let them swim in the harbor."

Drew smiled at the man. "Thanks, Joel. I promise I'll come get them tonight. The raccoons out here get them barking at night."

"Maybe they'll finally scare them away from my chickens," he said with a grumbly note in his voice. Joel certainly did love his fresh eggs and those clucky chickens.

"Breakfast?" his mother asked when Drew attempted to leave the kitchen.

"I'll stop at Duality on the way in." Part gas station and part eatery, the chefs at Duality made the best breakfast burritos Drew had ever tasted. He softened his rejection of her food with the biggest smile he could pull off and hooked his thumb over his shoulder. "I'm going to use the bathroom upstairs. I'll hang up my towel."

She didn't protest, and Drew took the steps two at a time to the mostly unused second floor. His old bedroom was up here, completely redone with the same luxurious hardwood Joel had gotten for next to nothing when a client decided they wanted something different. He'd painted the room in a light blue-gray and wispy white curtains had been added.

But the bedspread his mother had quilted still draped the bed, and Drew took a moment to run his fingertips along it. His favorite colors were green and blue, and he loved everything about being outside. So she'd carefully pieced together pine green pieces to make trees, dark brown pieces to make mountains, and several shades of blue to make the sky and ocean that surrounded this town Drew loved.

How he'd thought he could ever leave it and be happy plagued him. "Doesn't matter," he muttered to himself. He was back now, and happy helping around the farm as his parents got older, happy to have his old job back at the emergency services company that contracted with the hospital in Hawthorne Harbor, nearby Olympic National Park, and four other towns in the surrounding area.

After he showered, dressed, and let his dogs back outside, he climbed behind the wheel of his truck for the fifteen-minute drive into town. He loved the commute from farm to civilization. Though he didn't make it every day, the straight road and country stillness allowed his mind to wander along new flavor combinations for his ice cream fetish.

He'd been circling something new for a few days now, something he hadn't quite been able to put his taste buds on. He'd tried lavender and honey—that combination was as old as the Lavender Festival in town. White chocolate and lavender had been well-received among his paramedic teams, but he didn't think it special enough to enter the Festival's contest.

No, he definitely needed something special, something with that added oomph to make the Festival judges give him the coveted Lavender King title this year. He knew Augustus Hammond would enter the competition, and he'd won with ice cream three times out of the last six years. If Drew was going to take on the three-time Lavender King, it wasn't going to be with lavender and honey.

And he wasn't just competing against other food artisans. Oh, no. The town hosted the largest lavender festival in the entire country, and they gave out awards for revolutionary and best-use way of utilizing the plant that brought a new twist to old lavender traditions. He needed something special, but so far, it had eluded him.

He'd nearly arrived at the flavor that seemed to skip in and out of his mind when he saw a big, brown van on the side of the road up ahead. The vehicle looked older than him, and it sunk low on one corner, indicating a flat tire.

A blonde girl stood in the middle of the road, waving both of her arms. Drew immediately slowed and pulled to the gravel shoulder, giving plenty of distance between his truck and the van.

"Thank goodness." The girl ran up to his truck before he could get fully out. She looked to be ten or eleven, with big front teeth she hadn't quite grown into yet. She had dark green eyes that had probably come half from her mother and half from her father. "You're the first car that's come along in an hour."

"Not much going on out here in the mornings," he said, glancing past her to the front driver's side, where the van leaned.

"My mom blew her tire, and we need help." The girl sized him up as if she could tell by looking alone if he could help or not. "Can you change a tire?"

"Sure I can." He gave her a smile, noting that all the windows on the van were glazed dark. His defenses went up, especially because her "mom" still hadn't made an appearance. Crime was low in Hawthorne Harbor—one reason he hadn't gone to the police academy to make his certifications a trifecta in public service.

But still. This non-moving van, with all those black windows, and a little girl in the middle of the road... Drew proceeded with caution.

She played with the end of her pale ponytail. "My mom will try to tell you she can do it herself." Her voice pitched lower with every word and her eyes rounded. "But don't believe her. We've been out here for over an hour, and she's cried twice. 'The flowers,' she keeps saying." The girl turned and skipped toward the van. "Come on."

Drew took out his phone and tapped out a message to his boss. *On my way in, I ran across a motorist on the side of the road. Flat tire. Just north of mile marker seventeen on the Lavender Highway. Going to check it out.*

That way, if something happened, someone knew where

he was. He'd been on the Lavender Highway hundreds of times, and he'd only stopped once—to deliver a baby almost ten years ago.

He glanced around. It had been right around here too, closer to the farm than the town, out in the middle of nowhere. He wondered what had happened to Aaron and Gretchen Samuels, and the baby girl he'd wrapped in a towel before delivering the afterbirth.

Let us know if you need help came back, and Drew pocketed his phone and shelved his memories of the last time he'd been out of a car on this stretch of the road so his senses could be on full alert.

Read THE DAY HE DROVE BY, Book 1 in the Hawthorne Harbor Romance series right now! ***Available in paperback.***

BOOKS IN THE HOPE ETERNAL RANCH
ROMANCE SERIES

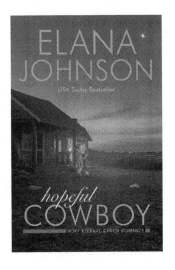

Hopeful Cowboy, Book 1: Can Ginger and Nate find their happily-ever-after, keep up their duties on the ranch, and build a family? Or will the risk be too great for them both?

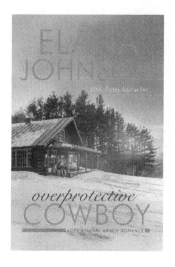

Overprotective Cowboy, Book 2: Can Ted and Emma face their pasts so they can truly be ready to step into the future together? Or will everything between them fall apart once the truth comes out?

Rugged Cowboy, Book 3: He's a cowboy mechanic with two kids and an ex-wife on the run. She connects better to horses than humans. Can Dallas and Jess find their way to each other at Hope Eternal Ranch?

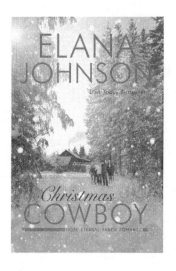

Christmas Cowboy, Book 4: He needs to start a new story for his life. She's dealing with a lot of family issues. This Christmas, can Slate and Jill find solace in each other at Hope Eternal Ranch?

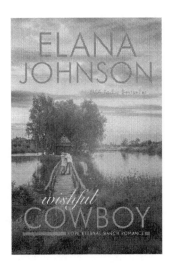

Wishful Cowboy, Book 5: He needs somewhere to belong. She has a heart as wide as the Texas sky. Can Luke and Hannah find their one true love in each other?

BOOKS IN THE HAWTHORNE HARBOR ROMANCE SERIES

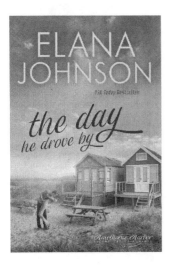

The Day He Drove By (Hawthorne Harbor Second Chance Romance, Book 1): A widowed florist, her ten-year-old daughter, and the paramedic who delivered the girl a decade earlier...

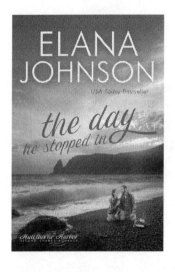

**The Day He Stopped In
(Hawthorne Harbor
Second Chance Romance,
Book 2):** Janey Germaine is
tired of entertaining tourists in
Olympic National Park all day
and trying to keep her twelve-
year-old son occupied at night.
When longtime friend and the
Chief of Police, Adam Herrin,
offers to take the boy on a ride-
along one fall evening, Janey starts to see him in a different
light. Do they have the courage to take their relationship out
of the friend zone?

The Day He Said Hello (Hawthorne Harbor Second Chance Romance, Book 3): Bennett Patterson is content with his boring fire-fighting job and his big great dane...until he comes face-to-face with his high school girlfriend, Jennie Zimmerman, who swore she'd never return to Hawthorne Harbor. Can they rekindle their old flame? Or will their opposite personalities keep them apart?

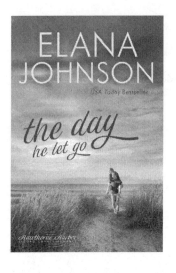

The Day He Let Go (Hawthorne Harbor Second Chance Romance, Book 4): Trent Baker is ready for another relationship, and he's hopeful he can find someone who wants him and to be a mother to his son. Lauren Michaels runs her own general contract company, and she's never thought she has a maternal bone in her body. But when she gets a second chance with the handsome K9 cop who blew her off when she first came to town, she can't say no... Can Trent and Lauren make their differences into strengths and build a family?

The Day He Came Home (Hawthorne Harbor Second Chance Romance, Book 5): A wounded Marine returns to Hawthorne Harbor years after the woman he was married to for exactly one week before she got an annulment...and then a baby nine months later. Can Hunter and Alice make a family out of past heartache?

The Day He Asked Again (Hawthorne Harbor Second Chance Romance, Book 6): A Coast Guard captain would rather spend his time on the sea...unless he's with the woman he's been crushing on for months. Can Brooklynn and Dave make their second chance stick?

BOOKS IN THE CARTER'S COVE ROMANCE SERIES

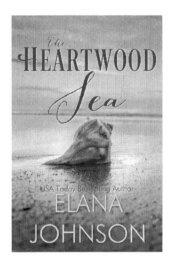

The Heartwood Sea (Book 1): She owns The Heartwood Inn. He needs the land the inn sits on to impress his boss. Neither one of them will give an inch. But will they give each other their hearts?

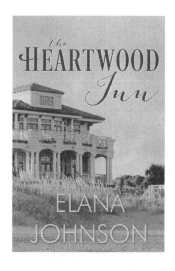

The Heartwood Inn (Book 2): She's excited to have a neighbor across the hall. He's got secrets he can never tell her. Will Olympia find a way to leave her past where it belongs so she can have a future with Chet?

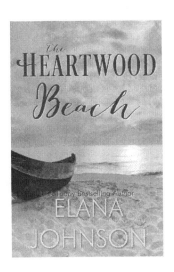

The Heartwood Beach (Book 3): She's got a stalker. He's got a loud bark. Can Sheryl tame her bodyguard into a boyfriend?

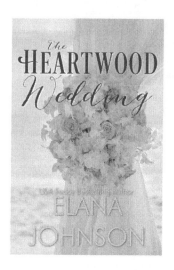

The Heartwood Wedding (Book 4): He needs a reason not to go out with a journalist. She'd like a guaranteed date for the summer. They don't get along, so keeping Brad in the not-her-real-fiancé category should be easy for Celeste. Totally easy.

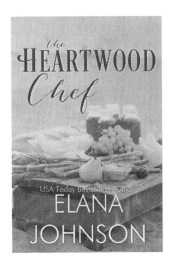

The Heartwood Chef (Book 5): They've been out before, and now they work in the same kitchen at The Heartwood Inn. Gwen isn't interested in getting anything filleted but fish, because Teagan's broken her heart before... Can Teagan and Gwen manage their professional relationship without letting feelings get in the way?

BOOKS IN THE GETAWAY BAY BILLIONAIRE ROMANCE SERIES

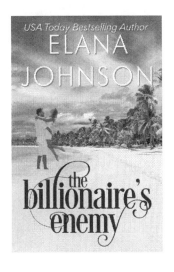

The Billionaire's Enemy (Book 1): A local island B&B owner hates the swanky highrise hotel down the beach...but not the billionaire who owns it. Can she deal with strange summer weather, tourists, and falling in love?

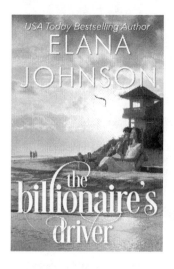

The Billionaire's Driver (Book 2): A car service owner who's been driving the billionaire pineapple plantation owner for years finally gives him a birthday gift that opens his eyes to see her, the woman who's literally been right in front of him all this time. Can he open his heart to the possibility of true love?

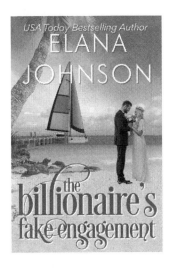

The Billionaire's Fake Engagement (Book 3): A former poker player turned beach bum billionaire needs a date to a hospital gala, so he asks the beach yoga instructor his dog can't seem to stay away from. At the event, they get "engaged" to deter her former boyfriend from pursuing her. Can he move his fake fiancée into a real relationship?

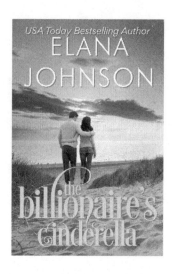

The Billionaire's Cinderella (Book 4): The owner of a beach-side drink stand has taken more bad advice from rich men than humanly possible, which requires her to take a second job cleaning the home of a billionaire and global diamond mine owner. Can she put aside her preconceptions about rich men and make a relationship with him work?

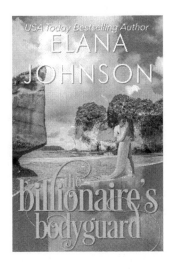

The Billionaire's Bodyguard (Book 5): Women can be rich too...and this female billionaire can usually take care of herself just fine, thank you very much. But she has no defense against her past...or the gorgeous man she hires to protect her from it. He's her bodyguard, not her boyfriend. Will she be able to keep those two B-words separate or will she take her second chance to get her tropical happily-ever-after?

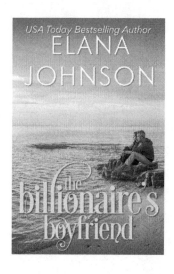

The Billionaire's Boyfriend (Book 6): Can a closet organizer fit herself into a single father's hectic life? Or will this female billionaire choose work over love...again?

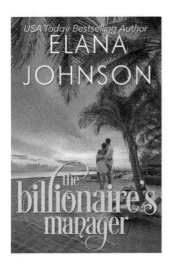

The Billionaire's Manager (Book 7): A billionaire who has a love affair with his job, his new bank manager, and how they bravely navigate the island of Getaway Bay...and their own ideas about each other.

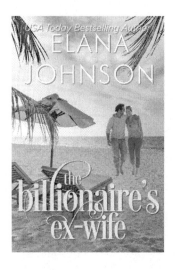

The Billionaire's Ex-Wife (Book 8): A silver fox, a dating app, and the mistaken identity that brings this billionaire faceto-face with his ex-wife...

BOOKS IN THE BRIDES & BEACHES ROMANCE SERIES

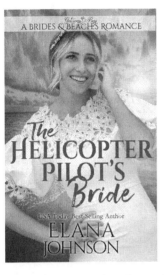

The Helicopter Pilot's Bride (Book 1): Charlotte Madsen's whole world came crashing down six months ago with the words, "I met someone else." Her marriage of eleven years dissolved, and she left one island on the east coast for the island of Getaway Bay. She was not expecting a tall, handsome man to be flat on his back under the kitchen sink when she arrives at the supposedly abandoned house. But former Air Force pilot, Dawson Dane, has a charming devil-may-care personality, and Charlotte could use some happiness in her life.

Can Charlotte navigate the healing process to find love again?

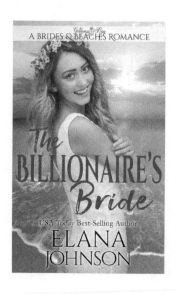

The Billionaire's Bride (Book 2): Two best friends, their hasty agreement, and the fake engagement that has the island of Getaway Bay in a tailspin...

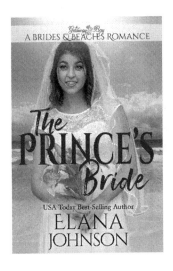

The Prince's Bride (Book 3): She's a synchronized swimmer looking to make some extra cash. He's a prince in hiding. When they meet in the "empty" mansion she's supposed to be housesitting, sparks fly. Can Noah and Zara stop arguing long enough to realize their feelings for each other might be romantic?

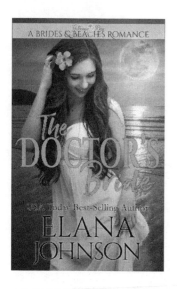

The Doctor's Bride (Book 4): A doctor, a wedding planner, and a flat tire... Can Shannon and Jeremiah make a love connection when they work next door to each other?

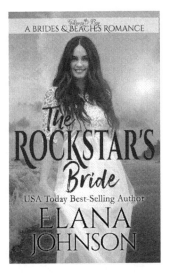

The Rockstar's Bride (Book 5): Riley finds a watch and contacts the owner, only to learn he's the lead singer and guitarist for a hugely popular band. Evan is only on the island of Getaway Bay for a friend's wedding, but he's intrigued by the gorgeous woman who returns his watch. Can they make a relationship work when they're from two different worlds?

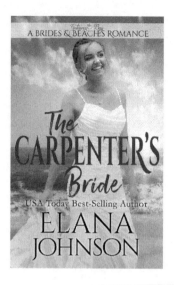

The Carpenter's Bride (Book 6): A wedding planner and the carpenter who's lost his wife... Can Lisa and Cal navigate the mishaps of a relationship in order to find themselves standing at the altar?

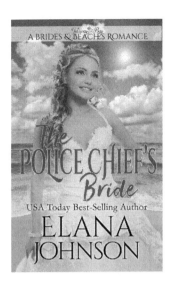

The Police Chief's Bride (Book 7): The Chief of Police and a woman with a restraining order against her... Can Wyatt and Deirdre try for their second chance at love? Or will their pasts keep them apart forever?

BOOKS IN THE STRANDED IN GETAWAY BAY ROMANCE SERIES

Love and Landslides (Book 1): A freak storm has her sliding down the mountain...right into the arms of her ex. As Eden and Holden spend time out in the wilds of Hawaii trying to survive, their old flame is rekindled. But with secrets and old feelings in the way, will Holden be able to take all the broken pieces of his life and put them back together in a way that makes sense? Or will he lose his heart and the reputation of his company because of a single landslide?

Kisses and Killer Whales (Book 2): Friends who ditch her. A pod of killer whales. A limping cruise ship. All reasons Iris finds herself stranded on an deserted island with the handsome Navy SEAL...

Storms and Sentiments (Book 3): He can throw a precision pass, but he's dead in the water in matters of the heart...

USA TODAY BESTSELLING AUTHOR
ELANA JOHNSON

Crushes and Cowboys (Book 4): Tired of the dating scene, a cowboy billionaire puts up an Internet ad to find a woman to come out to a deserted island with him to see if they can make a love connection...

ABOUT ELANA

Elana Johnson is the USA Today bestselling author of dozens of clean and wholesome contemporary romance novels. She lives in Utah, where she mothers two fur babies, taxis her daughter to theater several times a week, and eats a lot of Ferrero Rocher while writing. Find her on her website at elanajohnson.com.

Made in the USA
Columbia, SC
21 July 2024

38957778R00217